A seer's path

Liliana Lia

A seer's path

Does life ever go as planned?

Neither did this book.

Will that stop any of us?
No.
Keep fighting.

Contents:

Prologue

The droplets of blood were staining the fresh snow, and I stared horrified at them. I refused to look at the pool of blood close by, or to even consider looking towards her body, laying in the snow, a few feet away from me.

I had tears running down my face, and all that I could hear was the last sound she made, right as the sharp sword had slit her throat, merciless. I could not look away, just as she'd asked me, and I could not tear my eyes from her body. I was staring at the pool of red staining the snow, and I refused to think further than that...

This isn't happening right now; this could not be real... I rocked my body gently, hoping that someone would wake me from this awful dream, but no one did.

In the morning, father had decided that he needed to go hunting in the woods, so we could have some meat for a stew, while my mother said that we also needed to gather some branches, for the fire.

Normally, I would have gone with her, but this time, because I was sick, she decided to take my brother with her, instead.

I was left home with grandma, to feed the few young chickens and the pig that we had. They have gone quickly on separate ways, and I went in the small shed to grab some grains for the chickens.

Grandma's scream has stopped me dead in my track. She was on her knees, with her face towards the sky, but her eyes were closed. I knew then that she was having a vision and whatever she saw was awful enough to make her scream like that. She then straightened her head, opened her eyes, and looked straight at me.

'Astrid, come to me! Something terrible is about to happen, and we do not have much time left!'

The urgency in her voice made me drop the recipient that I was holding and run to her.

'What are you talking about? What is going to happen?'

She grabbed my shoulders, looked at me worried, kissed my forehead, then explained to me what she saw in her vision.

'King Magnus and few of his most trusted men are very close to us, and they will come so the king can talk to me. But he has done awful things in his lifetime, and he had angered the gods. I will be the one to deliver the warning of the gods to him, and unfortunately, he will not listen to my words. Astrid, King Magnus will kill me soon, and you my child, must stay hidden, where I will put you, and whatever you see or hear, do not make a sound, and do not come out until your parents return from the forest!'

I looked at her with my mouth opened wide. I heard clearly what she said, but I could not fully comprehend yet the cruelty of the things that were about to happen, and I could not tear my eyes from her worried face.

These awful things were about to happen, and all that I could think about was to tell her that we should run away from here, before the king reaches our house.

She hugged me tightly and held me in her arms for a little longer. Why would she accept this?

'Grandma let's run to the forest! That king doesn't know the paths like we know them, and there are so many caves in the forest, where we could hide. I will not let him hurt you!'

'Astrid, dear child, listen to me… Magnus has decided long time ago to find me so I will tell him about my visions, and running from him will only make him angry. If I stay, and he kills me it will only be one death, but if we run, and he takes revenge on the whole family, that would be worse. Remember, we choose our own fate by what we do in our lifetime, and revenge will come to Magnus for what he will do. I will not be here to see it, but his wickedness will catch up with him, and one day he will pay for everything; but for now, this is what I can see, and this will happen soon. There is not much time left!'

She grabbed me by my shoulders, and dragged me towards some bushes, behind the shed. She gathered some branches and threw some snow around me, doing her best to hide me. I stayed there, hugging my knees, and feeling the tears falling on my frozen face, understanding that something bad was about to happen.

She looked at me one more time, pleading with her eyes for me to stay hidden, and kissed me on my forehead.

'Astrid, my sweet child, I have told you what is going to happen. Please, I beg you, stay hidden here, until either one of your parents come home. Do not look at me, when King Magnus will kill me. You should not see this, but remember that the gods are always watching, and they will not allow for such cruelty to go unpunished. No one should hurt anyone; and a seer is the voice of the gods, that guides and wards humans from evil. Magnus is about to murder a seer, while the gods are watching, and they will not forget it, nor will forgive him. Stay hidden, and do not make a sound, it is only me that will die today. You and your mother will be heartbroken as it is, but if something happens to you as well, your parents and your little brother will have their hearts broken forever. Astrid, farewell my sweet child. Remember, whatever you see, and whatever you hear, you must stay hidden and don't make a sound!'

She wrapped her scarf around my neck, then covered my face, up to my eyes. Hastily, she threw more branches around me, to hide me better, and walked away. I only moved a few dried leaves, and from where I was hidden, I saw her throwing some seeds to the chickens.

I heard the horses, and I saw the men walking in our garden. One of them was dressed in black clothes, and had a red cloak made of fur, on his shoulders. He must be King Magnus, because the other four men were dressed as the soldiers that I saw sometimes walking through our little village.

I saw the king coming closer to my grandma and I squeezed my legs, bringing my knees closer to my body, in the sitting position that I was in, being afraid of what was going to happen next.

'Old woman, are you the seer that people are talking about? I am King Magnus. I demand you to come with me, in the capital. I could have a great use of a seer, to warn me before anyone would try to attack me, or the kingdom!'

'Yes, King Magnus, I am the seer, but I am living here, in this humble house. I would much rather stay here, but I could always come to bring you news if I have any visions that you should know about.'

'I'm the king, and you do not refuse me! If I told you to come with me, then you come with me, and you should be grateful that I let you live your miserable life. I will not ask you a second time, come with me, and I might let you live.'

'King Magnus, the gods are watching, and you've made them angry with your wrongdoings! Stop, before they come and deliver their justice to you!'

Grandma's words gave me goosebumps, but what scared me more were the three ravens flying above them, cawing loudly, then landed on the snow, close to Magnus and his soldiers, and seemed to be staring at them.

'Do you hear this old whore? If the gods are truly watching, then I will give them something to watch!'

King Magnus pulled his sword quickly, and in a rapid move, I saw the sword cutting my grandma's throat. I inhaled the cold air, fighting with myself not to scream, as she begged me to stay hidden and not make a sound.

I should have stopped them, I should have done something for this not to happen, but I didn't, and now I was looking at her lifeless body, and I was fighting with myself to listen to her pleas and stay hidden, instead of going over to her and hug her.

The men left the house soon, but not before searching the garden and looking through the house, to see if someone else was here. They went just past my hiding place, and now I understood why she hid me here.

I wanted so badly to go to her, but I didn't. I did as she asked me, and after I heard the horses going further away, I finally allowed myself to cry. I heard the ravens again, then I saw them flying away.

Why would gods allow something like this to happen?

Everyone knew that seers are chosen by gods to deliver their warning to humans; seers were chosen to help us, and no one ever dared to hurt a seer.

What King Magnus have just done to my grandma was something unheard of, no one would dare to kill a seer, no one would dare to anger the gods like that, and yet he just did that.

Why did the gods not stop him? Why would they only choose to watch him kill my grandma and not help her in any way?

I cried again, knowing that she was probably right, the ravens had witnessed everything, and they will tell the gods the terrible things that King Magnus did, and how he killed their seer.

She said, 'the gods are watching', and I knew that when grandma had a vision, the gods were showing her what will happen, and they were never wrong.

I started to rock my body, trying to keep calm.

The gods are watching, the gods are watching, the gods are watching...

Chapter 1
Zanos
The gods are watching

I could feel him, he was reaching out to me, and right before he materialised behind me, I could feel his powerful presence. While I was looking at my kingdom, I felt my father's presence, and turned around to face him, straight away. I bowed my head, in respect, then I waited for him to talk first.

'Zanos, my son, you do not have to bow your head before me.'

'Father, it's my choice.'

'I appreciate your respect, Zanos. I want to talk with you, for a bit. I know you are busy here, in your kingdom, and I can see how much you've worked in this world. You could have chosen to do less, and would have been less trouble for you, yet you are here, trying to build and organize this kingdom as best as you can, and I can see the results of your work. Everything here is arranged, everything runs perfectly, especially since you decide to ask the souls that come to your world to help you. And here you are, watching over everything, as things are running smoothly. I am proud of you. This world, full of mountains and rivers, reminds me of earth; only this eerie moonlight reminds me that I am not on earth, anymore.'

I looked at him and felt happiness that he was admiring my work. When he created the world under the earth, I did not imagine that I could make it look so nice, while serving its purpose.

The souls of humans came here after they passed away in their world, and from here, they could either be sent to the world above, where my father, my mother and my sisters lived, together with the souls of the worthy humans; or they could also be sent to the world below, where the evil spirits dwelled, ruled by my brother, Gurun.

Some souls could choose instead to stay here for a while, and when they were ready, I would send them to earth again, to be reborn, and live another life and have another chance to prove that they were worthy to be sent to the world above, to stay there with the gods, and their ancestors.

My kingdom was built after my own liking, and I felt so much pride and happiness seeing Father admiring my work of hundreds of winters. It was made like the human world, but instead of having the sunlight bringing the land to life, I chose the moonlight, without having the moon.

I made all of this for the souls that entered this world, to understand that something was different here; the leaves in the trees were dark green, almost black, and everything was a darker shade here, but somehow, they all looked perfect under the soft light of the moon that was always watching the land.

There were mountains, and some snow, but the grass was a dark green here, and the rivers were a dark blue, shining under the soft light. There were fewer animals here, and they were much different than the ones on earth, because these were no ordinary animals, these were the guardians and the watchers of the land, and they all were under my command.

The birds here were mostly ravens, much bigger that humans were used to, and some of them had feathers only on their wings, while their skeletons were exposed. Their eyes were dark and just their presence alone was enough to intimidate anyone. The ravens were one of my trusted guardians and they were watching every corner of my kingdom for me.

The wolves were much bigger, as well, ready to tear apart any soul that wanted to do harm here, or any creature that had no business being here. I had bears as well, one of the most feared of my guardians. They would communicate between them, and when they considered there was something important that I needed to be told about, they would send me the images that they've seen through their eyes straight to my mind.

No noises, no fuss. Everything was done quietly, and quickly; efficiently, if you'd like to call it like this, but this is how I like it, and it was working perfectly. My world was quiet but could have turned deadly for anything not meant to be here in less than a breath.

For the guidance of the souls passing here, I simply chose to allow the oldest souls living here to take charge. Even Father was impressed, and that made my immortal soul happy. To see him taking happiness and pride of the arrangement that I had done, was the proof that I need that I was ruling over this kingdom as I should.

He was watching over everything from the tallest mountain to the beautiful rivers running over the land, with a smile on his face. The throne he was seated on was made of branches, and it was made by me, just like the one that I was seated on.

I never thought of a queen to sit on this throne, I made it solely for my father to sit next to me and look over my world, next to me, every time he was vising. I had similar but smaller chairs for my siblings, and my mother, but they were not staying as much as Father was, when he was visiting.

'Zanos, aren't you feeling lonely here?'

For the first time, I fully turned my body towards him, not being sure where this question was coming from.

'I never thought of that Father, since you and Mother always visit me, and I also have my sisters coming over as well. I never thought of being lonely, I enjoy being here, and taking care of this world.'

'I see that you enjoy being the ruler of this world, but other than us visiting you, and your guardians and watchers, there is no one here, that you could share your immortality with. I am concerned, and I wish to know that you are happy; you are ruling over this world, all alone.'

'Father, I am happy.'

'What would you say to spend some time on earth, with humans? How would you like that?'

'Honestly, Father, I don't think I would like that, I am dealing with the human souls here, as well. I am content being in this world, and you know I don't spend as much time on earth like my siblings, or you.'

'You should try having some days on earth. Humans are interesting, and some of them, are simply amazing. They would entertain you.'

'They entertain me here, as well.'

'Agree, but Zanos, I think a small vacation, though I could not tell how long it will be, would do you good. Also, I need someone to watch over a human that I chose as the next seer, and I know you would do the best job. There will be some troubling times ahead for this human, and I need someone that I could trust, and someone powerful enough to protect her.'

'Father, if you want me to do anything for you, you know that I would gladly do it. Who would watch over my kingdom while I'm gone?'

'I have asked Mother to come here from time to time and check if everything is going as it should, and I will come as well. You don't need to worry about your kingdom, the way you created it, everything goes smoothly, and your guardians and watchers are doing their work wonderfully.'

'Alright, and regarding this human that you chose as seer, what would you want me to do? Just watch over her?'

'Yes, but I have some specific request; I want you to watch and only interfere if her life is in immediate danger; otherwise, just spend some time without worrying about your kingdom. Go on earth with your wolf form, the silver fur, and black eyes, so the humans around there will understand that you are a guardian sent by gods. If needed or more suitable, change to a raven, to watch from a distance, without other humans realising, but at the beginning I would rather have you walk on earth as a wolf.'

'Has the human visited the world below yet? I don't recall any guardian or watcher telling me something about a new seer, and the previous one that I remember was that woman who died some winters ago.'

'No, the new seer hasn't left earth yet, and I will need you to meet her, and explain to her that she is the new seer. She is the niece of the previous seer, the one that was killed by the king. I told humans that we are watching, and my seers are not to be touched, yet this king killed her, even after she delivered my warnings. This time, I am done watching, and I am angered by the king. I want you to protect my new seer, and I know you are powerful enough to wipe out an army on your own. My seers are not to be messed with, and my warnings are not to be ignored. The king will learn this soon enough.'

'I understand. I forgot that the previous seer was killed, the watchers told me, but you know I don't interfere in the mortal world.'

'I know, that's why I wanted you to watch over her. It will show you a bit of the life of humans, and you could have a break from your duties; we'll cover here for you. Spend some time on earth and will see what's going to happen with the new seer. I hope she will raise to the challenges she will have to face, but you know how it is with humans... sometimes they surprise you.'

'I know Father, they are one of your finest creations, and they never cease to amaze me, either. So much pain, and so much happiness in their souls... I can see the determination some have, and they deserve my respect. Some of them, though, fall to the temptation of the wicked so easily, while some are steadier than the mountains I have in this world, nothing will move them. They are something, I must give this to you.'

'Thank you Zanos, I care about every single being, alive or not. Speaking of the wicked creatures, your brother Gurun, will be the one to call the seer to a lake, but his intentions are not good; I think he is trying to get her drowned. In a few days, she will cave in and go to that lake, and I need you to step in and save her, while I drag your brother back to the world below and have a talk with him.'

As soon as he mentioned Gurun, I could see his face saddening, and I knew why. Gurun, my younger brother, was adored by all of us, but that did not make him happy.

Instead, he started to listen to the evil creatures, the ones that my father created to tempt humans so we could see their worthiness to live in the world above, and soon my brother experienced being jealous of others; he even tried to decapitate me.

Of course, my younger brother was no match for my strength, and I could tell something was wrong before he tried to make his move; I held him easily on the ground, and shouted for Father, deciding not to take revenge on Gurun, and letting Father to take over.

As expected, Father was disappointed in Gurun trying to cut my head, and dragged him to the world below, where the wicked one live, and made him stay there for all this time.

From time to time, he would go and check on him, just for him to realise that he was still listening to the wicked, instead of correcting his ways and be a god that will raise to his name. Gurun asked to be the ruler of the wicked, and Father granted him this, wanting him far away from both humans and gods.

Gurun will live in his own kingdom, where the souls that were corrupted by the wicked ones, were sent there for eternity, to learn from the mistakes that they made during their human life. Father would watch over Gurun, to make sure that he was doing his duties, but I could tell that he was not happy with my brother.

I was also saddened by my brother's choices, but I stepped aside and let Father decide, while I always offered my help, if he needed it; I know he could do everything on its own, since he created everything, but that did not meant that he had to do everything on its own, me and my sisters were always happy to support him with anything he would need.

I was surprised to hear that Gurun still did not learn his lesson and continued to mess with humans and not listened to Father, but I knew that Father would not interfere, unless it was necessary.

However, now, for the first time, I was requested to watch over a human, and I will gladly do it; my brother could try any trick he wanted, I will be there to stop him.

'Father, what would you want me to do regarding Gurun?'

'I will take care of him, but first, in order for everything to happen, I need Gurun to call the seer to the lake, and after that I will take over. You only need to watch over the human. Drag her out from the lake, be in your wolf form to keep her warm, then meet her in the world underneath, to let her know that she will become the next seer. After that, I will let you know about Gurun; I am sure he realised that the previous seer was related to her, and he is now trying to put her in danger, but I will not allow him to do that.'

I nodded, understanding why Gurun was trying to put the human in danger; Father would have chosen her as his next seer, and Gurun, as jealous as he was on everyone, wanted to make sure that there will not be another seer, so he could try to keep the humans away from the right path.

Maybe Father was right, and I needed to do something else for a while, and knowing how powerless humans were, comparing to us, it will probably be like a vacation to me, however, if Gurun decided to interfere with them, I will be there to sweep the ground with him, again.

'What about the human king, Father?'

'He made his choices in his life, and they will all led him to a tragic end, that I will personally deliver. Do not interfere with him, my seer had told him about my warning a long time ago, yet he still doesn't listen, nor changed his wicked ways. This time, I will not only watch him, this time, I will deliver to him what he deserves.'

'When you want me to go above, on earth?'

'Soon, I will call unto you before, so you know when the time has come. Thank you, Zanos. As always, I am happy to visit you, and I knew I could count on your help.'

I nodded my head in his direction, feeling already curious of the new seer and what will happen in the human world.

'You can always count on me, Father.'

Father's presence disappeared completely from the throne next to me, and I turned my attention towards my kingdom; I called with my mind on one of the watchers and soon, I could see the raven flying towards me. I stretched my right hand outwards, and the raven landed swiftly on my forearm. I pulled my hand closer, so I could look directly into the raven's eyes.

'Remind me of the last seer that Father had. Show me her journey, her death, and her staying in my kingdom.'

The raven tilted its head, and I could see everything in my mind; how the woman was born, her childhood, how her daughter, and after that, her niece and nephew were born. The raven showed me how she was killed by the human king. I felt sorry for the child watching everything hidden in a bush, then seeing the seer's family mourning her unjust death.

She did nothing wrong, she only listened to what Father asked her, and now I could understand and agree with Father's decision, it was time he interfere a little, change a few things. I saw the soul of the seer travelling in my world, and I remembered her immediately.

No matter how many souls I saw, she was one that stayed in my mind, and I personally watched over her, during her short stay in my kingdom; her pain, and her regret knowing that her niece had watched her being killed were tearing her apart, and I spent time with her, trying to make her understand that her time on earth was now over, and she needed to make peace with it, so her soul could travel further, where it was meant to be.

I was the one that sent her to the world above, or the world of the gods. She was deserving of living in peace alongside the gods and some of her ancestors. I watched her transform from a sad soul, to a happy one, glad to serve the gods on earth and the world above. She accepted her human life, and now she was at peace with her life, enjoying the wonders of living amongst gods. She was deserving of being in Father's gardens, the truly most beautiful places in his creation.

I opened my eyes and looked at the raven.

'Thank you, watcher.'

The raven bowed its head, then stretched its wing and flew away.

I turned my eyes to the world below me. I stood up and started to descend from the mountain. I had to prepare the guardians and the watchers for my absence, but I wasn't worried, knowing that they alone could handle everything that needed to be done, and especially since Father has told me that he will come here often to make sure that everything in my world was alright.

I haven't been away from my kingdom for as long as I could remember, and I did not necessarily want to go away on earth, but I wanted to help Father, so I looked at this as a chance to take a well-deserved break from my duties as the god of the world underneath.

The souls would be in good care with my guardians and watchers, and I trusted my parents and my sisters to take good care of my kingdom. Soon, it will be time for me to see the new seer, and I hope she will raise to her title; her grandmother has had a great life and died as a well-loved and respected seer.

I only hoped that Father will allow me to help him in delivering some justice to that low human king because I was enraged of how he killed the seer. I would love to help father and interfere a little myself, even though he didn't need my help; Father could have destroyed and rebuild a new world on its own just fine.

I took another look at my world, and I smiled.

Everything was alright here, and it will be alright when I will be done with what I needed to do on earth.

The time when gods were only watching, it's over.

Now, the gods are done watching.

Chapter 2
Astrid
The god of the souls

I put the cloak on my shoulders and headed outside, to feed the chickens. As always, I would stop and look a few more moments at the place where my grandma hid me ten winters ago...

Time has passed, but sometimes it felt like it happened yesterday; it still hurts me just as much, and there was nothing that I could do to make it better. That awful king was now better than ever, and we could not accuse him of the murder that he committed, since everyone was now afraid of him.

There were people saying that this is how he built his way towards the throne, on the bodies of people he killed one by one, to take them out of his way, for good. Most people lost someone because of the king, and everyone knew someone who disappeared because of the king.

Worst of all, he would send his soldiers to patrol around the villages, and every time they did, they took more of our animals, give them to the leader, who will then pay some coins in exchange for the goods taken by the soldiers, and the king's pockets grew larger every time his soldiers visited the villages, while we became poorer.

The few men and women who tried to fight against king's greed simply vanished from the face of earth and were never heard of again, so we just lowered our heads and tried to stay out and far away from the soldiers; you did not want to catch their attention. There was no hope for things to get better and all we could do was to keep our mouths shut and no matter how hard it was, allow the soldiers to take away the fruit of our hard labour.

The gods seemed to forget about us, and no matter how much I prayed to Father and Mother, I haven't received a sign from them. Since grandma died, there wasn't another seer chosen, so we had no way of knowing if gods were still looking our way. I believed that they were seeing everything that was happening, and I still hoped that one day, they would help us to get rid of King Magnus.

I looked at my mother sweeping the garden. She was sad as well, she did not like to come over this area of our garden, it reminded her of one of her worst days, when she discovered that her mother was killed, and her daughter was struggling to find words to tell her what happened. That day had aged her, and for some time after, I barely saw her smiling.

Birta, my beautiful mother, had managed to hold herself together, take care of me, and tried her best to make me forget what I saw, and insisted that my father would teach her, me, and my brother Vilmar how to defend ourselves.

Since that day, we all had a small, sharp knife tied to us, underneath our clothes, and we had different weapons, concealed in and around the house, so we could at least have a chance to defend ourselves.

My father spent days at a time making us hiding places, and teaching us the paths around our house, and we managed to find a cave in the forests nearby, hide some stuff in that cave, in case we needed to retreat there, and we made sure to keep it hidden from anyone else.

That awful day had destroyed my innocence and had made my younger brother feel more responsible than he should, at his young age. Vilmar stopped playing and started instead to learn how to fight, to sharpen blades alongside our father, and more than ever, was accompanying him on his hunting trips.

Now, we always stick together, no one was left alone anymore. One child with one parent, always. They would not leave us two alone again, out of fear of something horrible happening to both of us at the same time. I understood them, and I never argued about the new rules, because something has changed; I was afraid, too. I've seen something that has also changed me.

I stopped caring about other people, other than my own family. I knew, I was at the age that I should have thought of getting married and having my own children, but even though some men tried to propose me, I wasn't even considering them. Luckily, my family has not forced me to get married, and I choose to stay with them.

Marriage wasn't on my mind, but I would be happy if my brother would choose to get married and have his own family. He was too young now, not yet a man, but a few winters too old to be considered a child; yet he was so respectful and supporting of our family for his young age that I just knew that one day he would make a great father.

'Astrid, come to the lake...'

I heard this deep voice close to me, so I quickly turned around to see if there was anyone behind me; there wasn't.

My mother's face grew paler instantly and came to check what happened. I assured her quickly that it was the wind that startled me, but I did not tell her anything about what the voice was telling me.

Could it be the gods?

We knew that sometimes, one of the close relatives of the seer, could become the next chosen seer as well; I never considered that it could be me, but my mother had received no sign from the gods.

No one had been chosen as a seer in the last ten winters, and I would be surprised to be the next one, but I will not back away. If the gods chose you to be their voice on earth, that was one of the highest honours that anyone could receive.

Everything that was happening around us, was happening because of the people in power, but when gods were angry, they could help us. A new seer could awaken the faith and the courage in all of us, since we have been bowing our heads and kept our mouths shut for far too long.

People in the village have lost their faith in our gods few winters ago, but me and my family, we still believed in them. They saw what happened to their last seer, and this is why they thought we would not have another one: we weren't deserving of a seer. But when the gods will choose to come on earth again and set things right, I was sure that King Magnus will be punished for all his wrongdoings.

That night, after we ate our dinner, and I went to sleep, I heard that deep voice again, calling me to the lake. I opened my eyes wide and tried to find the source of the voice in the darkness around me. I must've made a bit of noise because my mother entered my room, sleepily.

'Astrid, is everything alright?'

She placed the candle on the small table and gave me a hug. She looked around the room, then looked back at my face.

'Mother, tomorrow I need to go to the lake.'

She frowned, then looked at me as if she wanted to ask me more but chose not to.

'It's alright. I'll come with you.'

'No mother, I need to go alone. I'll try to leave early in the morning, so I won't be gone for long, and I can come back quickly to help you around the house. Let my brother go hunting with father, we need to gather as much as possible before the winter comes. We could smoke the meat in the evening and keep some of it for the winter.'

I tried to talk about something else, but my mother realised why I wanted to go to the lake; I was called there. She knew that I did not had feelings from any man living in the village, and there would be no other reason that will make me leave her alone, even daytime.

'Astrid, it's the gods?'

I nodded, and I could see a beautiful smile blooming on her face. She still hasn't lost her hope in the gods, and the fact that I was called by them, it gave her hope that justice will be brought to her mother's cruel killer.

She kissed my forehead and left the room. I went back to my bed, deciding that tomorrow I will start to get ready and leave as soon as I wake up.

***

'Astrid, come to the lake...'

I opened my eyes, and I realised that I was in my room. I stood up sleepily, and removed the blanket, remembering the voice that I heard yesterday, as well. I started to get dressed, then I finally put my warm cloak on my shoulders.

In the kitchen, my mother was boiling some dried blueberries. She handed me a cup with her delicious warm tea, and I drank it, feeling grateful for the warm beverage that was waking me up.

'Good morning, Astrid.'

She looked at me, and she understood that I had to go. I saw her frowning, feeling her fear, but at the same time, I knew that she trusted the gods.

'Don't be afraid mother, the gods are always watching. I am sure that this time, they will not allow something awful to happen again. If they called me to the lake, I cannot delay this any longer, grandma would not like it if we will keep the gods waiting.'

I hugged her tight, hoping that I would see her again, soon, and I left the house. We did not have a horse anymore, since the last one we had was taken away by the soldiers, so I knew that I had some walking to do, in order to reach the lake.

It was cold this morning, and I could see small puddles of water already frozen, so it meant that it won't be long until we have our first snow this winter. I could see my own breath, and I could feel the cold air hurting my throat. I walked fast, not knowing what to expect once I will reach the lake, but I trusted the gods, so I knew that I must follow that voice.

I had the feeling that something was following me, and I looked around. Through the trees, I could see the biggest silver wolf. I stopped walking and looked at it. It was the biggest wolf I ever saw in my life, and its black eyes seemed to look straight at my soul.

I gasped and looked in awe at its size.

I have never seen such a breath-taking creature before, and I understood that it was sent by the gods, this was no ordinary animal. I felt that he was here to watch over me, and I had nothing to fear from him, so I continued my walk to reach the lake. The wolf kept walking, keeping some distance between us, while it was following me.

Soon, I reached the lake, and to my surprise the whole lake was frozen, its surface being covered in a thick layer of ice. In the middle of the lake, I saw a red flame burning, above the ice.

I knew instinctively that that is where I needed to go, so without having any doubts, or fear, I stepped on the ice. The wolf came near me, and started to howl, trying to push me away gently, towards the ground, instead of letting me go further on the ice. I placed my hand on its soft fur, and while my heart was beating strongly in my chest, I petted his head.

'I know guardian, but the voice called me here. I need to go to that flame.'

I kept walking with the wolf next to me, and I reached the flame quickly.

Why would the gods bring me here, in the middle of the lake? As soon as I touched the flame, I heard the cracking of the ice around me, and I fell in the cold water. I tried to grab onto something, to pull myself out, but I couldn't, as the ice broke as soon as I tried to hold onto it.

The last image that I saw, before I fell in the darkest, deepest water of the lake, was the wolf, looking at me from above and trying to pull me out, but my hand slipped through his teeth. I was frozen, and I could not fight the cold, as I was sinking deeper, in the dark water of the lake.

I closed my eyes and felt the cold water and the darkness embracing me.

***

When I opened my eyes again, I was back on the side of the river, on my own feet. I looked confused at the clothes that I had on; they were dry, and I was dry, as well. I knew that I fell in the lake, but strangely, I wasn't cold or wet.

Above me, I could hear a raven cawing. I looked up, and I saw the biggest, white raven, flying in circles, above me.

I gasped, realising that this was not earth anymore. Grandma told me long ago that when the gods are bringing a soul in the world underneath, to meet them, the guardians of the gods are usually large white animals, so the soul will know that is about to meet the gods. The guardians of the world underneath were different, so that meant that I was not dead yet, just that I was not on earth anymore.

I saw the raven flying towards the forest nearby, and cawing back at me, as if asking me to follow him. I started to walk towards the guardian, knowing that I have nothing to fear. As soon as I reach the edge of the forest, I saw a big, white wolf waiting for me.

This wolf had white eyes and came closer to me. I dropped to me knees, and I hugged its large throat, knowing that I don't have to be afraid of him. As soon as I let him go, he turned around, howled once, and started to walk away slowly. I followed him through the forest, not knowing where it will take me, but having faith that the gods were watching, and they were taking care of me.

I walked a long time, following the wolf, but I did not feel tired. The sun started to set, and the forest got dark, however, I felt no worry or fear, and I knew that I was meant to be there, so I continue walking behind the wolf.

At some point, the beautiful guardian stopped, and I could see in front of him, a large cave. Near the entrance there was a white bear waiting and I understood that the wolf had to bring me to the next guardian, the bear.

As soon as I came closer to the bear, I heard him making soft noises like he was welcoming me, then turned around and waited for me. I got closer to the bear, and he started to walk slowly, on his massive paws. I followed him through the cave, feeling grateful that from place to place, I could see a torch, illuminating the dark corridors of the cave.

I kept walking, following the bear, and soon, I saw him stopping in front of a pitch-black corridor. I understood that I had to go further on my own, and without any fear, I stepped into the darkness.

I could not see anything, and I had no idea which way I needed to go, so I extended my hands in front of me, trying to make sure that I will not hit my face on the walls of the cave.

As I kept walking in the darkness, I felt another hand catching mine and pulling me gently in one direction. This hand was much larger than mine, but it felt warm, and even though I could not see who was there in the cave, with me, I followed the direction in which I was pulled.

Somewhere, far away from me, I could see a throne made of branches, and illuminated by two torches, one on each side of the throne. I frowned, when I realised that the flames were blue, but I understood that this was not earth anymore; it must be the world underneath, the world of the god that was taking care of all the souls of the humans, the eldest son of Father and Mother. He was known as the god of the souls, and you would meet him only if you were dead, or a seer.

While he was pulling me towards the throne, I could see his back, as we were getting closer to the torches. He was so much taller than me, and even one head taller than the strongest soldiers that I saw in the village; I would only reach his chest, while the strongest soldiers would barely reach his shoulders.

I was impressed and a bit intimidated by his frame, and I could see his long, silver hair, going down, just under his bottom. His hair was let loose, covering the black cloak on his shoulders, and I could barely take my eyes away from him, admiring the long, silky strands, that were shining in the delicate light coming from the torches.

He let go of my hand and walked towards the throne. I stopped walking once I was behind him and watched him as he turned around and sat on the throne.

I gasped once I finally saw his face, never seeing such beauty before. His eyes were black, and his pale face was framed by the long, silver strands.

He had thick, silver brows, a bit darker than his hair, and his long, straight nose made me to stare for a few moments at his alluring lips, that were fitting his face perfectly. His sharp jaw was completing his unreal beauty, and while I was staring at him, I saw him looking at me.

I almost felt ashamed to look so plain in front of a god; I realised immediately that he was the god of souls, since his beauty was nothing alike the men of the earth.

I felt so plain and simple, small and unsignificant, in front of this perfect looking god. I felt my cheeks blushing, and lowered my head, feeling ashamed of my peasant like appearance.

'Astrid, look at me.'

His deep voice reverberated off the walls in the cave, and I felt my chest vibrating, like it was soothing me and vibrating deep, inside my body.

'We are watching, and we are here. Wake up, Astrid.'

As soon as he talked again, I felt gratitude to be able to look at his eyes for a few moments more. When he said that they were watching, I flinched and understood. He was indeed a god, just as I assumed.

When he told me to wake up, I started to blink rapidly, and I closed my eyes. I opened my eyes and saw that I was walking in a forest, and an awfully looking bear was near me. This bear seemed to be enraged, its fur was dirty and missing in some places, but from out of nowhere, a silver wolf jumped on him, put him down, and tore his throat with one swift move of its mouth.

I screamed, and when I blinked again, I saw something else. In front of me, there was a warrior whose face I could not see that was fighting a brown wolf, while behind me, I saw great crowd of people. I turned to look at the warrior fighting the wolf again, and I saw his dark blonde braided, his black clothes, and his armour shining in the moonlight.

I had a torch in my hand, and when I looked down, I saw the silver wolf staying protectively, in front of me. He was growling softly, but I placed a hand on his back, and he stopped growling. Standing on its paws, he was tall, up to my hips, and I could feel the warmth radiating from him being so close to me.

The wolf turned its head to look at me, and I froze, seeing his black eyes. They felt so familiar, just like the eyes of the god in the cave. Then, I saw the wolf turning his head to look at the warrior, just as the warrior was plunging his sword deep into the brown wolf. People behind me were cheering happily, celebrating the killing of the crazy wolf.

I blinked, and when I opened my eyes again, I woke up in my room. I saw my mother asleep on a chair, next to the table, while a small candle illuminating my room. Something wet and warm was touching my hand, and I looked to the side of the bed, with my eyes opened wide in shock, just to see the silver wolf with black eyes looking back at me.

'Are you a guardian?' I asked the wolf quietly, trying not to scare my mother.

To my surprise, I saw the wolf nodding his head once, and I understood everything. I met the god of the souls, and the dreams that I had, were two visions. He said that the gods are watching, and the gods are here. He must have sent his guardian, a wolf that was resembling him, to make sure that I was safe.

Wait, I had visions…

That meant that I was now, the next seer. I looked at the wolf, and saw him curling on the floor, next to my bed and closing his eyes. He was here, next to me, the whole time I was asleep, and he watched over me. I slowly rose from the bed, and touched my mother, that was sleeping and seemed uncomfortable, on the chair.

'Mom, wake up, are you alright?'

I saw mother opening her eyes sleepily and looking confused at me. Then, she smiled and hugged me tight.

'Astrid, my daughter, I was so worried for you, I thought we almost lost you'.

She stood up from the chair, and hug me so tight, that it brought tears to my eyes. I understood her, and I felt so sorry that she was afraid and went through this struggle, because of me.

'I'm so sorry, mother. I did not want to scare you, but I had to go to the lake. What happened after I fell into the lake?'

'After you left home, I waited some time, then I took your father and Vilmar and we all came to the lake to look out for you. When we got there, we found you on the side on the lake, and this silver wolf was covering you, keeping you warm. I know he must be a guardian sent from the gods; I never have, in my whole life, saw a wolf like this. He allowed us to check on you, then your father went to bring someone from the village with a horse so we can bring you home. You have been sick for almost three days; tomorrow morning will be the fourth day since you left to go the lake.'

'I'm so sorry you were worried, mother, it was never my intention to scare you.'

'Astrid, as soon as I saw the wolf, I knew you are protected. Gods are watching, I can feel it. I never felt my faith so strong like the last days. Yes, I am worried for my daughter, but at the same time, I can see that you are being taken care of, and I am only grateful to our gods for sending their guardian to watch over you. Have you had any vision, Astrid?'

I nodded my head, and told her about the cave, and the two dreams that I had. I told her about the god of the souls, that I saw in the cave, and while I was blushing, I admitted to her that I have never saw someone as beautiful as the god with silver hair, and I could have looked at him for days, and not be bored.

My mother took a long look at the wolf, then tilted her head and seemed to be lost, deep in her thoughts. The wolf was looking at her, but with a curious expression. I saw my mother talking, but she was talking to the wolf, not to me.

'Will you allow me to touch you?'

The wolf stood up and came to her. I looked shocked at him, as he seemed to understand that my mother was asking for his permission. He was taller and bigger than any of the wolves I have seen in the forest and was taking a lot of space in my room. I saw my mother kneeling in front of him, as she hugged his throat, and leaned her head on the wolf's head, completely trusting him.

'I beg you guardian, please take care of my daughter. My mother was killed by King Magnus, ten winters ago. I beg you guardian, do not allow something bad to happen to my daughter. I have faith in you, and I know the gods are watching. Please tell the gods that I am grateful to have my daughter being chosen as the next seer.'

The wolf nodded once and seemed to try to embrace my mother back. His black eyes were so unusual, but they were so expressive, that it felt my mother was talking to another person, and not to a wolf.

My mother stood up, looked at me and smiled.

'We knew that he is more than a wolf, we have never seen such a big wolf and one with black eyes before. Maybe the gods have sent your guardian to look like this, to remind you of the god you met in the cave, so you know that is sent by them. I know that we will have troubled times ahead, but have faith in them, my daughter.'

I nodded my head, realising that a few days have passed since I fell into the lake. Something was changed, and even though I was asleep for days, I felt stronger than I have felt in a long time. I felt protected, and looking at the massive wolf in my room, I understood that I was.

'Mother, please do not tell anyone but father that I had visions. Let him know, so he won't be worried, but for the time being, no one else needs to know.'

'I am afraid that Jon has seen us bringing you home. He tried to come closer, but the wolf chased him away with a few growls. He was saying that he only needed to borrow something from us, but I knew that he was scooping around.'

My mother's face was worried, but I tried to calm her.

'Do not worry, mom. He saw the wolf, so I know he won't dare to come too close to our house again; and even if he goes around talking about it, the wolf presence will keep the people away.'

'People will talk soon. The wolf was so protective of you, even your father realised that he was watching over you. I think he must have understood that you have become a seer. His friend was saying that our people did not have another seer in such a long time. You know that there are a lot of people that do not like King Magnus, and this time, if you see any soldiers coming close to you, run away with the wolf to our cave. You have everything you might need there for several days, and I trust the wolf to keep you safe. I don't know how to explain it myself, I know there are so many dangers in you being a seer, but I can see the gods trying to protect you, as well. I will let you sleep, my daughter; rest know, and we will talk tomorrow.'

My mother left the room, and I looked at the wolf, and ran my hand through its soft fur, touching its head gently. I saw the wolf closing its eyes, seeming to enjoy my touch. I giggled, realising that a nice, soft caress was appreciated even by the god's guardian.

38

I went to the table, and arranged the candle in its support, to make sure that it will run out on its own, without risking a fire, then went back to my bed, and covered myself with the blanket.

I saw the wolf climbing on the bed, then felt him curling its massive body next to my legs and watched as he was placing his head on my knees, closing his eyes, and starting to breathe slower. I closed my eyes and kept thinking about the gorgeous god that I saw in the cave.

Will I ever see him again?

Chapter 3
Valtyr
The army of hope

As always, we were on our horses, riding ahead to scout the area. We had to make sure there were none of King Magnus' soldiers in the area we chose to camp. I looked at my right and saw Gertrud scouting every tree around us, constantly watching the area.

Ahead of us, Tomas and Viktor were riding silently, looking constantly through the forest. Viktor signalled us to stop.

'Valtyr, we have been on our horses for some time. I told you, this area, north of Frostheim, is safe. I remember of some stories that the cave of gods is somewhere here, nearby, but we will not bother to find it. Instead, I will climb up that tree and look around us. I think it will be safe for us to camp here, for a few nights. When I signal you Tomas, just ride straight to the boys and tell them to camp here.'

Quickly, Viktor hopped from his horse, and we followed so we could stretch our legs a bit and allow the horses to rest. Just as he said, Viktor went straight to the tallest tree, and started to climb it, using the funny hooks he had, to have a safe grasp on the tree.

I'll be damned, I still could not understand how such a strong man like Viktor, that could send anyone straight to sleep with a punch, was able to climb the trees so quickly. I guess that's why they called him Viktor the Bear, he was amazing like that.

Gertrude was watching him, mesmerized, just like me. I couldn't blame her; the man had some tricks up his sleeve.

'You two, stop eyeing Viktor like that, I'm not sharing him', said Tomas, while smiling proudly.

'Honestly, I wouldn't share him either. You two are something else and I am happy to see you smiling, Tomas; really, I am happy for you and Viktor.'

'I know Gertrud, but remember, you will always be the mother of my child. Me and Viktor would give our lives to keep you and Petur safe, always know that.'

'And I will give my life to save all of you', I added looking at them.

I saw Tomas and Gertrud smiling, and I looked up at Viktor. We were united by the same goals, but we had love and respect for each other.

Gertrud nodded, and I never felt prouder of them. She married Tomas some time ago, but she decided to separate from him, after what happened to her. She never found someone else, but we all knew why.

We all understood and did not ask any more questions; we all knew why. King Magnus had kidnapped her, and has used her for his sick, demented pleasure. Gertrude has managed to escape, but she could not tolerate being touched by a man, and Tomas understood and gave space to his wife, while trying to do its best to help her.

I heard of the woman taken by the king that managed to escape, and I went to talk with Tomas and Gertrude. I proposed them to join my cause, and we were all united by our hate. I brought them closer to the village where I was raised by my aunt, Svartar, a safe village, away from Jotun; and that was how Tomas met Viktor.

While we all tried to rally against the king; we knew that we needed a big army to match the king's army of mercenaries. We were united by the wish to bring change to a kingdom ruled by a greedy and cruel king, and we soon found other people that joined us. We constantly recruited more, and constantly trained the people, teaching them how to fight.

In this situation, Gertrude was brilliant, and she dedicated every moment that she could spare to plan more strategies, more training, and more methods of having people joining us, without putting anyone in danger, and more importantly, without the king finding out about us.

I saw Viktor signalling from the top of the tree that the area was safe, and Tomas hopped back on his horse.

'Valtyr, I will bring the rest of us here, so we can camp. I will leave some to guard the area, so we know if anyone is approaching us, then we will come straight here. Make a fire for us, and I will meet you, back here, with the others.'

I nodded and went to tie the horses so they could rest for the time being.

'I will go around the trees and bring you some branches so we can start a fire. Try not to make too much noise, maybe I will stumble on a rabbit, or something. I know the boys have food with them, but I am hungry now.'

Gertrud left, and I watched Viktor coming down from the tree.

'Valtyr, there is a river nearby. I'll go and bring us some water.'

I nodded, and started to pile some branches together, to get the fire ready.

Lately, we were moving our camp often, never staying more than four nights in the same place, trying to travel from village to village, to find other people willing to fight against King Magnus, and join the Warrior's army. Only a few people knew that I was the Warrior, and we kept that a secret. The fewer people knew, the better.

Gertrude was the one to visit the villages and try to explain to people about what we wanted to do. She came up with the idea that our sign should be four small stones, left at the entrance of the houses, and that is how we knew who to approach.

Of course, we will all follow Gertrude around to make sure that she was safe, but we kept some distance between us, not to raise any suspicions, in case we met any of the king's soldiers.

There were people knowing already about us and our cause, before we even had the chance to speak, and our group grew larger as the days went by. Now, we only needed to travel to Frostheim, one of the few villages that we haven't been to yet and see if we can find any villagers that wanted to join us.

We will camp for the time being here, then we will join our main group, that already had five hundred people willing to fight against the king, safely hidden in the forest around Bolstadir, at a safe distance from Jotun, the capital of the kingdom.

I knew King Magnus, and I knew that he had all his army in and around Jotun, but he did not want to send them away from him, unless they were out to take whatever they could from people, just to exchange what they took for gold. Magnus knew that he was hated by so many people, so he turned Jotun into his personal fortress.

What Magnus did not know, was that more than half of his army was hating him just as much as the rest of the people, and they were ready to turn their weapons against him; they only needed someone to unite the people against him, and the Warrior was the one to bring everyone together against King Magnus.

Soon, I saw the rest of our small army, twenty more, joining us, led by Tomas. As soon as they unmounted their horses, they tied them to the trees around us, and they started to set the tents straight away.

There was no time to lose, and it was almost dark outside. The fire that I made was providing us with enough light so we could see what we were doing, and in no time, everything was set for the night, and I saw some men preparing the meat that we managed to save, so we could all eat something before going to sleep.

After everything we needed to do was done, we all gathered around the fire. It was cold outside, but the fire kept us warm, and the smell of the meat was bringing a smile on our faces.

'Valtyr, are we going tomorrow to the village to see if we can find more people?'

'Yes, we will do as we always did. Gertrud goes first, and we keep our distance from her, and between us. We will all meet in the market, but we will come from different directions, so it doesn't look like we all came together, at the same time.'

'There's so many people joining us, we weren't expecting so many men to want to leave everything and fight against Magnus.'

'It tells a lot about the kind of scum that Magnus really is, not that we did not know it already', added Gertrud, and we all nodded in silence, agreeing with her.

Meanwhile, the meat was ready, and we finished it quickly. We drank some fresh water and decided to stay around the fire a bit longer. Yes, wine or ale, would have been better, but we did not have the luxury to afford being caught drunk, in case we would have been attacked suddenly.

We all agreed it was painful to stay this long without drinking a drop of wine, but it was necessary for us to be able to fight at any moment.

I heard some commotion, and I saw one of the men stationed away from us to keep an eye of the area, dragging someone by the neck.

'Guys, I found this one snooping around. I brought him to you', said the man, then pushed forward the one he caught.

I stood up and came closer to him, trying to understand as much as I could about him, while I was looking at the man, head to toe; he was not a fighter, I realised as I was assessing his thin frame, and his clothes looked like something that most of the villagers would wear.

Maybe he was someone from Frostheim and he stumble upon our camp by mistake?

'Please, do not hurt me. I heard that you were sent here by the Warrior, and I have very important information to give you, but I also need some coins, I am poor and need them coins to buy me some food. Surely you will show me some generosity, because believe me, the Warrior would want to know what I have to say.'

Scum, he was a scum, I decided quickly, but I will not have him dismissed, until I will hear what he had to say.

I signalled for Viktor to give him sone coins.

'What information you have?'

'Great news, a new seer has been chosen, it's a girl from Frostheim, Astrid is her name. She went away from her house, and when her parents brought her back home, I saw it with my own eyes, there was a wolf like no other following her. Silver, with black eyes. The funny thing is that she was alive but in a deep sleep, and they put her on a horse so they could carry her, but I know something. Her grandmother was the previous seer. Surely, that was no ordinary wolf. Would not the great Warrior have a use of a seer, so she could tell him visions about how to defeat King Magnus? Told you, what I have to say, it's well worth the coins.'

The man was laughing and rubbing his hands together.

I do not like him; I decided straight away.

I went to Viktor and whispered quietly to him to send someone to follow this man and see what he was up to. Most of all, I was afraid of him turning us to king's soldiers, but the fact that he was willing to sell people like that for some coins was annoying me greatly.

Even if what he was saying was true, and the girl was the next seer, people should stick together and protect her, not sell her to the first stranger, especially people from her own village, since we all knew how much King Magnus hated anyone that still had faith in our gods.

'What is your name?'

'Jon, great sir. I live close to the girl's house, and I will come back if I see something else. Many thanks for your generosity.'

I dismissed him quickly, being disgusted by lows like him; he sold the girl in a blink of an eye for some coins, just like my parents were sold by a greedy neighbour, years ago. My father barely managed to save me, but him and my mother have paid the price, when King Magnus sent his mercenaries to silence them forever.

After King Ketiln was killed by Magnus, my father was in great danger, and he knew that, as he arranged quickly for my aunt Helga, to come and take me far away from Jotun, the capital of the kingdom.

Helga has managed to sneak on a horse with me, but my parents were killed by Magnus, as he would have been King's Ketiln favourite to be on the throne. Ketiln had no children, but everyone knew how much he liked my father and how much he trusted him, and that made Magnus to want to eliminate my father after King Ketiln.

All this effort, just for a greedy bastard to run and tell Magnus that he saw me being sneaked out in the middle of the night on a horse, and Magnus using this as pretext to have my parents assassinated.

Right now, I had another bastard selling information about a poor girl, and I promised myself that he will not go unpunished. For the moment, someone will keep an eye on him, but I will sort him out for good.

Gertrud took a seat next to me, close to the fire. I could see her frowning, and I knew she did not liked Jon, either.

'Don't worry Gertrud, I will make sure that the bastard will not go to King Magnus' soldiers. If he tries to, someone will take care of him, for me. I already know everything I need to about him, judging by how fast he sold his neighbours to the first unknown man that would open his purse.'

'Agreed. Jon is one shitty neighbour. Glad we are on the same page about him. I wanted to ask about something else, though… Shouldn't you go and meet the new seer?'

I turned to look at her, appreciating her clever mind.

While I was caught with my own emotions, I have not considered to meet the seer.

Gertrude was right; she could be an incredible help for us, sent by the gods, and I would have been a fool not to go and meet her, at least.

'Have I told you how much I appreciate your sharp mind, Gertrude? The gods have blessed me with your presence, woman.'

Gertrude giggled, and nodded her head, accepting my compliment. I saw her frowning, and I waited for her to finish her thoughts, knowing that she most likely saw a possibility that I didn't.

'Valtyr, while I will admit that the seer is not our responsibility, we still need to make sure that she is safe. Jon is the first to betray her, but what if there are more? The seer is chosen by the gods, and whatever happens, people need to make sure that she is safe. Regardless of her wanting to help us or not; that is something that will be decided by the gods, but do you think that she will be safe in her house? We need to hide her, if she doesn't want to help us, that's fine, but she is more than a girl, she is the voice of gods and she must be protected from King Magnus.'

I nodded, agreeing with Gertrude. She was right, the seer was a blessing that the gods sent to us, and we needed to make sure that she was safe, and she was hidden before the king will find out about her.

'I will go tomorrow to meet her, and we can go in the village after that. Just as you said, she is a blessing, and we need to make sure that she is safe, no matter what happens in the kingdom. I will try to talk with her and her family, and see what they think, maybe she will choose to join us.'

Gertrude nodded and looked around us.

Everyone had come closer to the fire, and they listened to our conversation, as we were not trying to hide our thoughts, since we were surrounded by people that I knew I could trust. They all agreed that the seer had to be protected, and if she chose not to come with us, maybe she will consider relocating to some of our secret hiding houses; somewhere where no one would know her, or her story.

I stood up and we all agree to take one more walk around the camp, to make sure that our location was not compromised; Jon had managed to find out about us, and I knew I could not trust him.

After I was satisfied knowing that our camp was still unknown and no one was snooping around, I went to sleep. People had already decided who will stay on guard at night, and how they will change each other during the night.

I went to my small tent, change to sleeping clothes, and fell asleep within moments.

***

As soon as I heard movements around my tent, I opened my eyes quickly, and my hand went straight to the dagger that I had underneath my pillow. I cracked the entrance from the tent just so I could see what was happening, and calmed instantly when I realised that Gertrude was waking up, and walking around the tent, sleepily.

'Good morning, Valtyr. How was your sleep?'

'Good morning, Gertrude. Good, thank you. Did you rest well?'

'Yes. Tomas and Viktor had me sleep with them, so they can make sure I will not be cold, and I slept like a baby, safe and warm.'

I giggled, knowing how persuasive Tomas and Viktor could be when it came to Gertrude. Even though Gertrude's marriage with Tomas had ended, the friendship between them was so beautiful, that it soothed my soul.

Not only that Viktor had no resentment towards her, but he liked her, and made sure that he and Tomas were Gertrude's shadows, always checking on her, and taking care of her; excepting the small, heated moments when Tomas and Viktor were sneaking out, the tree of them were inseparable.

They were a bigger family, and love, respect, and care for each other, were holding them together. Their fucking interest will separate them for some short moments, but otherwise, you will always find them together, and I made sure that whatever tasks they had to help me with, it could be done in three, so I could make sure that the two men will always watch over Gertrude.

Tomas and Viktor left the tent, and I could see Viktor looking around for Gertrude. Without saying a word, I pointed the direction in which Gertrude left, and Tomas followed. Soon, the three came back together, and we all stood next to the fire, so we can warm up a bit.

'Valtyr, shall we meet the seer first?', asked Viktor, and I nodded.

'First, we will go and meet her, then we will go to the village. Gertrude is right, even if she doesn't want to join us, we still need to make sure that she is safely hidden from the king.'

We all went inside our tents, to prepare for the road, and after we ate something, we went towards the horses, so we can meet the seer.

'As always, I will ride first, and you three will stay behind me. Make sure that no one is watching the seer's house and will see what happens from there.'

They nodded, and we hopped on our horses. I left the camp first, with them behind me. I followed the directions that Jon gave us, and soon after we came out of the forest, I could see the small houses that he described.

I could not see Gertrude, Tomas, or Viktor anymore, but knowing them, they had already hidden the horses somewhere, and they were close behind me, waiting to intervene, in case of something happened.

I wished I would have been more presentable, in front of a seer, but my black clothes and black cloak had to do. I had braided my hair, and had my beard long, just as I always kept it. As always, I had my sword with me, and my daggers, just in case.

I approached the house and saw a man coming out to meet me. He was as tall as I am, and I could tell that he was just wary of me, trying to decide if I was dangerous, or around his house by mistakes. His clothes were simple, much like the other people in the villages had, but I quickly took notice of the dagger at his waist.

'Good day, stranger, are you lost?'

'No. I wanted to come here, to this house, and if you give me a bit of your time, I will explain myself why.'

I quickly told him that I found out about the seer, and Orn, as he introduced his name to me, asked me panicked if I'm from the king's army. I wasn't sure how much I could trust him, but I told him that I had nothing to do with the king.

I could see his face relaxing straight away, and realised that he too, hated Magnus. Without telling too much, I explained to him that I was with the Warrior, and I could see relief on his face.

I told him that I wanted to meet the new seer, and above everything, I wanted to make sure that she is safe from the king's claws. Orn nodded and invited me to enter the small garden, then he showed me his house.

I did not know what to expect, but I was at peace knowing that my friends were close nearby, and they will make sure that no one will come closer to this house. I could protect myself just fine. The small hallway was leading me to a big kitchen, and I could see a woman cooking something, probably Orn's wife.

At the table, a girl was seated, and as soon as she heard me entered, she stood up and turned around to face me. My breath stopped for a few moments. She was so beautiful, and her dark hair complimented her pale face. I wanted to hug her, but instead I extended my hand, and she extended hers.

Her small hand was soft and warm, and I held her hand with great pleasure, while I was getting lost in her dark green eyes, reminding me of the trees from the forest. Her hair was dark, braided, and her braid was resting on her round shoulder.

I could see her curvy frame through the simple dress, and my mouth watered at the sight of her round hips, and her generous breasts. She looked like she was made to be held in tight hugs, and I had to remind myself why I was there.

'My name is Valtyr, and I am here to…', I started, but I stopped when I saw her looking through me, her eyes growing bigger, and her beautiful, round mouth opened slightly, like something was behind me, that surprised her. I turned to look around, without letting go of her hand, and I could only see Orn there.

I covered her hand, with my other hand, and kneel in front of her, understanding that she was having a vision. As soon as I kneeled, I saw the biggest silver wolf approaching me, and felt him sniffing me. I have never seen such a big beast, and I did not make a move, looking straight into the black eyes of the wolf. This was no regular wolf, this was a guardian sent by the gods, I realised.

Soon, she started blinking rapidly and looked at me again. I stood up and watch as the wolf laid lazily on the floor, with its black eyes on me.

'You had a vision, didn't you?'

She looked at me, frowned, then pulled her small hand away from mine.

'Who are you?'

'I'm Valtyr, and I came here to meet you, seer. What is your name?'

'Astrid', she answered, and I decided that her name fitted her perfectly.

It was a beautiful name, just like her. I knew now, deep in my heart, that she was indeed a seer, and I had no intention of hiding the truth from her, so I told her why I really came to her house.

'Astrid, I have no ill intentions towards you, otherwise I'm pretty sure that this silver wolf would have shredded me to pieces, already. I am here sent by the Warrior, who is raising an army against King Magnus. I want to know if you would consider joining us, and if you do not wish to do so, I want to make sure that you are safe. We did not have a seer in many winters, and me and my men want to make sure that King Magnus will not get his claws on you.'

As soon as I mentioned the king's name, I heard the wolf growling, and I honestly agreed with the beast.

'You are the Warrior.'

I raised my eyebrows in surprise, but I nodded my head. So, she was a seer, indeed, and she could tell who I really was. She could've been such a great help to me, against the king, but I will never dare to force her to join me...

'Astrid, what have you seen in your vision?'

'That's not for you to know, not yet. I am safe here, Valtyr, I have the wolf with me. I do not wish to join you, or your army; whatever you do, do not tell anyone about me. That's all I ask of you.'

I frowned, feeling upset that she seemed to not wish to have anything to do with me, but I refused to force a seer to do anything that she did not want. I respected the gods, and therefore, I respected the choices of their seer, even if I would much rather have Astrid with me, just to make sure that she was safe.

'Think about it, at least allow us to hide you in one of our secret houses, where no one knows you or who you are, while King Magnus is still on its throne. After that, you can do as you please but allow us to keep you safe. I will come again to visit you in a few days, let me know if you want our help. Think, Astrid, I just want to keep you safe from this corrupted king.'

'Thank you for visiting me, Valtyr, have a good day.'

And just like that, she dismissed me, and returned to sit at the table, while the wolf stood protectively around her, placing its massive head on her lap. I watched as she scratched his head with affection, and I was almost jealous of the beast, receiving so much attention from her.

I bid my goodbye to her father, Orn, then left the small house. As soon as I reached the forest, my friends met me, and I saw Gertrude, and her curious expression.

'So, how did it go? Is she really a seer?'

'Yes, she is a seer; no, she doesn't want to join us, or allow us to hide her.'

I saw Gertrude's disappointed face, and I fully agreed with her. I did not tell her about the vision that Astrid did not want to share with me, and I nodded towards the village, and we all headed there.

Maybe in a few days, Astrid will change her mind.

I refused, however, to force her hand in any way, but I really wished to have her with me. Her visions could have been useful to us, but just her presence alone was enough to brighten my mood, and I did not like it when she refused my offer of protection, but I did not want to force her.

Maybe she will change her mind...

Chapter 4
Astrid
Meeting the Warrior

Vilmar was so excited to explain everything to me; how they found me, how my father brought the neighbour with the horse, and how the wolf will not leave my side and always watch over me. He was so fascinated by the wolf, that he asked for permission out loud to touch him, and his expression of surprise when the guardian nodded, warmed my smile.

I could see through my little brother's eyes how blessed we were to have the gods choosing me as a seer, and he was so happy and grateful to be allowed to touch the big, great, silver wolf, that it warmed my heart. Vilmar made sure that I knew about every little thing that happened while I was in that deep sleep, and I was grateful for his effort to let me know.

While Vilmar went around the house to gather some branches for our fire, I had a surprise. We were visited by a man we did not knew. When I shook his hand, after he introduced himself to us, I realised that the blonde, tall man, sitting in front of me, was the one to fight the rabid beast, from my vision.

As soon as I remembered my vision, I had another one, and it left me shaken and surprised, not knowing how to react.

Valtyr, as he presented to us, was kneeled in front of me, and I was placing a crown on its head, giving him the blessing of the gods.

When I came back to my senses, I saw Valtyr kneeled in front of me, just like in the vision that I had, and felt my heart beating so much faster, that it was hard for me to find my words.

I knew now that he was the warrior from my vision, and the gods showed me that I will be the one to crown him as king. I just had to make sure that in the troubled times ahead, he would choose to fight, only as a last resort. I hated the thought of people dying, and I wished this could be avoided.

Valtyr was a tall man, and looking at his strong body, I could tell that he was a great fighter. His blonde hair was braided, and his light blue eyes were watching me intensely. He had a rich beard, that was hiding a bit his beautiful lips, but you could tell from his face, that he was a determined man.

It was not the time to join him yet, nor to share my vision with him. I felt the presence of the wolf near me, and I knew deep inside me, that the wolf would have given me a sign, if I did not make the right choice.

Valtyr insisted that he would come back to visit again, to see if I had changed my mind in joining his army, or accepting his help in have me hidden away, while King Magnus was still on the throne. I couldn't explain how, but I knew that I would see him again, and I knew that I would be guiding him in his fight against Magnus, just not yet.

As soon as he left and my father came back inside the kitchen, I saw his worried face.

'Astrid, are you sure you do not wish to think of his proposal to have you hidden in another village, while Magnus still seats on the throne? We could come with you, just to make sure that you are safe.'

I looked at my father and tried my best to console him. I felt that he was worried about my safety, but to make sure that the world was a safer place, the danger had to be removed first. I trusted the gods to keep me safe.

'Father, I cannot run and hide until the danger goes away. Look at the guardian that the gods have sent me, I have faith that this wolf could tear a whole army on its own, and this time, just as grandma warned, the gods are watching, and now, I feel them closer than ever. They are walking amongst us, and they will make sure we are safe. We must have faith in the gods, father. Right now, I can tell you that King Magnus' days are counted, and there aren't too many left. Have faith father, we will all have the chance to see a world where Magnus is not king anymore, but we cannot hide until it happens.'

My father nodded his head, and I saw hope in his eyes, for the first time in many winters. Things were happening, right before our eyes, and I thanked the gods for sending me their guardian, for its presence was reassuring, and was igniting the courage in our hearts.

'Vilmar it's taking a bit too long with those branches. I will go out to help him', said father and left the house to look for my brother.

'Astrid, you had a vision, didn't you?'

I nodded and looked at her.

'Mother, the man that visited us, Valtyr, will be king one day. I was the one that put the crown on his head. I believe that he has the best intentions for me, and I feel that somehow, I will be around him and his army to guide them. Whatever happens, have no fear; and if you think that father needs to know about this vision, let him know, otherwise, don't tell him yet. When time will be right, I will be joining Valtyr, but today wasn't the day.'

As I was explaining this to my mother, I saw the wolf sitting up and starting to pace through the kitchen. To my surprise, I heard him howling once, then it opened the door and went outside, in the forest. I got up and waited for him to return to the house, while my mother followed me. She was worried.

'Astrid, what's wrong?'

'I don't know yet, mother.'

As I waited, I saw a raven flying back to us, and out of instinct, I stretched my arm, and the raven landed on my forearm, grabbing it tightly with its strong claws. It looked at me, and through his eyes, I could see the wolf running through the woods, then turning into a raven.

From up high, I could see Jon pulling my brother through the woods, then taking him to a settlement of a few tents, deep into the woods. I saw Valtyr talking to Jon, then I followed the raven's flight back to our house.

Did Valtyr just dared to have my brother kidnapped!?

I was angry now, and my blood was boiling. I understood that I had to follow the path through the forest, just like the raven showed me.

'Mother, when father comes back home, tell him that you need to wait here. Both of you. I know where my brother is, and I will bring him back home.'

'Astrid, what is happening? Where is your brother?'

I turned to my mother, grabbed her shoulders, and tried my best to calm her.

'Mother, trust me, and have faith in the gods.'

She nodded, and I went back inside the house, grabbed my cloak, then started to walk. My blood was boiling, and I could have ripped Jon to pieces with my bare hands. That low scum took my brother away, and I was angry.

The raven was flying in front of me, showing me the direction. I tried to walk fast, as it was cold outside. The first snow was getting closer, and the weather was much harsher now. I could smell the winter in the cold air, but I was so determined to take my brother back, that I was not bothered by the cold, I only wanted to reach the camp as fast as I could.

I reached the camp of Valtyr soon, and I grabbed the dagger that was hidden in my sock, then hid it inside my sleeve. I saw the men from the camp gawking at me, but they all moved to allow me to pass, and near a fire I saw Valtyr warming up his hands.

As soon as he saw me, he stood up and came to greet me, surprised by my presence.

'Astrid, I wasn't expecting you so soon. Welcome to my...', he started, but I went closer to him and place the sharp edge of the dagger at his throat.

'Where is my brother?', I shouted angrily, and I pushed the sharp dagger against Valtyr's throat, to make sure that he understood that I was not to be messed with.

Valtyr expression changed, and he grabbed my hands, keeping my wrists firmly in his strong hands. He wasn't hurting me; he was making sure that I would not push the dagger in his throat.

'That piece of shit, Jon, has brought your brother to us, asking for money. He was the one that told me about you, and he keeps asking us for coins. Me, or any of my men, we had nothing to do with it, we did not ask him to do such thing. Fear not Astrid, he will be punished. Your brother is safe, don't worry.'

I allowed Valtyr to remove my hands, and for the first time, I realised how close I was to him. I could feel his body against my chest, and I could smell the forest and the cold, all wrapped in a nice scent, coming off his body; I almost got distracted by his charming presence, but I remembered quickly why I came to his camp.

I could and I would rip off his head for my little brother; warrior or not, he stands no chance against a sister looking for her little brother. My rage was making my blood boil and all I wanted to know for sure was that Vilmar was safe. I had to see him, right now.

'Bring Vilmar to me, right now!', I shouted in his face, while my hand was squeezing hard the dagger. I wouldn't hesitate to use it on Valtyr, and he probably realised that; he asked his men to bring the boy to me.

'Astrid!'

As soon as I heard my brother's voice, I turned to see him, and indeed, he seemed to be just fine. He hugged me, and I pushed him behind me, while I threw my nastiest glance towards Valtyr.

'Astrid, I told you, I had nothing to do with your brother being taken. Your neighbour, Jon has brought him to us, and he even asked me for money in exchange for Vilmar. If anything, we only kept the boy safe, until you arrived here.'

I nodded, then turned around, to leave the camp. After I turned, I sensed someone grabbing my hand. I turned my head and saw that Valtyr was the one.

'Astrid, stop. I cannot let you leave our camp. Look at what your neighbour did, you are not safe if King Magnus is on the throne. What if someone else tries to hurt your family, or tries to take you to the king?'

'Valtyr, that's my problem, not yours.'

'Actually, it is my problem. This kingdom hasn't had a seer in many winters, and now that the gods had finally chose another seer, I want to keep you safe. I will make sure that your brother is taken back home, but you should stay with us, where it's safe.'

I stopped and looked at my brother's worried face; Valtyr was right, but he did not bother to ask me what I wanted to do, he just decided instead, for me. I didn't want to worry my brother unnecessary and to argue with Valtyr in front of Vilmar, so for the moment, I accepted.

'Send my brother home, now, and we will talk.'

Valtyr nodded and arranged immediately for two of his men to come and accompany my brother back to our home.

'Vilmar, tell mother and father not to worry; I will come back home, but for the moment I will stay here a little longer. Take care.'

I hugged him, and watched as he went riding, with Valtyr men flanking him. I calmed down, knowing that he would reach home soon, but now, my anger on Valtyr was growing. I just waited for my brother to be out of sight, so I can properly shout at the man.

'Who the fuck you think you are to decide for me, Valtyr? It's this how you are going to rule the people once you remove Magnus? Oh, I know what is best for you, so you are just going to do what I tell you. What makes you think you are allowed to take decisions for others?'

I saw Valtyr frowning, and he stepped so close to me, that I had to tilt my head back, so I could still look at him in the eyes. He might have been a great warrior, and a beautiful man, but that gave him no right to make decisions for me.

'I have no intention to harm you, or hurt you in any way, seer. I will keep you safe, since you forget that you are so important.'

'I can keep myself safe, thank you. You forget that I have my guardian.'

Finally, I could see the raven circling and cawing above us, almost agreeing with what I just said.

Valtyr never broke eye contact with me, and I could tell he was just as upset as me.

Why couldn't he just ask me, instead of making his own decisions?

I would have accepted to stay in his camp, but I will not allow him to decide for me instead, completely ignoring my own will; I did not want this type of men to rule over people, everyone had the right to decide for themselves, even if they took the wrong path.

'Really? And how did that keep your brother safe from your neighbour? Gods are watching, but they are letting people chose, and your neighbour chose to put your brother in danger.'

I frowned as well, realising that he was right; Jon was able to take my brother away, and even if I saw that, Vilmar could have been in great danger, by the time I managed to reach him.

'That still doesn't give you the right to decide for me!', I shouted angrily, knowing that I was right.

Valtyr had to learn to ask me, instead of ordering me.

He took one more step, and now our bodies were touching; I could feel the smell of forest and wood coming from his clothes, just as I could feel his warm breath on my face.

None of us was going to back down, and for a second, I was worried about where this was heading, but I decided to stand my ground; Valtyr had to ask me to stay in the camp, not to order me.

'You will stay with me, where I can keep you safe, until Magnus is removed from the throne. After that, you can do as you wish. You are too important to be left where you are.'

Valtyr seemed to decide to stand his ground, as well, and I was angry now.

What can I say to get it through his thick head, that I was not an object, and I had every right to decide what I wanted to do?

'Valtyr, can I talk to you for a moment?', I saw a blonde woman asking him, while she placed her arm between us, and pulled him away from me.

She was beautiful, dressed in black clothes, and had trousers, just like men had. I could see the armour protecting her chest, and the arrows and the bow strapped to her back.

Just like Valtyr, she had a big sword, and had her hair braided. She seemed to be just as fierce as any of the men in his army, while having a delicate touch that only women could have.

Soon, she pushed Valtyr enough, for her to place her own body between me and him. She was blocking him to come any closer, and somehow, I could feel that she understood me, and she probably wanted to pull him aside to explain to his thick head why I was so angry.

'Gertrud, not now. We can talk later, as much as you wish.'

'I think that right now is the perfect moment, Valtyr. Leave the seer for a few moments and hear what I need to tell you.'

Valtyr frowned but seemed to accept Gertrud's request. I saw him looking around the camp for something.

'Tomas and Viktor, I want you both to stay on either side of Astrid. Make sure she is not trying to leave and make sure that no strand of hair on her head is hurt. Keep her safe while I talk to Gertrud, please.'

The two men that he talked with nodded, and just as he asked, one came and stood to my right, and the other one to my left side. I saw Valtyr leaving with Gertrud to talk with her in his tent, while one of the men, the one wearing what seemed to be a bear's fur on his shoulders, talked to me first.

'Hello seer, I am Viktor, and this one here is Tomas. What is your name?'

'Astrid', I answered, looking at the tall man.

Viktor had long, black hair, that was draping over his shoulders, brown eyes, and a rich beard that was framing his face nicely; the fur on his shoulders seemed to match his personality, and I had a hunch that most probably he got that fur after he fought the bear.

The other man, Tomas, was just as tall as him, with blonde hair and green eyes. Tomas had the sides of his head shaven, and a long, thick braid was holding the hair on the top of his head that he chose not to shave. His beard was shorter than Viktor's, but it matched him. Tomas was smiling at me.

'Do not worry Astrid, I know that Valtyr seemed angry earlier, but he has your best interests at heart, and we will keep you safe. No harm will come your way, you don't need to be afraid of us.'

'I'm not afraid, I want Valtyr to understand that I am a human that has its own will, and not an object that he can decide what to do with. I'm sure that none of you want to hurt me, otherwise you would have done it already, and I thank you for taking care of my brother and me.'

Tomas nodded, then looked towards the tent.

'I'm sure the Gertrud is explaining that to him, better than we can. She'll get through his thick head, don't worry. Let's sit next to the fire, so you can keep warm.'

They allowed me to sit, then, as instructed, they sat again on either side of me. Viktor had chosen to sit with his back to the fire, while looking in the direction of Valtyr's tent.

Viktor was the one to speak this time, while glancing quickly towards me.

'What a great neighbour you have. Why is he like this, trying to sell you and your family to strangers? Has he always been this shitty?'

'I'm not sure, but since my mother rejected his marriage proposals, he seemed to have something against my family. He always hated my father, and he was never welcomed on our land.'

'Ah, there you go, the jealous shitty neighbour. This bastard really wants to harm you and your family and is greedy enough to try to make a profit out of it. I don't like him at all.'

I agreed with Tomas and nodded my head. Jon has been a headache to my family lately and is trying hard to destroy us. I hope that Vilmar will warn my parents, and they will keep him away.

'I will make sure he won't mess with you, or your family', added Viktor. The anger in his voice gave my goosebumps, and I frowned.

'Is Jon still in the camp?'

'Yes, Valtyr will not let him go this time. If he kidnapped your brother to try and sell him to us, Valtyr doesn't trust him not to hurt you, if he releases him.'

I nodded, feeling a wave of relief that at least for the moment, I will not have to worry about Jon trying to do something to my family. If he was being held in this camp, at least my family was safe, for the moment.

Viktor stood up, then looked at Tomas.

'You stay with Astrid; I will be back.'

Tomas nodded, and I watched as Viktor went to Valtyr's tent. Will he tell Valtyr what I told them about Jon?

'Don't worry, Astrid. When Jon took your brother away, he did not care about anything. Now, you don't need to care about what will happen to Jon.'

Chapter 5
Valtyr
The Warrior

'Valtyr, instead of arguing with Astrid, just ask her to stay with us. I don't think you have asked her what she wants to do, you just ordered her around. She is a seer, after all.'

I looked at Gertrud, feeling the anger rolling from my body.

What was wrong with the women in this camp? I only wanted to keep the seer safe, and now they were all angry at me.

'Gertrude, she doesn't want to stay in the camp. Let's say that I let her go back home, and Magnus finds out about her. How long will it be until he kills her? You know that Magnus doesn't want people to believe in the gods, and a new seer will be just a new target for him. Gertrude, Magnus has had all the servants of the gods executed across the kingdom, do not forget that.'

'I know Valtyr, but try to ask Astrid to stay, instead of ordering her. That's the only difference. Otherwise, you are just forcing her to do something that she doesn't want to.'

'Gertrude, she is too special, and we have to make sure that she is kept safe.'

'Valtyr, just ask her!'

73

Gertrude shouted at me, and I was shocked since I hadn't heard her shouting in a long time. Suddenly, I stopped arguing with her, remembering about her own past, and understanding why she was so angry with me.

King Magnus has asked Gertrude to be his lover, and she refused. Gertrude was kidnapped by the king, and kept by force for days at his castle, and we all knew that he forced himself on Gertrude. She had managed to escape, but what she went through was the reason why Gertrude's marriage has fallen apart, and why she was terrified of any man that tried to touch her.

We all knew how much Tomas still cared about her, and he would have probably still been with her, if the king hasn't done what he did. Tomas was hurt because his wife could not stand to be touched by a man, and no matter how much he tried to help her, their marriage was broken, as she could not stand to be around any man.

Tomas had met Viktor when he joined my army, and we all noticed how well they got along, until we noticed that the two men were often disappearing together, for short times. Gertrud had also joined my army, and the three of them had become inseparable.

I loved them deeply, and I trusted them. I understood now why Gertrude insisted for me to talk with Astrid, but before I had the chance to say anything to her, I saw Viktor entering the tent, and he was angry.

'Valtyr, the neighbour has always hated the seer's family, after Astrid's mother had refused to marry him. If we let that scum go away, he will try something again.'

Gertrud turned to him, frowning.

'That's why he was selling information about the seer to us, then kidnapped her brother? Because her mother will not marry him? Piece of shit!'

We all looked at each other, and without speaking anything, we understood each other.

We had to take care of the neighbour.

'I'll take care of him.'

'Valtyr, maybe you should talk to her about it. Otherwise, she will hate you.'

'Yes, but she will be alive and safe, and when all this is over and King Magnus removed from the throne, she can be free and safe to hate me as much as she wants to. I'd rather have her safe and alive with us, than release that imbecile and knowing that if something happened to her family or her, it will be our fault.'

'Valtyr, I'm not sure that we should decide what will happen to another person's life', added Gertrud, trying to be the voice of reason in all this mess, as always.

I looked at her and nodded, then placed my hand on her shoulder.

'That's why I will be the one to do it. You and Viktor will have nothing to do with it, anyway. And if Astrid wants to hate me for it, then so be it, I'd rather have her alive, no matter what.'

I frowned and saw Gertrud looking worried at me. She realised already that everything that happened today was reminding me about my own parents, how my father realised how dangerous Magnus had become, just after Magnus had King Ketiln killed, and how he asked Helga, his sister, to come and take me away to her village, Svartar, just to make sure that I will have a chance to live.

My father, Bjorn, has tried to prepare an escape for him and my mother, and they only managed to reach Vatnar, the village near the Old Bridge, before mercenaries sent by Magnus had caught up with them and killed them.

My parents, just like Astrid's brother, had been sold by a neighbour who was always jealous of how well they were doing in life, and how much King Ketiln liked my father, making him a favourite to the throne. All this time, I was left an orphan, just because a neighbour was jealous of our family.

I knew better than anyone that Jon will not stop until he will cause Astrid's mother a great pain, so he could have his revenge on the woman who refused to marry him.

Years ago, I had no power to save my parents, and I had to run with my aunt, in the middle of the night, but now, the situation was different, and I will not sit and watch how Jon will try to destroy the seer's family, just so he can have his revenge.

Astrid might hate me for this, but at least, her family will be safe. She will be safe as well, and maybe in time she will forgive me.

After all, in front of the gods, I was the one that will be taking Jon's life, and not her, or anyone else. Jon will have to face the consequences of his acts, and if he will not stop, then I will stop him, all to make sure that the new seer was safe.

'Gertrud, try to stay around Astrid, because I know that she will be a lot angrier at me soon. Viktor, have Jon being brought to the fire, and gather everyone from the camp, so they will see it; I will not hide from my men.'

Viktor nodded and went away. I left the tent and went towards the fire. I saw Astrid sitting calmly, with Tomas next to her. Soon, the people had started to gather around us, and Tomas looked at me.

'Valtyr, why are the people gathering?'

Astrid turned around to look at me when she heard my name.

How could I explain to her, that I was not a monster, and everything that I will do next I will do it for her, and for her safety?

I couldn't, and I knew that this would make her angrier.

'Seer, you will not like what is going to happen next, but I must do it. If the gods are watching, I hope they will forgive me for this, because I am doing it hoping that it will keep innocent people safe. I know that if I don't, you and your family will always be in danger.'

'What are you talking about?', asked Astrid, not knowing what to expect.

Her voice was unsure, and she seemed to be a little afraid of my words. I just wanted to hug her, and tell her not to worry, but I didn't, since I wasn't sure if my hug would be welcomed by her.

Meanwhile, Viktor has managed to bring Jon. He was trying to fight Viktor but had no chance against him. Everyone was now looking at me, as they felt that something important was about to happen.

'As you all know', I started loudly, to get everyone's attention, 'I'm not hiding myself or my actions from you. This man, Jon is the neighbour of the seer and her family, and instead of respecting her, and help them, he decided to sell information about Astrid to me. More, he did not stop here and had Astrid's brother kidnapped, and brought here, and asked us for coins for the boy's life. Vilmar is back with his family, but I refuse to release Jon.'

I looked around to see the faces of my men, and I saw them nodding, agreeing with me.

Someone shouted that seers should be protected, and gods told people to not mess with their seer, and I nodded as well.

I continued with my speech, knowing what I will do next, and hoping that Astrid will understand that this was the best choice, so I could keep her safe.

'As we know, we cannot give him to the leader of the village, since they are all corrupted and they all report back to King Magnus. If any of them would find out about Astrid, that will put our seer's life in danger.'

My men nodded again, agreeing with my words.

'Jon, Astrid's mother had refused your marriage proposal, and you have tried for a long time to mess with her family, just out of jealousy. You have tried to do harm to a woman that had done nothing wrong, and you have taken her son, and tried to have him sold for coins. You are not to be trusted, and you are an awful man. I will refuse to provide food for you, and I refuse to burden my men with watching over you, so you won't try to harm Astrid or her family. Your action has brought you here and may the gods be the judges of mine.'

I took out my sword, and with one swift move, I aimed for Jon's throat. I heard someone's screaming, but I kept my eyes on Jon, watching the drops of blood coming towards my face, then saw his shirt stained with blood.

I saw him gasping for air, then trying to lift his hands, but suddenly falling, collapsing on the ground. I looked towards Astrid and saw her horrified expression. Her mouth was opened wide, and her eyes were shocked by the scene that she just witnessed.

Some men had come and took Jon's body away, and I knew that they were going to bury him, somewhere, in the forest. Others were still looking at me, and one of them shouted my name, and lifted his sword, to show his support for me. Soon, all of them did the same, and I bowed my head.

I went to Gertrud, and whispered in her ear to watch over Astrid, knowing that she will not want to be close to me, after she just saw me killing her neighbour. I knew that one day she will agree that this was the safest choice for her, but for the moment I realised that she will not agree with me, and will not want me next to her.

Gertrud nodded, and I saw her walking to Astrid, then hugging her, and walking her slowly, but firmly towards her tent. For the moment, Astrid will be alright with Gertrud, and I only needed to look at Tomas and then, back towards Gertrude and Astrid, while they were walking away; and he understood my message straight away.

Tomas signalled Viktor, and they left, following the women. Later, I will join Tomas and Viktor, but for the moment, I had to wash Jon's blood from my face. I started to walk towards the river, thinking that I wished I could have killed the neighbour that betrayed my parents, as well, but he had died before I had the chance to do so.

I walked through the forest, until I could hear the river, that I knew it was close to our camp. I thought about my parents, and wished that they had someone to protect them, like Astrid had me.

They were long dead, and I could not change their fate anymore, but I will keep the seer safe, even if I had to give my life to protect her.

I knew that the gods were watching us, and I was ready to face the gods and answer in front of them for what I have done in my life. I knew the gods would understand that I was keeping their seer safe.

I remembered how Viktor, that was living in Helga's village, had taught me how to fight, right before I became a man. Viktor was the one to encourage me to raise an army against Magnus and revenge my innocent parents and remove the king from the throne. I couldn't care less who was on the throne, I wanted a better life for the people living in the Kingdom of Kulta, and I wanted to make sure that Magnus could not kill whoever he wanted, just like he was doing now.

Along the years, many had tried to fight against him, and they all failed. I was advised by Viktor to gather as many people as I could first, trained them, then fight against Magnus.

I knew that the king had managed to destroy the lives of many people, and far too many were ready to fight against Magnus or die trying. Even the men in his army, agreed that Magnus had reached a level of evil that was not seen before. More and more people agreed that the king had to be stopped.

I had managed to fight some of his soldiers, and soon the stories about the Warrior had started to travel from village to village and most of the people from the northern villages wanted to join the Warrior in his fight against King Magnus.

It did not take long until I found Tomas, then Gertrud had joined, as well. They were the people I trusted the most, and they had reasons to wish for the rule of Magnus to end, as well as I did.

I reached the river and washed my face, then my hair, in case I had blood in my hair. I also cleaned my shirt as good as I could, then started to walk back towards the camp. I hoped that Gertrud have managed to calm Astrid, since I was waiting for the gods to send us a sign that we were going in the right direction.

I believed that Astrid was that sign, and I vowed to myself to let her go free, wherever she wanted, the day when Magnus will be removed. I know that she must be thinking that I am a monster right now, but I hope that one day, she will understand my actions and she will not hate me as much she hated me today.

I wish I could hug her and ask for her forgiveness, because she had to witness such an awful scene, but I wanted to do everything in front of my men, so they will know that I will not hide away, like others. Everyone had to learn who Jon was, what he did, and they also had to know about the reason why Jon did everything.

I reached the camp and stopped by the fire to warm myself. I wanted to go and talk with Astrid, but I was afraid that she could not bear to be in my company, right now, and honestly, I could not blame her. I saw Tomas sitting next to me and turned towards him.

'I agree with you and what you did, but I am afraid that our little seer is a bit shocked, right now. Gertrud has managed to calm her, but I would leave her alone until tomorrow. We don't want to force her to eat. Let her sleep in Gertrude's tent tonight, let her get some rest, and try to talk to her tomorrow. You know, everything is better, after a bit of rest. Let her rest tonight, Valtyr.'

'I will leave Astrid alone tonight. Thank you for helping me, Tomas.'

'Don't worry about Astrid, I will check over them. Viktor is moving our tent next to theirs, so we will be able to hear them through the night. You go, eat something, and get some rest. You need to rest as well, Valtyr.'

I stood up, and this time, I went quickly to eat something with the other men. It seemed that even though Astrid looked terrified by what I did, everyone else agreed. The seer was important, and trying to disrespect her like her neighbour did, was against everyone's belief.

To my surprise, not only that they agreed with me killing Jon, but my men have decided that having Astrid in our camp was a good sign from the gods, that they are supporting our case. I could barely swallow my food once I realised that if Astrid would go away from the camp, the people will not like it.

I finished the food and went towards the tent, hoping that by tomorrow, Astrid will have changed her mind and accept to stay with us, so we could keep her safe. I frowned, when I realised that I didn't ask her to stay, I just told her that we are her best choice.

Then, I thought about the first time when I met her, and realised that I had asked her, back then, but she refused.

Fuck it, she was too important to risk her safety. Even though she didn't know it, everyone looked at her like she was the living proof that the gods were still thinking about us, and everything will be alright with our attempt of dethroning Magnus.

It was all dark and scary around us, and Astrid was our little star that shone light and hope into our hearts. Truth to be told, her dim light wasn't enough for us to see the path, but it was enough to give us courage to face the darkness.

I'd be damned if I will allow her to put herself in danger, or anyone else to put her in danger. I will give her time to think about it and if her choice wasn't to stay with us, I will allow her a few more days to reconsider her decisions.

I laid in my makeshift bed, feeling thankful for meeting her.

Before I saw her for the first time, I was curious of how she would look like. Well, she looked like she would fit perfectly in my arms, and I could not stop staring for a few moments, at her perfect curves. I hoped I wasn't drooling in front of her, but I would have loved it if I could hug her small and curvy frame.

I remember how she seemed to look through me; then, I asked her about the vision that she had. She had a vision the first time I saw her, and she still not told me about it.

I grinned in my bed, thinking that now, I could try and pest her tomorrow until she tells me more. She had seen something, and she saw it when I touched her, but the sneaky little seer, had managed to keep her lovely mouth shut, and I completely forgot about it.

I just hoped that I did not scare her too much when she saw me executing her neighbour, otherwise it will a bit harder to talk with her, but I could always insist about her telling me what she saw the very first day when I met her.

Could she have seen us sleeping together?

Because I could not take out from my mind the roundness of her hips, her large beast; the nice curve of her delicate throat...

I could kiss her all night until she moaned my name. I felt my blood running faster through my veins and my heart beating stronger. I had to find out what she saw, I just had to know.

Patience, I had to have patience with her, but I was hard already just when I thought about her; I just wanted to kiss her soft skin and feel her body underneath mine. I lowered my hand and squeezed, and barely managed not to moan her name, while my hand was working hard and fast, up, and down.

I could have died in peace if I had the chance to kiss her naked body, bury my face between her breasts, and bury my cock deep inside her warm and soft body. I could have her, again and again, until she milked the last drop of life from me. I wanted to see her from all angles, kiss every spot on her body, and taste her. I would have love to kiss her lips until they would be red and swollen.

I wanted to have her taste on my lips, and I wanted to make her scream my name in pleasure; and while I was thinking at every way that I could possibly make her mine, I finally tensed and felt the wave of pleasure taking over my body, and barely managed myself to stop from moaning her name out loud.

I laid on my back for a few moments, feeling grateful that I could contain myself from calling out her name, otherwise I could be heard by the others. I could not stop myself from wanting her, and it was driving me insane.

There is no way I will let her go; she will have to come with us.

Chapter 6
Astrid
What happens in the cave…

I gasped when I saw the sword slashing at Jon's neck. I didn't expect Valtyr to do this, and I couldn't believe that no one said anything to stop him. Yes, he did wrong, but surely, Valtyr had no right to decide if someone else lives or dies…

I looked at Valtyr and could see no regret in his face, only determination. He looked straight in my eyes and had probably noticed how shocked I was.

I knew he was right, and we could not turn to the leader of the village to judge Jon for trying to put me and my family in danger, but from there to kill him coldly like that, there was a long way, full of wrong steps and Valtyr has walked them all with one swing of his sword.

Gertrude had pulled me away from there and took me to her tent. She tried to calm me, as I was shaking and could barely register anything from what she was saying. I tried to look at her, but still could not understand any words. I felt her pity and sympathy for me.

She was so gentle with me, but I just needed a moment to understand the things that I just saw. I held my palm open to make her understand that I needed to calm down and sat on the edge of the mattress.

I lowered my head, then lifted my arms to support it, and I stayed like this, while memories were invading my mind.

I could see grandma's face when she was killed by Magnus, alternating with images of Jon's face killed by Valtyr.

It wasn't the same, I tried to repeat to myself, grandma had done nothing wrong, while Jon had put me in danger. It's not the same, Jon was guilty of betraying me and my family, while my grandma was killed for warning the king about his wrongdoings...

'Astrid, are you alright?'

'I can't believe that Valtyr killed Jon like that...'

'Astrid looked at me', Gertrude asked me, then I saw her kneeling in front of me so she could look into my eyes, 'Jon was the kind of person to put everyone in danger. I can see that you are a kind soul but think of what could have happened if Valtyr had let him go. What if Jon had gone to the leader and told him about our camp? All the people here would have been in danger, including you and your family; and you know he would have done it for money.'

'He could have kept him as a prisoner', I said, trying to find the simplest solution that would not require Jon to be killed in cold blood.

'Oh, dear child, I can tell you are still innocent. I know it sounds harsh, but Jon would have been one more mouth to feed, and someone should have always watched over him, since he cannot be trusted. He would have cost us food and people to watch over him when we don't have that much to begin with. Astrid, we are preparing to dethrone a king, we need to train, not to watch over a scumbag that could put us all in danger. And what if he managed to escape? All of us would be in danger.'

I did not say anything more; she was right, but I wasn't convinced that this was the best solution. I wished I could talk with Valtyr, before he killed Jon, maybe there was something else that we could have done, instead of what he did.

There was no way to know which was the right thing to do, but even I could understand that Gertrud was right, still there was a part of me that wished Jon was not killed, but locked and kept alive, so he could live everyday regretting what he's done.

Gods were watching, and I remembered about my vision when I crowned Valtyr as king; maybe our gods were agreeing with Valtyr punishing Jon, so if anyone else who wanted to do the same and betray other for personal gains, will think twice.

This has happened already, and no matter how many times I would try to come with better ways, I still couldn't change anything, anymore.

It wasn't the best way, I decided, but maybe this will be an example for anyone who would be tempted to make the same mistakes as Jon; maybe this will be a warning lesson for everyone.

I only hoped that Valtyr would not become corrupted like Magnus, because he would be someone who would have the power to decide for the whole kingdom, and I wanted people to have a better life.

I knew that I had to talk with Valtyr about his ways, but I couldn't stand the thought of seeing him right now. I would rather stay here for a while, to try and calm myself down; I could not be seeing Valtyr right now, since the image of his face stained with Jon's blood was too painfully fresh in my mind.

I heard Gertrud asking someone for some hot tea, then I saw her coming closer to me again, and sitting on the mattress, next to me.

'Astrid, you are still young, and I know you haven't seen or lived half of the awful things I did. I know that what Valtyr did today might look cruel to you, but the world we live in, it's like that. This, and I promise you, will not be the only horrible thing you'll see, and years from today, you might accept that Valtyr has done the right thing.'

'I just want Valtyr to choose his ways wisely, and if it's possible, I'd want him to avoid people being killed. It's important for him to understand that.'

'Then why don't you go and tell him?'

'I couldn't look at him right now, Gertrud. I... maybe I will explain to you one day, but I hate to see people being killed in front of me, I don't like it.'

'No one likes it, Astrid, but you must understand that these things happen a lot in our kingdom. Magnus would have killed someone for less than that, so think about this for a second. In a world ruled by men, cruelty is something common, maybe it would have been different if this kingdom was ruled by a woman, but what can we do, other than trying to advise the men to do better?'

She handed me the cup, and I started to drink some tea, feeling the hot liquid warming my body. I felt so tired, I just wanted to go home and lay down on my bed, but I did not have this option.

'Would you like to eat something before you go to sleep?', Gertrud asked me.

'I don't think I could', I answered her.

'I would bring you some bread and cheese. You must eat, you are still alive, and you need food to keep you going, regardless of your feelings. You will sleep tonight in my tent; if you have bad dreams, I'll be here with you.'

I nodded, then, after some time, she handed me some slices of bread and cheese. I didn't feel hungry, but I forced myself to eat the food, not wanting it to be wasted. After I finished eating, Gertrude handed me a nightgown, and turned around, so she would give me some privacy. I change quickly, then got under the thick blanket, feeling grateful to be able to rest my body.

I heard Gertrude talking with Tomas, then she lit a small candle in a lamp and placed it on the table near the bed. She took another nightgown from a small trunk for herself, and I watched her removing her body armour, then I turned my head to give her privacy.

'Astrid, if you don't mind, I will sleep in the bed with you. Is that alright?'

'Yes, it's alright.'

'If you need anything, let me know, and if you need to talk about anything, don't be shy; at least, I could help you with this.'

'I actually wanted to ask you a question, why do you think Valtyr wants so badly to keep me here?'

'Well, besides the fact that Magnus might want to kill you if he finds out that you are a seer now; I think that you inspire everyone... We haven't had a seer in such a long time and having one in our camp feels like the gods are looking at us and sending us a sign that everything is going to be alright.'

I felt the blanket moving, and Gertrud lay in the bed, while turning her back to me. We were back-to-back, but I was grateful for her warmth, and while I was listening to her, I agreed that people needed to feel that the gods were supporting them.

'How did you know that your brother was here, Astrid? You came quickly to our camp.'

'I had a vision.'

92

'See, if you have even one vision about what is going to happen, that could help our army so much... even if you don't, just your presence alone gives us courage. It's not about trapping you in a cage, like a bird; it's about the fact that we all want to make sure that you are safe, and any of us will fight for you, if needed; Valtyr as well, you know. A seer must be protected, you are meant to be the voice of gods amongst our people, and we do take your safety, very seriously. I think that I speak in the name of us all, when I say that you are considered our treasure, sent from the gods. Will you just leave a treasure at the side of the road, or will you take it with you, to make sure that no one is messing with it, or worse, using it with wicked intentions?'

'I understand your point, but Valtyr needs to learn to ask for permission, first. I also want a better life for all the people in the kingdom, and I don't think Magnus is the one that could make everything better. I want to make sure that Valtyr is the right person to rule a kingdom.'

'I agree with you; just give Valtyr a chance, once you'll get to know him, you'll see that he could be a great leader; that's why we all joined him, because we all believe in him.'

I thought about what she said for a few moments, then I turned my head towards her.

'Sleep well, Gertrude.'

'Have a good sleep, Astrid.'

I felt my body relaxing, and heard Gertrud's breath changing, so she must be falling asleep, quickly.

I understood her, and I agreed with her, but I still wasn't happy with how Valtyr had just decided to do the things the way he wanted; he needed to learn a lesson, he needed to learn to ask.

Truth to be told, he did ask me to join the camp at the beginning, but I said 'no'. He should've waited until my answer changed. I decided to sneak out of the camp as soon as I made sure that Gertrude was truly asleep. I heard the cawing outside and the flap of wings of the raven and I knew that the guardian was trying to communicate with me.

I prayed to the guardian to make them all fall asleep, so I could sneak out and say goodbye to my family, just to assure them that I was safe. I heard Gertrud next to me snoring loudly, and I smiled.

Sure, the gods were watching. I sneaked out of the bed slowly, then changed back into my clothes, feeling thankful for the small candle that was giving me the light I needed, otherwise I would have stumbled and fell in the tent, in the dark.

The raven was sending me images with Valtyr, and his men fallen asleep around the fire, and I knew that this was the moment for me to sneak out. I didn't wait too long, and managed to untie a horse, so I could get home fast, and maybe come back, just after sunrise. I will let the men from the camp to realise that I sneaked out, but I will come back; they needed me.

When I reached home, I tied the horse to our small fence, then looked at the raven that landed on the roof, watching over the area; if someone approached the house, the raven would let me know. I knew that I could count on my guardian, as the gods prove me once more how strong was the connection between me, the guardian, and them.

I entered the house, and saw my mother staying at the table, looking worried. When she lifted her head, and saw me, her whole face brightened.

'Astrid, my child!'

She crushed me into the strongest embrace, and I held her just as tight in my arms. I hear her crying softly, and it broke my heart.

'Mother don't cry. I am safe, and I will be safe, but I cannot stay home, for the moment, if King Magnus finds out about me...'

She nodded, understanding. She knew about my visions and knew that there would be some troubled times ahead.

'Mother, look at me. I cannot stay too long; I just came to tell you that I am safe. I am with the future king, and I will be away from home for some time, I don't know for how long, though. When you hear that King Magnus has been dethroned, it means that my visions have been fulfilled. As soon as I can, I will come back home, but if I come any sooner than that, I might put you, father, and Vilmar, in great danger. Hear me, Jon has tried to sell us to Valtyr already, so I am afraid that there might be others who would try to do the same. Don't tell people what I told you, say to them that I managed to save Vilmar from Jon, but you haven't seen me or Jon since, and you don't know what happened. Like this, no one will try to put you in danger, because no one will know what happened to me. I want you and father to spread the news that you are afraid that I might be dead; it's for the best, for the moment.'

My mother nodded, understanding everything I told her. I hugged her one more time, and stood a bit with her, before I left. When I looked through the small windows, I saw that the darkness of the night was replaced by the first rays of the sun, and I decided that it was time to leave, so no one will see me.

When we left the house, it started to snow, and before I went in the saddle again, my mother insisted to give me a bag with some bread and cheese, and gave me her black cloak, and the two daggers that my father had them done for me. I looked at her one more time, waved her goodbye, then headed towards the forest, riding at a slow pace, while the raven was flying above us.

While I was riding through the forest, I had a vision of a wolf cutting in front of us and scaring the horse, then I saw myself falling from the horse. I stopped, then unmounted the horse, and after I walked for a bit, I saw the wolf.

The horse has started to neigh, nervous, and I couldn't calm him, so I allow him to run away. From behind me, I saw the silver wolf appearing and growling at the animal. As expected, the other wolf ran away, and I was left with the silver guardian, that reminded me so much of the god of souls. I kneeled in from of him and started to caress his soft fur.

'Thank you for keeping me safe, I wouldn't manage without you helping me and warning me of the dangers ahead.'

Through my surprise, the wolf was showing me affection, licking my face, and I started to giggle. I saw the wolf going in a bush, and after a few moments I saw the raven flying out. I had a feeling that the wolf and the raven where the same guardian, and wondered if my guardian could also turn into a bear; that might be useful at times...

I stood up and decided that it was time to head towards the camp; it started to snow heavily, and I could barely find my way in the forest. At least, now, it was daytime, and I could see where I was heading, but the snow falling was making everything much more difficult for me. I started to walk, feeling upset that I could not find the path anymore.

After some time, I felt tired, and I still didn't find my way back to camp, so I stopped to eat a bit of the bread and the cheese that my mother has packed from me. I thanked the gods for the fact that I was lucky enough to have some food, then I started to look up, at the raven, begging the guardian for some guidance.

From up there, from the raven's eyes, everything looked even more confusing; there was an endless sea of trees and snow falling everywhere around us. I was fucked; I managed to get lost in the forest, while it was snowing. I knew from what my father had teacher me that I had to keep moving, so I could stay warm; maybe I could find a cave nearby so I could make a fire, until then, I had to keep on walking.

After walking for what it felt like hours, I had to stop and eat some more bread. I was scared now; as it seemed to get darker outside, and I still didn't find a cave.

I knew that I could be in danger, at night, and I had to find shelter, before it was night. I should've talked with Valtyr, before I sneaked out of the camp, but no, I thought that I knew better and now, I was looking hopeless around me, while realising that I just managed to put myself in danger.

I heard someone calling my name, then the horses. Someone had found me, and I really hoped it was Valtyr, or anyone else from his army. Soon, I saw Gertrud, Tomas, and Viktor, and I thanked the gods for keeping me safe.

If they managed to find me, I knew I would be safe.

'Astrid, you scared the life out of us! Why have you runed away?'

'I'm sorry Gertrud, I had to talk to my family, before I joined your cause.'

'Valtyr has sent us to look for you, but this snowstorm is worrying me', said Gertrud frowning, and looking concerned.

They dismounted and came closer to me. Viktor was the first to speak.

'We need to take shelter in that cave, soon it will be dark, and it's still snowing. Let's stop for one night, and tomorrow we can find our way back to the camp. There is no point walking at nighttime, while it's snowing. We need to stop, make a fire, eat a bit of bread, warm up, sleep, then we can go back to camp tomorrow. Valtyr will wait for us to return for three days, before he sends everyone after us.'

Tomas nodded, and Gertrud seemed to think about it. I felt bad for putting myself, and them, in danger.

'I should've talked with Valtyr before. I'm sorry that you are here in the snowstorm, because of me.'

I felt bad for putting them in danger and hoped they won't be upset on me.

Gertrud hugged me straight away, and I never felt more gratitude for her being so nice to me.

'Don't say this, Astrid, thank the gods that we found you. We are all safe, and tomorrow we will all go back to the camp. For the moment, we'll stop in the cave that we saw, right before we found you. It will be alright, don't worry.'

We all headed to the cave that Viktor was talking about. I saw Viktor tying the horses to a tree, and taking a blanket from underneath his saddle, then unfolding it, and placing it on them. Tomas and Gertrud went inside the cave. Gertrud lighted a candle, then took out a torch that she had wrapped safely and strapped to her back. She lighted the torch, while Tomas decided to go outside and look for some branches.

To my surprise, even though the cave entrance was small, after a few steps, the cave had a very tall ceiling, a nice flat area in the middle, and I discovered happily that there was a small lake on one of the sides, with warm water. I haven't come across a warm lake in such a long time, that I felt truly lucky to find one now, after I have been walking aimlessly, all day, through a snowstorm.

Soon, there was a small fire going in the cave, while me and Gertrude arranged all our cloaks so we can all have something to sleep on. I brought the bread and the cheese that I had left, and they brought some more food, from the camp.

'I have some water, then I think we can all have a sip of this. It's strong, but it will keep us warm.'

Viktor showed us the small bottle that he had hidden in his bag, and I could guess that the drink he was talking about would be something strong, but at this point, I didn't care anymore; I was happy and grateful to be found by them, and I felt bad for putting them in danger…

'I'm sorry that you had to start searching me through a snowstorm. I feel bad for putting you all in danger.'

'Astrid, even if you weren't a seer, I would still go through every snowstorm to help finding a friend', said Viktor, and I felt so much gratitude for their support.

Tomas nodded, and Gertrud hugged me again. I smiled and at the same time, I promised myself to not put them at risk again.

We started to eat the food that we had, then finally Viktor handed me his small bottle. I took a sip and started to cough as soon as the liquid fire touched my neck.

'What on earth is that? Fire?'

They were all laughing, and I passed the bottle to Gertrud. She didn't cough, and she had taken a good sip of the strong liquor. Tomas was next to drink, and Viktor was last. I felt my body warming up, and slightly lightheaded; I felt like giggling, and suddenly, I felt the tensions leaving my body.

I was looking intensely at the lake in the cave, and I saw Gertrud looking at me, then at the lake.

'Should we end this cold day with a hot bath?'

'It will be a sin not to bathe in hot water', added Tomas.

I was shy, but when I saw Gertrude and Tomas standing up and getting naked, I threw my fears out the window. Tomas had his back turned so we could take our clothes out, then I saw Viktor joining us, as well.

In less than a moment, all of us were naked, in the hot water, and giggling.

The lake was almost up to my shoulders, so much deeper than I expected, but it warmed up my cold body, making me so happy, that it put a stupid grin on my face. Gertrud was splashing Tomas and Viktor, while I was watching them.

Soon, she came next to me, and I could tell that Viktor's drink had made her tipsy, as well. We were smiling at each other, when I saw a surprised expression on her face; I followed her eyes to see Tomas and Viktor kissing each other passionately, just an arm's length away from us.

I turned to look at Gertrude, and I had suddenly a wicked idea; I turned to look at her, and as I was watching her beautiful face, I was wondering what it was like to kiss someone, and how it felt like to kiss a woman. I got closer to her, close enough to feel her body against mine, and underneath the water, I hugged her.

'Can I kiss you, Astrid?', she asked me, with her voice deeper than usual.

'Yes', I answered, wanting to taste her sweet lips.

There was a weird feeling in my belly; nervousness mixed with excitement and curiosity. Gertrud touched my face, then kissed me gently on my lips, and I felt my body reacting to the touch of her lips on mine. She was so delicate, and her body was so soft, that I was curious of feeling her curves, under my touch.

I closed my eyes and moaned as our kiss deepened…

Chapter 7
Zanos
...stays in the cave

What were they doing now?!

I watched the humans entering the cave, and as a raven, I sneaked past them and went to a darker corner. Astrid was happy to have been found by the other three, and I could read the relief on her face, but at the same time, I was upset that she did not realise that she could communicate so much more with me, and in my raven form, I could guide her, while being able to answer her whispered requests and pleas.

The humans were making some kind of place to sleep, using their cloaks, then ate some food. Up until then, I almost fell asleep, thinking that the day must be over now, that they found shelter and had a fire going, and some food in their bellies.

They must have been tired wandering all day through the cold, and worse yet, through the snowstorm. I thought that they would be happy to warm up and go straight to sleep.

I was a god, I was much stronger than they were, and even I wanted to be able to close my eyes and have some rest for a few moments.

But no, the real fun started when they drank some strong alcohol from a bottle. I watched them as they were slowly getting undressed and going into the hot water lake.

I had savoured every moment of seeing her getting undressed and admiring her full and round body in the dim light inside the cave. I rarely took lovers, but I was now curious of her and craving to touch her soft breasts and round hips.

I saw her undoing her long hair, and felt something inside of me, urging me to take her. Instead, I stayed in my raven form and watched Astrid getting in the lake, with the other humans.

At first, the men kissed each other, then I saw her looking intently at the other woman, and they started to kiss. I would have been jealous if one of the men would be kissing her, but looking at the other woman kissing her, I felt suddenly very intrigued.

Maybe at some point, another man would be kissing her, but I wasn't ready to witness it just yet; instead, I watched as Astrid and Gertrud were kissing each other, and Gertrud was caressing her face, then her hands went slowly underneath the water playing with her breast and massaging her nipples.

Next to them, Tomas and Viktor were kissing as well, and I saw Tomas hand going down, straight at Viktor's manhood and stroking it slowly, until Viktor tilted his head back, and opened his mouth slowly, tasting the pleasure that the other man was bringing him. Tomas then started to kiss Viktor's throat passionately, while his hand was moving faster, underneath the water.

It only took a few moments until the men started moaning, and I could see that the other woman had her hand near Astrid legs, then I heard our little seer moaning, and I watched her with my beak opened in shock. I was sure that my raven eyes were bulging out of my little raven head, as I looked at the humans having what looked like really good fun.

I saw them exiting the lake, then laying on the cloaks. I still had my beak opened, and for the first time in my immortal life, I tilted and lowered my raven head to one side and opened my beak a little more, watching them in shock, as they were making love to each other...

How was this even possible?

How could I have never thought of this?

Astrid was lying on her back, while Gertrud was caressing her breasts and sucking her nipples. I saw her throwing her head back and abandoning her body to Gertrud's touch, while the woman's head was going slowly lower, stopping right between her legs, licking, and sucking.

I saw Gertrud stopping for a few moments and looking behind her at one of the men.

'Tomas, I want to feel your dick inside me.'

Tomas nodded, then came closer to Gertrud, started to caress her breasts, kissed her back, while she was busy licking and sucking Astrid's pussy. The man started to touch Gertrud, then slowly placed two fingers between her legs, and moved them at a steady pace. When he heard Gertrude moaning, he penetrated her from behind, holding his hands firmly on her hips.

Viktor got closer to Tomas and started to penetrate him, while gently biting his shoulder. They were moving slowly, but at the same rhythm, and while I was watching from my place, I looked at them bewildered, feeling humbled by how creative humans could get, and how well their extended arrangement was working.

Astrid was moaning loudly, massaging her breasts and Gertrud was slowly massaging her hips while her tongue was tasting her most private parts. The men were moving first at a slow pace, then a little faster. I heard Gertrud moaning Tomas's name, and I watched them enjoying each other and wishing I could be there and joining them.

They were effectively and passionately fucking each other, while I, the immortal god, was staring at them with my eyes bulging out and quite surprised of their lovemaking.

Their naked bodies, moving close to each other were doing something to my mind, and I watched them hypnotised, while their rhythm increased, and moans were getting louder.

They were so close to each other, and I could hear their rapid breaths, their moans, and the sounds that their bodies were making.

I watched hypnotised as they were rubbing against each other in pure pleasure and ecstasy, while caressing their own bodies, at the same time.

Astrid was moaning the loudest, while Gertrude had her head buried between her legs; I could tell that she was unexperienced, and this was too much pleasure for her. Her face was red, and her mouth was opened, while her eyes were closed, enjoying every touch she got from Gertrud.

I wanted to show her what real pleasure meant, but I was stuck here, watching, and hearing her moaning, without being able to touch her. This was torture to me, as I my body was thirsty of hers…

I felt another raven next to me, and almost forgot how to stand on my raven feet, while I realised that my lovely sister, Sera, had decided to join me.

'Oh, you are having some fun here, brother', she said through my mind, while turning to look at the humans fucking passionately, few feet away from us, 'my days, I have never tried this combination before, it looks like it would feel really good.'

I rolled my eyes, irritated at my sister's presence. Normally, I would be happy to see her, but now it was really a bad moment, as I was really enjoying the spectacle in front of my eyes before she decided to appear.

'I thought that they would be going to sleep, but look at them, they are fucking like rabbits now', I said, hearing the irritation in my voice.

Really, I was just upset that my sister was distracting me from what was happening in front of us.

Sera was now laughing loudly in my mind.

'Brother, I have to go and find myself three humans.'

'Why?', I asked surprised.

'I have to try what they are doing, it looks like really good fun', and just like that, she disappeared and left me alone.

I couldn't sneak out since I promised to watch over Astrid. Speaking of Astrid, I watched her as she was moaning loudly, then tensing her whole body, as she was shaken by the pleasure Gertrud was giving to her.

Gertrud had collapsed over Astrid, while the man was taking her faster now. They were both moaning, and then I saw Viktor collapsing on top of Tomas. Soon, they were all laying on their back, tired and sweaty from their lovemaking.

I was sitting here, as a raven, admiring the ravished seer, and wishing I could have been in my real form, so I could join them. Surprised, I realised that this was the first time that I was lusting for a human, and that didn't happen to me in a long time.

I saw Gertrud rolling to look at Astrid, as she was giggling.

'Astrid, what happened in the cave, will always stay in this cave. We are the only ones to know about this. We all needed a bit of happiness since life has been shitty lately. This is between us, our little secret; no one else saw us.'

Astrid nodded, and I humph from where I was. Yeah, I saw that, and my sister too...

They went back to the lake, washed their bodies, then I saw them getting dressed and almost crawling to their cloaks.

Of course, they were tired now, after they have walked all day through a snowstorm, then fucked in the cave until they weren't able to move anymore.

Soon, the humans were sleeping soundly, with the small fire burning at a safe distance from them. I was stuck in a raven form, looking at them sleeping and still wishing I could have joined them earlier.

I heard another flapping of wings and saw the raven landing next to me. I didn't need to hear anything to know who it was, since I could feel Father's strong presence from miles away.

Unfortunately for him, he just missed the best part of this evening.

'Son, Sera told me that something really important was happening in the cave and I had to know about it; what have I missed?', he asked me, and even though we were not talking out loud, I could hear his curiosity, in my mind.

I sent him the images that I just saw, and his voice was laughing loud now, through our mind connection. I rolled my raven eyes at him, and watched as his raven form was crouched in a funny position. The raven quickly gained its serious posture, then looked back at me.

'I see that you are learning great things from them. Do you need a small break to… you know…cool a bit? Roll out in the snow, or go and lay down with some humans?'

I rolled my eyes again, and again he was laughing loudly in my mind.

'Father, I thought I was supposed to keep her safe. So far, they are having more fun than I am.'

'Well, you are immortal, son, you have so many human lives to try out what you've learned from them.'

I wasn't sure if my father was trying to console me or trying to point out that I was spending too much time alone. Right now, it could be both, as he always was telling me that I should find someone to be with.

'Let them have their fun, for the moment… They will soon face difficult times, and these moments will help them to get through the dark days coming. I'll go and tell your mother about this, maybe we will have a good night, too.'

As soon as he said that his raven flew away, while I was left here, to watch over the sleeping humans.

Great, now that the humans have finished their fucking, the gods were starting theirs, and I refused to imagine or think further about my sister or Father. It was too much for my mind, and instead, I turned my attention to Astrid.

110

She was sleeping deeply, between Gertrude and Viktor. Tomas was holding Gertrud in his arms, and they all seemed at peace.

Of course they were at peace, I mumbled to myself, they have sextenuated themselves tonight; and I wasn't sure why I felt jealous of them; I was a god, and I had all the time and energy to do what they did, but I would have really liked to join them tonight. Instead, I had to stay on the side and watch them from my raven form.

Maybe one day, I will meet her again in my real form, face to face...

Chapter 8
Astrid
Chained

Why does my head hurt so badly?

I opened my eyes, and realised I was in someone's arms, and someone else was snoring loudly in my face. Viktor was the one snoring loudly in my face, and after I turned my head, I realised that Gertrud was holding me in her arms, and Tomas was sleeping peacefully, next to her.

I moved gently and slowly, to not wake them up, and remembered about what happened last night, while I was adding some more branches to the fire. Oh dear, I felt my face going red when I remembered the things that Gertrud did to me.

Viktor was the next to wake up, followed by Gertrud, and they come to join me next to the fire. They seemed to be fighting their own headaches as well, judging by how slowly and clumsy they were moving.

'That drink was strong, but last night was good', said Viktor, then started to laugh softly.

I blushed stronger, and looked down, feeling a bit shy, when more memories came to me about the things that we did last night.

'What happened in the cave, stays in the cave. Is that clear?', asked Gertrud, and we both nodded immediately.

'Good, now we can come back to what we must do today. Astrid, would you like to come back to the camp with us?'

'Yes', I answered, and appreciated Gertrud's question, feeling happy that at least someone understood my desire to have my will respected.

'Prepare yourself to meet Valtyr, he is half angry, half scared that something must have happened to you. Honestly, I don't know how you managed to sneak past all of us, it felt like the whole camp was under a spell, we were all asleep. It had to be a spell, otherwise I would have felt you getting out of bed.'

Gertrud was perplexed, and I decided to confirm her suspicions. There was no point in letting her worry about something that she couldn't control.

'It wasn't just a sleep, sometimes things will happen the way they do, and this is not human's doing. We are being watched, and I got help, so I could sneak out. That wasn't something any of you could stop or control, so it's just for the best to leave it like that.'

Gertrud looked at me but did not try to ask me more about what happened before I ran away.

Meanwhile, Tomas had finally awakened as well, and he looked just as confused as I was, when I woke up. He managed to shake the sleep away quickly, and we got our cloaks on, then we got on the horses, and started to ride back to the camp.

Since there were four of us, and only three horses, I got on the same horse as Gertrud, holding tight onto her, while she was following Tomas. Viktor was riding close, behind us.

As soon as we got into the camp, we were greeted by an angry Valtyr. His eyes seemed to be throwing daggers at me, as he was walking towards me at a fast pace. I will not get intimidated by him, I decided, and I will be ready for a fight if he wanted so.

When I got down from the horse, he came near me, and stopped a few inches away from me. He scanned me worried for a second, then, after he realised that I was safe and sound, the angered expression came back on his face.

'We need to talk', I said not blinking and looking straight into his eyes.

He nodded, turned around and gestured for me to follow him, while he was leading me to his tent. This could either turn bad or good, and I hoped that he would finally learn a lesson, and change his ways.

Inside the tent, he finally faced me.

'You got me worried sick for you, Astrid. I thought that something had happened to you, or someone had taken you.'

'You need to ask me something, Valtyr.'

'I don't understand what you mean...', he said, looking confused at me, so I decided to enlighten him.

'I'm not your puppy, so if you want me to stay in your camp, you need to ASK ME! If I want to leave, I am free to do so, and you have no right to stop me. Do you understand?'

I saw Valtyr taking a step back, when I shouted at him, and felt proud of myself. That should teach him a lesson, and he should finally understand that I had my own will, and he had to respect my decisions, whether he liked it or not. I saw him smiling, but a wicked smile, like an idea that I would not like, was blooming in his thick head, and now I was the one to take a step back, feeling worried.

Valtyr came closer, and I was blessed with his most beautiful smile, while he looked at me, just the way a wolf would look at a deer.

Prey. I felt like I was his prey, and he was ready to pounce at me, at any moment.

'Astrid, would you want to stay with us and give us your help?'

I frowned, not expecting him to give up so easily.

'Yes', I answered hesitantly, not knowing what to expect from Valtyr.

That was the answered that he wanted and set him in motion, straight away. With a quick move, he threw me on his shoulders, while I started to scream and punch his back, and to my indignation, I felt him slapping my ass.

'VALTYR! Put me down, now! You will apologise for this, on your knees!'

'Oh, Astrid, if I get on my knees in front of you, I'll make sure you'll enjoy it!', he said laughing, then he left the tent, with me still on his shoulders.

I saw Gertrud's feet and started to shout.

'Gertrud! Tell him to put me down!'

'Gertrud, don't you even try! I will make sure I won't lose her from my sight again, I promised you I won't do anything to her, unless she asks me for it', said Valtyr, and I saw Gertrud nodding, and staying away from us.

'Valtyr, everyone is staring at us. Put me down.'

'I will, once I make sure you won't run away anymore.'

He kept walking past the tents, until he stopped at the edge of the camp where a man was sharpening a sword, and I realised, to my horror, that this man must be the blacksmith.

Valtyr finally put me down, only to hug me close to his body. I was crushed against his chest, while I was trying to push him away. I gave up; it felt like his arms were made of steel and no matter how much I pushed him away; he was tightening his embrace.

My face was too close to his chest, and I could hear his heart beating strongly. I tried to ignore how nice he was smelling, of forest, winter, and something else, his own smell, that was making me take another deep breath. I could have enjoyed his hugs, but right now, this one was unplanned and unasked for, yet his warmth and his heart beating fast were affecting me, and somehow, I felt myself calming down.

'I need to ask you a favour, make me a chain, long about six feet, and I want the best handcuff that you can make. Take a rope out to take a measurement.'

Valtyr has search for my hand, and while holding me close to his body with one hand, he extended my left hand to the blacksmith, so he can measure my wrist.

'You wouldn't dare, you beast! What am I, your dog?'

'No, you're one of the most important person in this camp, you are our guidance from the gods; and I will keep you chained to me if I have to, but I promised you, I will not lose sight of you again.'

I looked up at him, trying to meet his eyes; I could tell from his expression that he was serious, but I could see something else on his face, an expression of worry that wasn't there until today.

Was he worried for me?

'Valtyr, I already told you that I am going to stay with you. Sometimes, bad things happen, and something could happen to me, even if I am chained to you or not, and even if it does, that doesn't mean that it's your fault, unless you are the one hurting me; then it will be your fault. There are not enough chains or walls in this world to stop bad things happening; and if anything, it might be better for me not to be chained to you, I might be an obstacle in your way, instead of helping you.'

He looked at me, and I could see the blue sky in his eyes, while he was listening to me. He seemed to have taken my safety too serious, and he needed to understand that not everything was his responsibility.

Valtyr placed his hand carefully on my face, and it startled me, not expecting his delicate gesture. He caressed my cheek slowly, then retracted his hand quickly, seeming just as surprised of the way he touched me, as I was. I could see him trying to say something, then hesitating, and finally, looking at me.

'Astrid, it will only be for a little while, I promise you.'

I frowned, not being happy with his decision, but in the end, I decided to allow him to do it for the moment. Whatever evil creatures were torturing his mind, it looked like they got to him, for the moment. I will ask him to remove the chains, but for the moment, I will leave it like this.

I looked at the blacksmith, and the way he respectfully placed the handcuff on my right wrist, then he attached the long chain to it, just as Valtyr requested him. Valtyr had taken the other end of the chain and opened his belt, then attached it straight to his belt.

Oddly, he looked just as uncomfortable as I felt, yet he went on with his chain. I lifted my right hand and looked disgusted at it, while he was studying my face. I felt like shouting, but I knew there was no point. I dangled the chain, and felt more upset than I could remember, in the last few days.

'I feel like a dog', I added sad, and then let the chain fell on the ground, in the snow.

I didn't say anything else, and watched as Valtyr lowered his head, and looked down at the ground, not wanting to meet my eyes.

He started to walk, and I followed him. He was leading me to a part of the camp that I haven't seen until now, the training area. I watched, standing next to him as the men were training, and understood how motivated they were to fight against King Magnus.

At some point, someone has asked Valtyr to join them, but he refused, then looked at the chain fallen at our feet. I could feel that he wanted to join his men, but he realised that it would have been harder than usual to train, when I was chained to him. Ha! I told him, but his thick head refused to understand.

After some time, we headed back to the main fire, the one near the sleeping tents, and I saw most of the people were gathering there as well. I saw other people looking at the chain and frowning, and for the first time in days, Valtyr seemed uncomfortable.

He swore, then I saw him undoing his belt, letting go of the chain, then taking my right hand and working out the mechanism so he can open the cuff at my wrist. He took the chain, and threw it aside, looking angry with himself for doing something like this. Valtyr step in front in front of me, placed his hands on my shoulders, then looked at me intently.

'I'm sorry Astrid, you were right; I shouldn't have done this to you or to anyone. Please stay.'

I nodded my head, and for the first time, I smiled at him, happy that he finally understood. It took him some good hours, but better later than never. He smiled back at me, and I had to fight the urge to hug him, I never wanted so much to touch him, and it surprised me. He came closer to me, still with his hands on my shoulders, and whispered in my ear.

'Tonight, you will sleep in my tent. I will not let you out of my sight, Astrid.'

He let go of my shoulders, then walked away to bring us something to eat. I saw Gertrud, Tomas and Viktor sitting next to the fire, so I went to sit down with them, next to Gertrud. As soon as she saw me approaching, she looked at me and smiled, and I smiled back at her.

Meanwhile, Valtyr returned with food, and he passed some to all of us, then he stood down, next to me.

'How are you feeling, Astrid?', asked Gertrud, with a cheeky smile on her face.

'Better, now that I'm not in chains anymore', I answered to her, looking at Valtyr.

Gertrud frowned, then look at Valtyr.

'Did you put her in chains?', she asked him straight away.

'Yes, but I took them out. I realised that it was a stupid idea', he added then looked at me, with regret written on his face.

I saw Gertrud threatening him with her fork.

'If you ever do that to her again...' she started with a low voice, and saw Valtyr, looking down, shame written all over his face.

Good, I thought, he should be ashamed of what he did, and I was happy to see that others didn't agree with him. I realised that Gertrud had no problem of speaking up her mind to Valtyr and felt that any leader should be able to take criticism for his decisions, instead of assuming that his decisions were just the best choices.

I decided that Valtyr showed potential for a good king, with a bit of chiselling here and there, he could have made the kingdom better, and he would have been a better leader than Magnus was. I hoped, for the first time, that this world would be better, and I hoped that Valtyr would succeed in his attempt of dethroning Magnus.

That's when the small flames in front of me, started to flicker away, and I saw from somewhere up, a pack of mad wolves, with their furs dirty and patchy, trying to attack Valtyr and his army. I saw the white bear coming out of the forest and simply launching himself at the wolves, tearing into them, while the white wolf was near Valtyr, defending him from the other wolves. I saw myself fighting with a sword and managing to hurt a rabid wolf, while a white raven was flying above me, and cawing.

I heard the raven cawing, then I looked at it while the raven started to attack the other wolves, going straight for their eyes; I was helping the guardian and went to the wolf's neck with the sword. The battle seemed to keep going for some time, but all the rabid wolves were killed, while we were celebrating the victory. I saw myself cheering with the others, and the flames reappeared in front of my eyes, only that this time, Valtyr was shouting my name worried, while Gertrud was holding my shoulders and tried trying to wash my face with some water.

'It's alright, it was a vision', I added trying to calm them, as I realised that they feared something happening to me.

'What did you saw?', asked Valtyr and looked at me, waiting for an answer.

'The gods will watch our fight', I said, trying to pick my words carefully, so they could not be interpreted, 'and they will help us'.

As soon as I said this, I saw the raven flying above me, then sitting on my shoulder, and cawing three times, as if it was trying to show the people, that this time, we were not alone anymore and their suffering was seen by the gods, and they will receive the help that they deserved. After that, it flew away into the trees close to the camp.

I saw Gertrud's face filling with joy, while Valtyr seems to be shocked. Tomas smiled with genuine happiness, while Viktor was shouting and lifting his sword.

There was an air of happiness spreading through the people, and I heard my words being repeated, and I could feel that they motivated everyone, while bringing hope, like never before.

Gertrud was the first to speak, and I saw tears rolling on her face, while she spoke loud and clear, for everyone to hear.

'It's time for King Magnus to pay for his countless crimes. He kidnapped me and raped me for days. I barely managed to get away, but I will not let him destroy me. I will have no peace, until I will see him paying for what he has done.'

Tomas was the next to speak, and I felt his pain through his words.

'Magnus has hurt Gertrud deeply, and my family. I will fight for Gertrud, and I will fight to make sure that he never hurts another woman, like he hurt my previous wife.'

'King Magnus has murdered my parents, and I barely managed to escape; being sent away by my father. I will not live in vain, and I will fight against him, so I can stop him from killing other innocent people', said Valtyr, and I looked shocked at him, feeling sorry for him, losing his parents, because of Magnus.

This time, it was my turn to speak as well, and I looked at the faces around me, and realised that they all had been affected by the wickedness of our king.

'My grandmother was the previous seer. She warned Magnus that the gods are watching, and he must stop his wrongdoings, but he killed her regardless. I was just a child when I watched him killing someone I love, with no remorse. I will not have peace until Magnus is punished for everything he had done.'

To my surprise, there were other men who had similar stories to ours, people that have watched their dear ones being butchered by Magnus, or men that had their wives or daughters being taken away by Magnus, and they never heard from them again.

I was shocked to hear how evil Magnus really was; and when I realised that every single person gathered tonight, around the fire, had a painful reason to choose to fight against Magnus I felt my blood boiling with anger.

We were all brought together by pain and injustice, and we all vowed not to stop fighting until Magnus will answer for his wrongdoings. There was so much pain in our lives, so many different people, having their lives turned upside down, by one single person; it was time for a change, and it was time for King Magnus to be punished.

'I am Viktor the Bear, and I have heard all of you. Tonight, I have decided that my next cloak will be made from Magnus' skin. From tonight, you may all call me Viktor the Magnus!'

I watched as everyone laughed, and the mood lightening once Viktor spoke. We all sat down at the fire and finished out food.

There was a feeling of peace in the air, of people feeling united for a cause, more than ever. I understood why we were all here; even if we had different reasons, we will be the ones to stop Magnus from continuing with his wicked and corrupted rule on the kingdom.

People deserved better, and people were ready to fight against a tyrant so they would finally have the good ruler that they needed so desperately. I looked at Valtyr eating his food slowly, while talking with other men, and I realised that he could make a good ruler for Kulta.

Valtyr could bring the peace that everyone needed so badly, instead of the life they had now, living in fear and feeling scared of their king. No king should be allowed to do the things that Magnus did, and now the worst ruler that Kulta had seen in generations, will be dethroned by the people he hurt in the past.

I yawned, feeling tired and looked at Valtyr, that was coming closer to me.

'Feeling sleepy, seer? I personally invite you to my bed, not with bad intentions, I just want to make sure that you are safe and warm, while you're sleeping.'

I looked at him and I blushed, but I nodded. I wanted to sleep in his arms, and I will not be the one to shy away from what I wanted.

Gertrud has come closer to us, and she looked at me.

'Astrid, where will you be sleeping tonight?'

'In my bed', answered Valtyr, while looking straight at me, without blinking.

I swallowed hard, feeling too hot, suddenly. I saw Gertrud looking at me, then I nodded, not taking my eyes away from Valtyr.

'Ah, it looks like you'll be warm tonight', added Gertrud giggling, then walked away smiling.

Valtyr walked past me, then, at the last moment, extended his arm and circled my waist, spinning me around and pulling me towards him.

I followed him in his tent, and I looked at him, turning around to face me, with an expression hard to read on his face. He was looking in my eyes, and I wanted to feel his skin on mine, I wanted to hug him and loose myself in his embrace.

'Astrid, I will not touch you, unless you want me to; if you want me to, come to me.'

I looked at Valtyr, as he was waiting for me to decide; he opened his arms, and I was overwhelmed with my desire of kissing him, right now. I did not know what will happen tomorrow, but tonight I wanted Valtyr, every inch of him, and I wanted to enjoy every moment that I had with him.

I came closer to him, and felt his arms wrapping around my waist, while I placed my hands on his chest, and I tried to reach his face. He leaned in, closer to me, and I kissed him. I heard him moaning softly, while I was exploring his soft lips.

He hugged me tighter, then returned my kiss. This time, it was my turn to moan, as his hands were removing the cloak from my shoulders. I heard the cloak falling on the floor, and I reached for his, opening it and letting it fall.

I took a step back, then watched as he was removing his body armour, then his sword and his belt. My eyes were following his hand, as he removed his shirt slowly, followed by his trousers. I had to stop my mouth hanging open, when I saw his manhood standing straight, and I understood that he wanted me, just as much as I wanted him.

I watched his leaned body as he was moving closer to me, and caressed his chest, while he was untying my long skirt, then started to remove my blouse. I was left in a thin large, white dress, that was underneath my clothes to keep me warm. I grabbed the dress and pulled it over my head, exposing my naked body to him.

I saw Valtyr licking his lips watching my full breasts, then I saw him looking down at my hips and my legs. I saw the desire in his eyes and felt my body answering to his hungry eyes; I felt myself getting wetter down there, while wanting to have his hands all over my body.

He came closer to me, and kissed me again, but this time more slowly and passionately, then pushed me gently and guided me towards the table in his tent. I saw him lowering his head and starting to suck on my nipples, while I grabbed his hair and pulled his hungry mouth closer to me.

Valtyr kneeled in front of me, and lowered his head between my legs, while kissing me on my most sensitive part of my body. I felt his tongue exploring and his mouth sucking, while I threw my head back and felt my heart beating out of control, in response to what he was doing to me.

I felt his hair touching my thighs, while his hands were pulling me closer to his face. I grabbed his shoulders, and crunched towards him, while I had my eyes closed and I could taste the stars in front of my eyes. I felt him lifting me off the table, and laying me gently on the bed, and I opened my eyes to look at him.

Valtyr looked hungry, as he was once more returning to my breasts and massaging my hips slowly. I felt his erection between my legs, and I moved my hips so I could rub myself against it.

I felt him pressing his face against my neck and moaning, then he kissed my neck, and looked in my eyes.

'Astrid, are you sure you want this?'

I nodded, looking straight into his eyes. I was just as hungry for him, as he was me, right now.

'I want to hear you saying it, Astrid.'

'I want you, Valtyr', I said, and I closed my eyes and moaned gently as I felt his cock rubbing against my delicate skin.

I was wet and ready for him, and I gently move my hips, to be able to feel his length against my wet, hungry pussy. I wasn't ashamed of wanting him, and I was moving my body as close as I could to his, biting my lips when I felt how warm and hard his member was.

I wanted him, and when I felt his cock starting to push, I squeezed his shoulders, while my breath deepened. I saw his surprised expression, as he realised that he was the first man that I was sleeping with, and I kissed him, while he was penetrating me. At the beginning, he was moving slowly, but I could feel him moving deeper, in and out of me, while our bodies were rubbing against each other.

I started to tense my body, anticipating the pleasure, and he started to kiss me, as a moan was escaping my lips. He moved deeper inside me, and faster, then I felt the sweetest pleasure taking over me, while Valtyr was pulling my hair gently and kissing me. He was moaning against my lips, while we were riding the waves of pure bliss, together.

He stayed on top of me for a few more moments and looked at my ravished face. I was sweaty, and I could see his hair was just as messy as mine, while a few strands of his hair were caressing my face. Valtyr kissed me again, but this time slower, and I answered back.

He laid next to me and covered us with the blankets. Underneath the blankets, his hand pulled me closer to him, and I rested my head on his chest, while he was playing with a long strand of my hair.

'Astrid, I do not know what the future will bring us, but I want you to know that this was one of the best moments in my life. Thank you for choosing me.'

I looked at Valtyr and could see happiness on his face, and I was amazed that I was the reason for his smile.

'Same, Valtyr. I wanted to be with you, and I am grateful for the moments we shared together, tonight.'

I hugged him, and I started to feel sleepy, being held so close to him, and feeling safe in his strong arms.

The last thing that I remembered before drifting to sleep was Valtyr kissing me gently on my forehead, while he turned on his side, effectively managing to pull me even closer to him; from my head to my toes, I could feel every inch of my body against his warm body, and I was lulled into a deep sleep by the steady rhythm of his heart and his breathing.

Chapter 9
Valtyr
Sweat and swords

I woke up with Astrid in my arms and smiled remembering what happened the previous night. I nudged her gently, and I laughed as I heard her growling in protest, then I felt her arms and legs wrapping around my body.

It's been a long time since I felt so happy, and I was thanking the gods for their decisions to bring her in my path. I nudged her again, feeling her going back to sleep. I felt sorry for my beautiful seer, but today, we had a long day ahead of us.

We had to start preparing, and we really needed to get some clothes on us, until I changed my mind and made her mine, again. I had to control myself around her; now I took advantage of being able to run my hands all over her naked body.

'Astrid, you must wake up beautiful. Look, you ravished my hair last night, now you must braid it.'

I looked smiling at her sleepy face, the way she was struggling to open her eyes, and trying to understand what I was telling her. She looked at me, then smiled.

'I'll braid yours if you braid mine.'

'Deal.'

I kissed her, then got out of bed slowly, and watched her, as she was stretching her body. Soon, she followed me, and I watched with regret as she was putting clothes back on her tempting, voluptuous body. I looked at her and realised that we had to ride for long hours today.

I went around the tent and presented her with a set of clean clothes, undergarments, a blouse, and a shirt.

'Take these, then go to Gertrud, and see if she has some trousers that will fit you. I'm sorry, but I think it will be better for you if you have trousers on you to keep you warm. We will go back to the main camp today, and we will ride for hours. I'm afraid that your skirt will not keep you warm enough.'

I saw her nodding, then preparing to leave the tent, while I called her name, and showed her my hair. She smiled and came back to braid my hair, and after that I braided hers. I was quick enough to see her raising her eyebrows, surprised, and I felt proud.

My aunt Helga insisted for me to learn everything, and she was the one to teach me how to braid, and now I couldn't thank her enough, as I saw how impressed Astrid was with me. Who could've thought that I could impress a woman while I was braiding her hair?

I watched Astrid as she left the tent and going straight to Gertrud's tent. Meanwhile, I went to the fire and decided to wait for her there. It was still early morning, and the men in the camp were awake, but just as sleepy as I was.

I talked with everyone about what we needed to do this morning, to get us ready for the road. Everything needed to be left just the way we found it, and we needed to make sure that it was little proof left of us being here. We have already moved around a few times, while recruiting more people for our cause, so everyone knew exactly what preparations needed to be done.

First, we would have something to eat and make sure we had some food prepared for the road, in case we needed to stop for the night, and we couldn't cook, then we would pack everything in the wagons. The men were ready to join our main camp and start training there.

I hoped that we would be ready by the third full moon from now. It seemed like we had plenty of time, but I knew how quickly time went away, when such an important event was ahead of us; what we were preparing to do, could and would change the fate of a whole kingdom, and I only hoped that it would change it for the better.

Everyone was moving fast and efficiently around me, and all the tents were already dismantled and packed; the wagons that we had were being prepared for the journey, and some food that was cooked for the trip ahead of us, was already being packed.

I gathered my friends around to discuss how we were going to move, until we reached the main camp. We will go ahead all the time to check the roads for any danger, and the wagons will stay behind us, since they were moving much slower.

Two of the wagons were filled with men ready to fight at our signal, and they were in the middle of the convoy. We tried to disguise the rest of the wagons to make them look as unsuspicious as possible, while the best fighters were riding ahead and behind the wagon convoy. We had the archers flanking the convoy, from a distance, and they were ready as well to defend, in case they were needed.

I tried to convince Astrid to stay with the wagons, so we could protect her better, but she insisted on riding with me, Thomas, Viktor, and Gertrud. Gertrud had found some of her spare armour and had already equipped Astrid. I was nervous when I thought of Astrid's safety, but I realised that she was right; if she had any vision, or if she could see anything, it was best to have her close, so we would know and try to act as quickly as possible.

Soon, we started to move, and although I was worried about everyone's safety, we were moving faster than I had anticipated. The convoy was organised, and we were moving quietly through the woods, not wanting to draw attention to us.

I saw the raven landing on Astrid's shoulder, and I was surprised at the connection that seemed to exist between her and this bird. It felt like the gods were present amongst us, and I looked at the bird flying away, ahead of us; we had another pair of eyes checking the road, with us.

We had only stopped for some brief moments, to allow the horses to rest, and we all agreed to continue through the night, but at a slower pace. I knew it was a difficult day for everyone, but by the time the sun rises, we could reach our camp, and finally be back to safety; everyone else agreed with me and we all decided to go on with the journey and not stop until we reached our destination.

We would take turns into riding back and forth between our small group and the wagons, just to make sure that everything was alright, and before I knew it, the darkness of the night was pierced by the morning, and I knew that we had to be getting close. The raven was flying around us all the time, but it would stop from time to time to rest on Astrid's shoulders, as it seemed that it was its favourite place.

When I finally saw our camp, I whistled three times. I signalled to Viktor and Tomas that I would go first, and they nodded. I went quickly to the camp and breathed out in relief when I saw the same men that I left, in charge; thankfully, our location hasn't been discovered by King Magnus, and I thank the servants of the gods that had the inspiration, many winters ago, to build this blessed sanctuary in the mountains, close enough to Jotun.

From where we were, we could barely see Jotun and its surrounding gates, but we could conveniently reach the king's fortress just by walking, not needing the horses.

This place had been kept secret by the few people that knew of it, and because it was situated in the mountains, it was easy to hide from Magnus. I watched as they opened the gates, and the wagons finally entered the camp; now we were safe.

Astrid was looking surprised around her; I have gone to great lengths to disguise the gates with rocks and cover the walls of the building sheltering us with rocks and stones; it was hard to spot the building from a distance, and because the yard was filled with men and weapons, you knew straight away that this place will not go down easily.

There were many puppets made of straws that we were using to practice on, and the yard was carefully organised; the stables, the arenas, the shooting areas, the puppets, and the weapons were all arranged to make sure that we took advantage of every little space we had. We had outposts that looked like trees from a distance, but they had stairs built in, so we could climb them easily.

Astrid was now taking it all in, and I saw the smile on her face widening when she understood how well organised this place really was. We took the horses to the stables, and I could see that all the men around me seemed to be just as relieved as I was that we reached the camp safely.

'What will happen next?', asked Astrid looking at me.

'Today, we rest, and tomorrow the training will start. There is still plenty of time, but I want us to be prepared for what we will do. We will train every day, until we descend upon Magnus. When he is gone, then we will truly rest.'

'I want to train, as well.'

I looked at her and sighed. Under no circumstances, I will not allow Astrid near weapons. I wanted her to be safe, and away from anything that could cut her, or worse, kill her.

'No, Astrid. You will stay away from weapons.'

'Valtyr, you do not get to decide this! Have you heard me? When I joined you and your army, I willingly put myself in front of danger. I want to be able to defend myself if it's needed. What if something happens, and no one is around me, to protect me? You want me to be helpless, or you would rather know that I can defend myself?'

I looked at her and how fierce she was, and I understood that, once again, she was right. It was better for her to be able to fight, but that was making me nervous about her safety. I nodded my head, and saw her beautiful lips turning up, into a smile.

She got what she wanted, while I was promising myself to give her a few lessons in handling a sword and a dagger. Until now, I only made her sweat between the sheets, but now I had a few exercises in my mind…

I showed her the bedrooms and the way around the camp, the hallways, and the secret-not-so-secret tunnel that we all knew about in case we needed to leave the camp quickly and head towards the mountains for escape.

I explained to her about the people that were always watching the surrounding area in turns from the outposts, and everyone got a turn, either day or night, us included. No one was spared from any job, be it cleaning, cooking, stables, or the outposts; we all took turns.

After everyone had settled in the spare bedrooms, I took Astrid to mine, and I decided to have the one across from mine being assigned to her. The bedrooms were all small, but they were enough to have the minimum necessities in there. Since the camp was originally built by the servants of gods, that used to be many, long time ago, they decided to keep everything to the minimum.

We kept in great condition the original furniture that they made, and only changed the mattresses; the bed frames, the tables, the chairs, and the trunks for clothes were made by them, and we made sure we took care of everything. There was no luxury here, but our needs were met, and we were all safe. This was a cherished placed, and we made sure to take great care of it.

I left Astrid to arrange her belongings in her room and told her to make her way to the dining room to eat something before she goes to sleep.

I went to my room, and removed my armour, then changed to more comfortable clothes. I've shown her already everything in the camp, then after I finished with changing my clothes, I knocked on her door.

Just as I expected, she had changed to some lighter clothes as well, and I walked with her.

This time, she let her long hair down, and I couldn't help to caress her soft locks. I saw her blushing, but she did not take her eyes away from mine. Playing with a long strand, I wrapped it around my hand gently, and I look at her intensely.

'I cannot wait to have your hair falling down on my naked body.'

She smiled and looked defiantly at me.

'Be careful what you wish for, you might get it.'

'I cannot wait for it', I answered, admiring her, head to toe. I already knew what was hiding underneath her clothes, and I was yearning to feel her body in my arms, again.

We found the others at the table, and we sat down and ate with them. Tomas, Viktor, and Gertrud were just as relieved as I was that we managed to reach back here safely, and I could see their happy faces, despite travelling for so long. We cleaned our plates quickly, and I saw Astrid going with Gertrud, to the women bathing room. I might have been staring a little too long, and Viktor noticed it.

'Valtyr, you're drooling all over your food; close your mouth, captain.'

I turned my head and frowned at him, while he and Tomas were laughing quietly. We were the only ones that heard him, and I did take his advice and closed my mouth. Yes, I forgot I was drooling, while I was staring at Astrid's nice and round bottom, that was looking so tempting in trousers.

I finished my food, then went to shower myself. I knew I was stinking after so much riding, and I tried to wash myself as quickly as I could. With my hair down and wet, I went towards my bedroom; I had lost the notion of time, but I knew it was just after mid-day.

I opened the door, and my mouth fell wide open, in shocked. A gorgeous, naked Astrid was laying on my bed, smiling at me. I closed the door as fast as I could, and looked at her, admiring her naked body, while approaching the bed. I threw my clothes on the floor, and without taking my eyes off hers, I buried my face straight between her legs.

I smiled when I heard her gasping; she wasn't expecting it, but soon I heard her gasp turning into moans, then I felt her hands pulling at my hair; that's it, Astrid, I'm not going to stop until I hear you screaming my name. I felt her hips moving in rhythm with my tongue, and while I was tasting her most vulnerable parts, I finally heard her moaning my name, but I still not stopped until I felt her body tensing, while she was facing the waves of pleasure.

She was ravished, but she was beautiful, still panting from the wonderful things my tongue did to her. I laid on top of her, kissed her gently, while she was responding to me, and caressing my body. I hugged her tight to my body, then flipped her quickly. I almost laughed when I saw her confused expression, but I saw her moaning, when she felt how hard I was.

'Now it's time for you to work, princess. Let's see how good you are with riding', I told her defiantly, but I had no idea what was awaiting me.

140

At first, I helped her to hop onto me and watched her wiggling her hips, while she arranged her body, then I guided her hips with my hand, and watch her mouth opening slightly, while she tilted her head back and enjoyed the feeling of my hard cock filling her. She was slow at the beginning, but her hips have started to move faster, as she bent down to kiss me.

I finally felt her silky hair falling on me, while she was riding me without mercy. It was my turn now to moan her name, while I saw her increasing the pace; I could barely stop myself and caught her delicate nipple in my mouth, while she was tensing from the pleasure, and I was holding her hips into place while burying myself deep inside her and facing the wave of pleasure with her nipple between my teeth; I filled her quickly, and looked between us, at the shiny nectar on her tights.

I helped her to come next to me and looked at her nestling on my side. I caressed her face and kissed her gently. I turned to my side, and pulled her closer to me, and I felt her drifting to sleep; I pulled the blankets on top of us, not wanting to disturb her well-deserved sleep, and while I was holding her close to me, I understood how much she meant to me.

In such a short time, Astrid had become one of the most important people of my life; I realised that my obsession of keeping her safe wasn't just because she was the seer, no; I had feeling for her, and it was my instinct to make sure that the woman I hold most dear is safe.

I was so adamant to make sure that she is alright, because I cared deeply for her, and I would have gone insane if something had happened to her. While I was admiring her beautiful face, I heard the flapping of wings, and I saw the raven watching us, from outside. I wondered if the gods were watching everything we did, but then I turned my attention back to her.

I took another look at her sleeping face, trying to make sure that I will always have this memory of her, sleeping peacefully next to me, after our lovemaking. I closed my eyes, and drifted to sleep, as well.

***

When I opened my eyes, I was alone in the bed. I got up quickly, remembering how I fell asleep with Astrid in my arms, and wondering where she was. I got dressed quickly, then I went to her room.

I knocked, I entered, but she wasn't there. I went to her window, knowing that it had a view over the inner yard; I saw almost everyone gathered in a circle, and when I looked to the middle of the circle, I almost panicked.

Gertrud was on her knees, looking at Viktor, while he was trying to fight Astrid; it took me a moment to realise that Gertrud was in fists, laughing her soul out, while Viktor was trying to get an advantage over Astrid. Viktor's heavy sword had cut many throats, and I was witness to that, but in front of Astrid's speed, he had no chance.

Even I smiled when I saw her evading him quickly, and managing to dance around him so fast, that it made everyone laugh. It was like watching a bear, trying to catch an eagle; Astrid was dancing around him, while Viktor was getting frustrated, trying to catch up with her.

Constantly, she avoided his large and heavy sword, while she was using her dagger and a lighter sword to stop his attacks. Eventually, Viktor had enough, threw his sword on the ground, and went to Astrid, and lifted her on his shoulders. I saw Astrid dropping her weapons and laughing, while Tomas and Gertrud were laughing from the side, as well.

I left her room and went straight to them; Astrid was still on Viktor's shoulder, while Gertrud was laughing at him. When I reached them, I saw Viktor looking shocked at me, then smiling, happy to see me.

'Valtyr, good morning, princess! You'd have no clue, but our little seer is quite good with her sword. She made me sweat a little, but nah, I got her.'

'Viktor, you can put me down now', said Astrid, and I watched as Viktor dropped her gently.

She turned to look at me, and I saw her face brighten when her eyes met mine. I don't know what tomorrow will bring me, but I had every intention of enjoying today.

'I want you to teach me how to defend myself, how to fight, and how to attack; I need to be able to do this, Valtyr.'

I nodded, and while others were pairing up to resume their training, I picked up a sword and started to explain to Astrid everything I knew about fighting. She wasn't as strong as I was, but she was fast in her movements, and I begged the gods to protect her, so she never has to fight to defend herself.

If she was near me, I would have defended her, but I hated the thought of not being near her, and not being able to help her if she needed me. I corrected her posture and showed her some sneaky moves, so she could be aware of them. Soon, she was moving even better than on her training with Viktor; I had to ask the blacksmith to forge her a sword, she needed one made specially for her.

We all took a break from training and moved to the dining table to eat. The room was once again full of people, of laughter, and you could almost feel the hope in the air. Astrid was sitting next to Gertrud, in front of me, while Tomas and Viktor were on either side of me.

Together, we talked about the plans for training and how we will organise so we could keep everything in check: the building, the yard, the stables, the kitchen, our wellbeing, and teach the new people that have joined us.

Everyone was eating, and while we talked about what we needed to do, I felt proud seeing people getting involved, trying to come in and help with their own ideas; the men were willing to take any of the tasks that needed to be done, and I was moved to see how well things were being sorted out, when there was a wish to cooperate, amongst people.

This, this right here, was something that King Magnus could not possibly understand, as he was the one to call the orders and everyone had to follow his orders blindly. There was really no way in which someone could force their will onto other people; sooner or later, people always rebelled.

Instead, to have people involved in what was happening, and having them to express their opinions was strengthening any decision taken in this manner. No one was forced here to do anything that they did not wish to do so, and every person present here was willing to contribute in any way they could to our cause.

I looked around us, trying to lock these moments in my mind, so I can always remember how hope looked like to me. These people, and the ones that were hounded by Magnus, deserved to live peacefully, but instead they lived in fear, for their own lives and the lives of the people close to them.

Magnus has managed to destroy the kingdom that was made before him, when people could farm their lands in peace and not be afraid of the greedy king that send his army to reap the result of hard work. I was tired of looking over my shoulder and I would rather die trying to stop this, then be afraid for the rest of my life.

Living in fear was not viable for anyone, and I was proud of the men and the women that decided to join our army; people were tired of the miserable life that Magnus had created for them and decided to risk everything to fight against him.

I looked around the room and registered in my mind every face that was here today. I could feel hope brightening the room and giving an invisible motivation to all of us. People were united here, and we only had ourselves.

Either we rise together, or we fall together; but we were done waiting for a miracle to happen, we will make it happen.

Chapter 10
Zanos
The god that is watching

Day after day, I had to look at them. In the beginning, when they first arrived at the camp, I did not care about what was happening, but slowly, I was feeling something that I did not use to.

Astrid was beautiful and lovely, and I could not blame Valtyr for being attracted to her, since I started to like her, as well. At first, I did not care that they were also sleeping together, but now, I felt annoyed because he had the opportunity to be near her, as a man, while I was stuck in raven form, having to watch over her; every time they were sleeping, I choose to turn around, so I would not see them.

I would not see them making love, but I could still hear them, and it was eating me away. I could have been there with her, instead of him, but I was stuck on the outside, hearing her moans of pleasure, while I was trying to fly further away from the window. It was saddening to see how happy she was with him, but at the same time, I felt some sort of peace knowing that she was happy; she deserved to be happy.

I wonder how she will react to me if I was able to show her my true form.

Would she look at me the same she was looking at Valtyr? Would she blush if I kissed her?

I tried not to care, but I could not help it, and I ended up caring. I wanted to be the one to hold her in my arms, and I wanted to be the one to have the chance to fall asleep next to her.

Instead, I was watching another man hugging and kissing her. Again, I had to turn my back, to give them some privacy.

Sure, what I saw in the cave was a sight, but now, I was not interested in watching him making her, his, again and again. I was almost angry at my father for not allowing me to show my true form to her; I was wondering if she would have looked at me just a bit longer, or if she would want to do with me the things that she was doing with him.

Every time I saw Valtyr hugging Astrid, I wanted to reveal myself to them, and I wanted to take her away, but how could I have done that to her, knowing that she was happy with him?

Every moan that I heard from her started to feel like a hot knife going straight through my heart; it was hurting me more every day, but I will stand by the promise I made to Father and I will watch over her, for as long as he needed me to.

I never wanted to feel this way, and I was still considering flying over to my kingdom, but since my father hasn't said anything else to me, I understood that he still wanted to watch me over Astrid.

I ruffled my feathers annoyed; the raven form was one of my favourite, apart from my wolf form that was intimidating for humans.

As a raven, I was able to go around unnoticed by most people, but somehow, she could almost feel me around her. She will always turn her head to the place where I was hiding, and I could see her smiling towards me. She felt my presence, and she was always welcoming me around her, but what she didn't know was that I was craving for more.

The first time she extended her right arm to allow me to land on it, I did not think too much, and I landed as softly as I could, so I wouldn't scratch her skin. Next thing she did was to move her arm closer, so she could look straight in my eyes. I looked in her beautiful eyes, and I could see the dark green of the forest looking back at me, and her beautiful lips rewarded me with one of her most charming smiles.

Timidly, she touched my wings then petted my head, and without realising, a small sound like a cat's purring escaped my beak. Yes, I was in my raven form, but her hands on my feathers felt so good, that I leaned my head into her palm. She started to scratch my head gently, and I made another sound to express my appreciation, which made her giggle.

I decided that I was getting a little too comfortable with her, and just like that, I flew away from her arm, which made her look almost sad towards me.

I looked at her, following me with her sad eyes, and decided that I did not like to see her upset, so I landed on her as gently as I could, but this time, on her left shoulder, and I was finally satisfied when I saw her smiling again.

After that day, I became used to landing on her shoulder, and staying there for some time; I would only fly away from her if I saw Valtyr coming. It was upsetting me, see him hugging her, when I was craving for so long to do it, but there was nothing I could do... for the moment.

I hope that I will get the chance to talk with her, and I was annoyed that Valtyr was so blessed to have her next to him every day. I had nothing against him, I only wished I was as lucky as he was, and have the chance to be around her, as a man, every day. I was asked to protect her, and I will not break my promise to my father, but I craved to hug her, and at the beginning it was just a thought, but now it was a thought that was torturing me...

To be around her every day, and not be able to speak with her, was eating me alive. Maybe I will have the chance to show my true form to her. I know she only saw me once, and I was curious to know what she thought about me, or if she even remembered me.

Meanwhile, I had the pleasure of watching her relationship with Valtyr blooming into something more serious; I wondered if he would sacrifice everything for her, I knew I barely managed to stay quiet on the side and just protect her. I was too close to come to her in my true form, but I had to wait. Maybe one day, I will be able to talk with her.

Now, as I was comfortable sat on a branch, I watched her training with one of the men, in the yard. She was laughing and trying to defend herself from the fast sword of the man.

From where I was, it looked like she was dancing. Astrid was moving so graciously and fast, that I felt proud of her; she was our seer, and even the other humans were impressed with her agility and her ability to foresee the next movements of her adversary.

I frowned thinking that maybe one day, she might need to defend herself from men trying to harm her. I would wipe the ground with anyone who would even think of hurting her, faster than they could understand what happened to them.

I understood why my father wanted me to be near her; as they were all preparing to dethrone Magnus, the king ruling over the kingdom now, they could find themselves in dangerous situations, and I agreed with father now, she had to be protected.

I knew that she wasn't aware, but we, the gods, still remembered what Magnus did to the previous seer, her grandmother. It made my blood boil to think how corrupted and vicious one human could be, and I knew exactly where Magnus will go, after his death.

He would pay for his wrongdoings, but he was still alive now, and I wanted badly to see him dead, so I would be the one to send him where he belongs, amongst the evil monsters, who were created to make human repent for all their wrongdoings.

Now, I had to wait and see what would happen next. I felt Sera's presence, long before I heard the flapping of the wings. She landed on the same branch that I was standing on, and I looked at her, in her raven form. I heard her voice, in my mind, immediately.

'How are you, brother? Having fun in the world of humans?'

'As a raven, not that much fun, Sera. I must admit, they are quite interesting. I understand now why you and father like to spend time with them.'

'How about the one that father chose as seer? How is she doing?'

'She is being trained and she is learning how to defend herself. I believe she is one of the good humans. I watched her for quite some time, and I am happy with her as a seer. She inspires others and manages to strengthen their faith in us. She will be a good seer.'

'You were never interested in the previous seers, brother. Is there something special about her?'

'Sera, don't exaggerate. You know I was asked to watch over Astrid, it's normal that I see and understand a lot more now, rather than when I was in my kingdom and minding my own business.'

I saw Sera looking again at Astrid; in that moment Valtyr chose to appear, and give her a hug, which draw an annoyed huff from me. Of course, Sera heard it, and she did not miss my mood changing straight away.

'Annoyed by the competition, brother? Is it me, or you like this seer a bit too much?'

I wish I was in my normal form, so Sera could see me rolling my eyes at her. I stopped for a second, realising that she was right, and for the first time, in hundreds of winters, I was paying more attention to a human, than I ever did before. She was right, I realised.

'Brother, you are jealous on the man.'

I nodded my head once. She looked at them, then looked at me.

'Good luck to you.'

She flew away, as quickly as she came, leaving me with the realisation that for the first time, I was feeling something, and I was stuck on looking from the side at another man getting closer than I could, to the woman that I had feelings for.

I drew a sharp breath and tried to concentrate and remember that I was there only to watch over Astrid for the moment, and there was nothing else that I could do. Maybe one day, I will be blessed to just hold her in my arms for a few moments, but until then, there was nothing else left for me; I had to watch over her.

Days passed while the humans were training, and I watched as Astrid was getting better at fighting as the time went by. She didn't know, but I was proud of her, watching as she turned from a shy girl, into the strong woman that managed to amaze people with her fighting skills.

I wished these days would last forever, because I was worried of what will happen when they would try to dethrone Magnus, and I knew that important day was getting closer.

I have decided to take my raven form, while they were marching to the capital city, but as soon as they face anyone from Magnus's army, I would turn into my wolf form, and I will not leave her side.

I had a few moments when I could be closer to her, when she extended her arm, to allow me to land on. I looked into her eyes, as I was training her to open her mind towards me; in the beginning, she thought she was having visions, but after some time, she understood that I could show her everything that I saw, from the raven's eyes.

Astrid was amazed by the landscape from such a great height and seemed to be excited for me to show her more, but as I was flying above the training yard, she understood. It hurt me to see the saddened expression on her face as she understood that I was showing her these things now, so I would prepare her for the day when she would need to know where the danger was lying ahead.

Her saddened face was wreaking havoc in my immortal heart, as I wanted so badly to be able to tell her that I would be there to protect her, but I wasn't able to. I watched as the corners of her lovely mouth went down a bit, as she seemed about to cry.

I leaned forward so my forehead would touch hers, to comfort her, and I felt her soft fingers caressing my feathers. I cawed softly, then looked at her, as she was trying to calm herself. I extended my wings, and she understood that I wanted to fly away, but this time, I flew in circles around her, again and again, while she stood still, with a sad smile on her face.

I was trying to show her how beautiful she was, to distract her from her dark thoughts, and I was working with her to strengthen the bond between us, so she could have a real advantage, while I was showing her everything that I was able to see.

I started to fly higher, and faster, while I was pushing everything that I saw at her mind. I tried my best to show her the beautiful forest and the mountains around the camp, then I started to plunge from a height, straight towards the ground, repeating it. I started to fly as fast as I could through the trees, so she could get used to see the world at a greater speed, as fast as the raven was able to fly.

I turned to her, and I sent her the image of her looking at me, while I was seeing her through my eyes. She extended her arm, and I landed softly. I looked at her face, and this time she was in awe, and she looked at me, like she was struggling to find her words, to express what she felt.

'Thank you for what you showed me, it felt like I was the one flying.'

I saw the timid smile appearing on her face, and I wished I could smile back at her, and be able to talk to her. I saw her friends approaching, and I flew away, towards a tree, while she started to talk with them.

That night, as soon as I saw her kissing Valtyr, I flew away. Again, I could feel the knife piercing my heart, while I was trying hard to accept that no matter how much I loved her, she had her own life, and she would probably never know anything about how much I wanted her.

I came back to the window, after some time, and I watched her, as she was lying on her side, with only the blanket to cover her. Valtyr was playing with her beautiful, long strands of hair.

Suddenly, I saw Valtyr kneeling at the bed, before Astrid, and he asked her to marry him, and Astrid accepted. She asked him not to tell anyone for the moment, as everyone needed to concentrate on the fight they had ahead.

I heard them talking about how they could get married after everything settled down, and Magnus was no longer king. I haven't seen Astrid smiling so happy in a long time, and I felt jealousy eating me away, as I watched Valtyr coming back in the bed, and hugging her, while making plans with her.

I looked from the window, and envied their moment of happiness, and wished I would not be so selfish, as a god, but for the first time in hundreds of winters, I was being hit by emotions that I never felt before.

For the first time, I could understand why so many humans were not strong enough, and ended up doing wrong things out of jealousy, but I fought and managed to calm myself down. I was a god and had to accept that there was a chance that I could never be with the woman I had such strong feelings for.

I couldn't be with her, but I will protect her, and I will personally make sure that no one will touch her. Valtyr was the luckiest man, holding her in his arms, and kissing her, and I felt a wave of sadness hitting me, when I saw how happy she looked back at him.

I could only watch from distance, but at least I was grateful that she was happy. Even if I wasn't the one that made her happy, at least she was smiling. It broke me that I wasn't the one to make her smile, but at least I could be at peace, knowing that someone else was brightening her life. Valtyr was a charming man, as much as it pained me to admit, and he looked like the kind of human that could take care of her and treat her nice.

I watched as they finally fell asleep and wondered what was like to live as a human. They were so fragile, and so strong at the same time...

I could finally understand why Elia had married a human. I blame myself for looking down upon him, but now that I saw how hard their life was, I understood him so much better. Now, I could finally understand why my sister was relieved when Father decided to bless the human that she loved with immortality.

It pained me to think that one day Astrid will be old, that she will be in pain, and she will die.

I knew that she would enter my kingdom after she will die, but it pained me deeply not to be able to ever see her again. I was able to handle seeing her in another's man arms, as long as I knew that this was what she wanted, but to not see her again at all, would have broken me.

There were just a few days left until they will start marching towards the capital, and even I was nervous, thinking of what could happen.

I knew, at least, that Father wanted to make sure that no one would hurt her, since he sent me to watch over her, so that meant that she was one of the humans that would live after the fight against the king.

I was dreading that day, as much as the humans were dreading it. Sure, they were training hard, every day, and they were ready to give up their life for what they believed in, even though they knew that some of them might not live to see another day. I looked at them watching every interaction between me, in my raven form, and Astrid.

They understood quickly that I was more than a raven, and it seemed to give them courage, as they knew that the gods were still watching. I made sure that I was always announcing my presence around the humans, and I watched as they bowed their head at me, and moving out of my way, even when I was flying above them.

It seemed that my presence and Astrid's were raising the spirits in the camp, and I made sure, every day, that the humans could see me and hear me. I smiled when I saw them leaving two bowls outside, one with water, and one with grains, for me.

I made sure that I always emptied them, even though I didn't need the food, in my animal form. I appreciated their efforts, and it made me care about them even more, when I saw how kind and thoughtful they were. I saw them treating their horses with respect, and taking care of them, every day. I saw the humans caring for themselves, and for everyone around them, and I understood.

This time, I truly understood why my parents and my siblings were so invested in them, and why they would watch them up close, for long time. I know my brother was comparing them to cockroaches, but I agree with the other members of my family; humans were so precious.

Their life was short, and they had to fight every day, in a way or another, to stay alive. They worked hard for their food, they were building their homes with hard work, and when they thought that things were finally settling, the corruption and the greed of their king was reducing their efforts to nothing. And to make matters worse, they had to watch their loved ones dying, knowing very well that they will never see them again.

For the first time, I was grateful to Father for asking me to watch over Astrid, as I finally had the chance to truly explore humanity so close. I wondered what would happen after they started to attack King Magnus, and I called upon Father, knowing that he would soon show up.

This time, not only that I felt Father's presence, but I felt Mother closer, as well. They were both in their raven forms. I watched them as they landed on either side of me. I felt grateful for their presences, and how fast they come to see me. I heard Father's voice in my head, after I thanked him.

'Zanos, we need to talk about what's going to happen next.'

Chapter 11
Astrid
The gods are done watching

There wasn't much time left, just three days. Three days until we start marching towards the capital, in our effort to dethrone Magnus.

Valtyr and the men had done everything in their power to make sure that we were all ready for what was about to happen. We trained daily, and after we ate our dinner, we spent time to discuss about how we are going to lead our offensive against Magnus and what will happen on that day.

Gertrud had spent a long time drawing a big map of the capital, and she managed to gather some buttons, to be able to explain to people how we are going to organise the attack, while placing the buttons on the map. A few of us will go ahead, to assist with opening the gates, right before sunset.

I had no idea how Valtyr had managed to gather so much information about the capital and the defenses that Magnus had installed, but he was the one who explained to Gertrud how to draw the map. The greatest help that we had, were the men in Magnus's army, that had enough of his cruelty. People had enough of the cruel leader, and the men at the gates will be our way in.

We went over the plan again, how the main gate will be opened from the inside, while some men will go in the secret tunnel to block it, while others will set fire to the king's ships, that were anchored in Jotun's port. That will be the signal for us to enter the capital, and while most people will have their attention diverted towards the ships and the boats, we will enter the city and attack Magnus, hoping that we will be victorious.

In theory, the plan was alright, but we were all aware that things could go wrong at any time, and we were prepared for it. Valtyr was pointing on the map, explaining to the men where the guards are gathering, which areas to avoid, and what to do in case that we were captured and everyone else needed to retreat.

While we were all listening, I felt the pull, and I closed my eyes, knowing that I was about to see something. I saw swords being swung around, people dead, our men fighting against the guards, and I saw one of the guards coming closer to Tomas, who was already fighting another guard, and saw the coward soldier getting closer to him, and with a quick move, the blade touched his neck.

I gasped as I saw Tomas falling on the ground, with blood oozing from his wound. I saw him fighting to breathe, but soon, his body became numb, and he gave his last breath.

When I opened my eyes again, I heard Valtyr explaining about the streets in the capital, and from which directions they could expect the guards to come from.

I realised that since I was a bit further away from the map that was lying on the table, no one had seen that I just had a vision, and because Valtyr was talking, they were all facing him and paying attention to what he was saying.

I stepped outside the dining room and waited for all the people to leave. I saw Tomas soon, accompanied by Gertrud and Viktor. I knew that the three of them were most of the time together, so I went to Tomas and asked him if we could talk. Gertrud and Viktor walked away without asking me why, and I pulled Tomas back into the dining room, that was now empty.

'Astrid, is everything all right?'

'Tomas, I had a vision, and you were in it.'

I knew that I was struggling to find my words, and as I was explaining to him what happened in my vision, I saw his face darkening, understanding why I chose to warn him.

'Astrid, thank you for telling me. I will try my best to stay alive, but I will make sure that I will cherish the days that I have left with Viktor and Gertrud.'

'Tomas, I'm so sorry to be the one that tells you this, but I don't know what else to do. Would you consider instead to not coming to Jotun? That way, we would be sure that you will be alright.'

I was desperate to convince him to stay away from the capital, knowing that my vision would come true.

'I know you want to save me, dear girl, but there is no way that I will leave them two alone in this fight, just so I can hide somewhere. If this is my fate, then so be it. I lived a good life, and I trust Viktor to always watch over Gertrud and Petur, for me. I'm only sorry that I cannot see my son, again, but I will make sure to leave you a letter for him.'

I nodded my head.

'I will keep the letter to your son, Tomas.'

'I will write another, one for Gertrud and one for Viktor. I will give them to you, but promise to give them those letters, only after the battle.'

'I promise.'

Tomas gave me a quick hug, then walked away. I looked after him, still wishing that he would choose not to fight, but understanding completely why he couldn't stay away from this fight; if I were in his place, I would have done the same. I still hoped that gods will choose to interfere this time, and his life will be spared, but I knew very well that the visions were never wrong.

I walked towards Valtyr's bedroom doing my best to hide the sadness, but as soon as I entered, I saw him looking carefully at me, as if he knew that something was wrong.

'Astrid, what happened? What is wrong?'

'It's about the fight, Valtyr. I'm nervous; when I think that some of us might get hurt, and others...'

I did not finish my sentence, and I felt Valtyr's arms hugging me tight. I leaned into his embrace, and I did my best to hug him back as tight as I could. There was nothing better than his embrace, while he was caressing my hair.

'Astrid, look at me.'

I lifted my head, then looked into his lovely blue eyes. It was like seeing the sky looking back at me, and I could not get enough of it.

'Even if we are defeated, each and any of us, are ready to die for what we believe in, rather than hiding in our homes and watching Magnus destroying everything around him. I know we could get killed, but I hope that we won't. I can't stay and watch Magnus killing so many innocent people without trying to do something to stop him, no matter how much this will cost me. I will willingly choose to die on my own feet rather than living my life in fear and hiding somewhere.'

'I know Valtyr, and I feel the same. You know very well why I want to see Magnus gone.'

Valtyr nodded, and caressed my face, then kissed my forehead gently, without releasing me from his warm hug.

I was grateful for how gentle he was with me, right now, when I needed it.

'Astrid, I would prefer to know you safe. I would rather have you staying here, away from any danger.'

'Valtyr, no. I will come as well, and I will be riding with you, Gertrud, Tomas, and Viktor. I am the seer, and I will not hide. If something happens to me, then I will tell the gods what I saw, and if we manage to dethrone Magnus, I will still pray to the gods and tell them how brave we were.'

I saw Valtyr trying to say something, then changed his mind and nodded his head, instead.

Just like I understood him, he understood me as well. There was no hiding from this fight, there was no going back. Once we started this, we had to finish it.

Tonight, we went straight to sleep, both of us being pensive about what will happen. I enjoyed staying in the arms of the man that I loved and admired.

I turned my head to look at the window, and I saw the raven, sitting on the window ledge. I wondered for a moment, how many times the raven stood there, watching what was happening in the bedroom, and hoped that it did not saw everything…

It was weird, but at the same time, now, when I was nervous and worried about what was going to happen, the presence of the raven was reassuring, to me. I was still amazed by how the raven managed to show me everything that it saw, while it was flying, but now I realised what advantage it gave us, in front of the king's army.

I knew that the raven would help us that day, and I knew that it would watch over us. Right before I fell asleep, I prayed to the gods that Magnus will be defeated, and the next king will care about its people. I knew it was Valtyr, I remembered about the vision that I had, long ago, when I was the one that put the crown on his head.

Valtyr was a good man, and I knew he will not treat his people the way Magnus did. He would have made a great king, and I knew that Valtyr was the kind of person that would put another before him.

I smiled, knowing that in the end, things will be alright, and trying not to think how many of us will end up wounded and how many will end up dead.

I finally closed my eyes and fell asleep quickly.

***

I inhaled deeply, welcoming the cold, crisp air into my lungs.

This is it.

I looked around me, at the men on their horses, getting ready to ride towards the capital. The day of the battle had come, finally, and we were all gathered in front of the main gates of the camp, ready to march towards Jotun.

Valtyr was ahead of us, waiting for us to get into formation. I looked at him and could see the determination on his face. He was looking at each of us, and waited patiently until we were all ready to start the short journey.

'My friends!', shouted Valtyr, getting everyone to look at him, curious about what he had to say.

'Today is the day when our fate will be decided. We ride now, together, to put a stop to the evil that is corrupting and destroying our lives. I am done waiting for a better day, I will take my sword and make the day better myself! I am done watching and waiting, today is the day we put a stop to Magnus' wrongdoings!'

People nodded their heads and murmured in agreement with him.

'We walk together, as one, and we will stand together to face and destroy this corruption that has brought us so much misery; I know I had enough! I will raise my sword against Magnus, and I will rather die for what I believe in, than watch him destroying his own people completely. Who stands with me against Magnus?'

I lifted my own sword and shouted, just like everyone else around me. Our voices were loud and piercing through the silent woods around us. I saw the raven flying above us, then circling me, and landing on my shoulder.

Valtyr turned his horse around and started the journey to Jotun. We all followed him. I looked at Gertrud, that came to ride next to me. She smiled at me. Behind us, I could see Tomas and Viktor.

We had to move quietly through the forest, and we had to make sure that we will not be seen before we reached the capital. It was still dark outside, and the moon was lighting the road ahead of us. You could still hear the hooves of the horses and gentle movement of the wagons, but people were quiet while riding.

Jotun had a great wall surrounding it on land, build by Magnus. Around the capital, all trees were put down, so once we will be out of the forest, the soldiers from the watchtowers could see us.

That's when the soldiers at the gate will come into play. Those were in fact soldiers that were supporting Valtyr and had chosen to infiltrate willingly into Magnus' army so they would be the key to open the surprise attack against the king.

As we reached the forest close to Jotun, we stopped. It was early in the morning, and somewhere, far ahead of us, we could see the first rays of sun. We had to move fast.

The plan was already set in motion. Some of the men had started to walk away, through the forest. They would set the ships on fire, while we were waiting to hear the bells ringing, a clear sign that our little diversion had worked. That will be our signal to march towards the main gate.

I saw the raven flying above us, then going towards the city. Just like the practices at the camp, I saw everything, almost the same way I had my visions. The images in my mind were moving fast, but I could see the small flames that started on the king's boats.

'Valtyr, they managed to set the ships on fire, it won't be long from now.'

Valtyr nodded.

We all got into position and waited. Sometime after the men walked away, I finally heard the bells. Instantly, I looked at the main gates of the city being opened, then I heard Valtyr giving the order.

'To the main gate!'

As soon as Valtyr gave the order, everyone started running.

I lifted my sword, and inhaled deeply, then I started running as well.

That's when I saw the raven flying above, then circling the city. Trough the raven's eyes I could see Jotun, and I saw the soldiers moving in the city.

A part of them stayed at the main gate, while most of them headed towards the house where most probably Magnus was living, so they could defend him.

The men that opened the gates were the ones supporting our cause, but the other soldiers around them draw their swords out, getting ready to fight against us.

All the pain I felt when I saw my grandmother brutally executed, has now resurfaced as anger, pure and untamed. As I plunged my sword deep into a soldier's chest, I prayed that the gods would forgive me for taking another life. I had to fight with them, I had to do something to stop the evil that destroyed so many people.

I went closer to Valtyr, then I shouted, while I was defending myself against one of the mercenaries.

'Valtyr, we need to move from here, most of the soldiers have gone to protect Magnus!'

Valtyr was fighting two mercenaries on its own, but I heard him shouting, to let everyone know.

'As soon as are finished here, we are all heading towards Magnus' house!'

I thanked the gods for sending me the raven, as it was giving me a complete view of the city, and letting me know in time how the troops moved.

As I prepared to fight another soldier, I saw Tomas beside me, coming to help me, and fighting against the man, alongside me. I remembered about my vision, and I felt a pang of fear gripping my heart.

The place that we were in, right now, looked like the one that I saw in my vision, and I knew what was about to happen. I felt tears in my eyes, knowing that this will be the place where Tomas will be murdered.

'Tomas, go away from here!'

I shouted desperately, knowing what will happen soon. I could not tell him that this was the place that I saw in my vision, but I hope he realised that something was wrong.

'I'm here to help you, Astrid.'

'Tomas, I want you far from this place!'

I tried to convince him again, and I saw him frowning, hearing the desperation in my voice.

'Astrid, if this is how I die, then so be it, but I will not leave you alone!'

As we fought the soldier, two more appeared, and I heard Viktor and Gertrud shouting, and coming towards us, to help. I looked at the soldiers concentrating on Tomas, and I saw one going behind him, ready to deliver what I knew it was the fatal blow to his neck.

I tried to distract the soldier behind Tomas, but he shoved me aside. I fell, and as soon as I managed to get up I started to shout at Tomas, trying to warn him; but my shout came a split second too late, and as I was shouting his name, I saw the sword cutting his neck, then blood poured from the wound.

Tomas fell on his knees, as Viktor and Gertrud were approaching him.

'Tomas!'

Viktor has shouted his name as well, but he reached too late. With fast moves, he killed the soldiers gathered around Tomas's body, and Gertrud ran to him. I had tears in my eyes as I watched Gertrud hugging his lifeless body.

Viktor was shielding us, roaring and effectively wiping out from existence anyone who approached us.

'No, please come back to us! Open your eyes, Tomas, look at me...'

For the first time, I saw Gertrud crying in front of me, and it broke my heart. I heard Viktor swearing and cursing at Magnus, while he was fighting.

'Astrid, take Gertrud, we need to keep on moving!'

I pulled Gertrud up, and looked at her face, seeing the sorrow written on her features. I knew Viktor was right, so I called her name, forcing her to look at me, instead of Tomas's lifeless body.

'Gertrud, we must keep on moving, we cannot stay here. We will come back to Tomas, once this is over, and give him a proper burial, but right now we have to keep on fighting.'

Gertrud nodded, and I took a step back when I saw her face. All the pain that was written on her face moments ago, had turned into anger, raw and untamed anger. I knew that right now, she was no longer herself, and she was driven by pure rage.

'Viktor, Astrid', she shouted, 'let's kill these bastards; every single one of them!'

They put me in the middle, and we draw our swords out. Together, we made our way through the soldiers, and we managed to reach Valtyr.

Most of Magnus' soldiers were lying dead around us, in pools of blood. Valtyr had taken a quick look at us, stopped for a second, when he realised Tomas was missing, then I heard his ferocious growl, when he understood what happened.

'Follow me', he shouted, 'we are close to Magnus' house.'

Just as we came around the corner, I saw Magnus, and a young boy standing next to him, most likely Matthias, his son. The boy looked like his father, a younger version of him. Both had dark hair, and blue eyes. Magnus looked older than the last time I saw him, when he killed my grandmother. I felt my heart beating faster, as all I wanted to do was to bury my sword straight into his heart.

They were surrounded by a small army of mercenaries, and I understood that we were so close to removing him from his throne. We have already fought against the biggest part of his army, but from now on, we had to fight against the men that were left.

'Magnus, enough with you and your bloody rule over the kingdom! You have killed too many people, done too many wrongs, it's time you pay for everything you've done!'

Magnus did not even bother to answer Valtyr, but instead, looked at his mercenaries, as he gave the order.

'Kill them, then bring me their heads!'

Half of the mercenaries drew their swords and approached us. We started fighting them, and while I was busy staining my sword with more blood, I heard the rest of our people closing in; and now, there were two other men, fighting alongside me, killing any mercenary that approached us.

There was nowhere to go for Magnus, as he and his little army were surrounded by us. The mercenaries that tried to attack us were now lying on the ground, lifeless. Magnus and his son were protected by the remaining half, about twenty people left, while we were four times over.

They had no chance. Valtyr took a few steps forward.

'It's over now, Magnus. Spare the lives of people and surrender yourself.'

'You, filthy peasant, you will not…'

Just as Magnus started to speak, I heard the most terrifying howls, and I looked behind us. My mouth hung opened, as I saw a pack of white wolves. What drew my attention was their huge bodies, and their full black eyes. There were so many, easily more than thirty, and they all looked the same.

They moved slowly, and they headed towards Magnus. I saw people moving out of their way and staring with their mouths open. I was surprised as well, and I realised that they must have been sent here by the gods.

When they reached near me, the pack stopped. The wolf leading the pack turned towards me and as I was staring into the abys of darkness that were his eyes, I heard a loud voice in my head.

'We are here, and we are done watching. We will decide what happens to them. Tell this to the people.'

I nodded and turned towards the soldiers that were mesmerised by the wolves.

'The gods are done watching. They are here and they will decide what happens to Magnus and his acolytes.'

As I finished talking, I saw the pack surrounding Magnus and his men, but what happened next had made me take a step back.

It was bloodshed.

Each wolf had jumped on one of them, and as I was watching in horror, they ripped their throats open. No one was spared, and two wolves were jumping now on Magnus, ripping him to pieces. His son was quickly taken out by a third one.

In a few moments, I watched as the gods have effectively wipe out Magnus and his mercenaries. Their white furs were now stained red with the blood of the people ripped apart.

I froze, and everyone around me froze as well, as we watched the carnage that was left. The wolves turned towards us, and just as quickly as they come, they left. For a few moments, I was too stunned to speak, or to move, so I turned to look at Valtyr.

He was just as shocked as everyone else, but he was the first to break the silence.

'Let this be a warning for every person from now on. For the first time, gods themselves had come and punished people for their wrongdoings. Let us be better and make the gods proud of us!'

People murmured in approvement.

I knew what I had to do. I took a step forward, and everyone looked at me, including Valtyr.

'Today marks the day of a great success. Valtyr, you had led the fight against Magnus, and the gods ended it. You are our leader, and starting this very moment, you are the king of Kulta.'

I kneeled in front of Valtyr, and following my lead, so did everyone else.

Valtyr looked at me, with a bittersweet expression on his face. Just like him, I felt the joy of knowing that Magnus was defeated, while at the same time, I felt the pain of knowing how many people have died today, including our dear friend, Tomas.

Valtyr approached me and offered me his hand. I stood up, next to him, and looked into his eyes.

'Today we mourn our losses, tomorrow we celebrate the start of a better life for all of us!'

Chapter 12
Astrid
Picking up the pieces

The cleaning of the city has begun. While some of us cleared the carnage that the gods left behind, and burned the dead bodies of the mercenaries, the rest of us had started to dug holes next to Jotun, right in the field between the city and the forest. I was the one to gather as many rocks as I could to mark the burial places of our friends.

I saw Viktor approaching me, and I looked at his saddened face.

'Astrid, some of us have decided to give the honours of a true warrior to Tomas. I already took his body to the port, and soon, we will begin his funeral. We want you to be present, as well.'

'Thank you for letting me know, Viktor. I'm so sorry that it happened this way.'

'I know. He told me about your vision, he knew, and he chose not to back down. Thank you for warning him.'

I started crying, and looked down, feeling ashamed for not being able to convince Tomas to stay away from the battle.

'I tried to convince him to stay away from this fight. I'm so sorry, Viktor.'

Viktor hugged me, then, as gentle as he could, he touched my chin and lifted my head, so I will look him in the eyes.

'It's not your fault, Astrid. I would have done the same. I would have still come and joined the battle, even if the gods themselves would tell me that I will die doing so. This fight was something worth dying for.'

I hugged him back, knowing that he was right. It didn't matter what could have happened to me, I would still choose, just like Tomas, to be present here, today.

'I will finish here soon, then I will come.'

Viktor left, and I continued to arrange the stones. I will come back here one day, to make sure that more stones were added, so the following generations will know how important these men were for us; the heroes that gave their lives to fight a corrupt king.

I started to walk through Jotun so I could help on the preparations for Tomas's funeral. I looked around the city, feeling empty. I looked at the small houses surrounding the one that kings used to live in, including Magnus. All others were small, and showed how poor people were, while the building occupied by Magnus was well maintained.

I entered the building and saw Valtyr tearing out the flags of Magnus from the walls. I have taken one look at him, and I realised how upset he was.

'Valtyr, they are preparing the sending for Tomas, on the beach. It's time for us to join them and say goodbye to our friend.'

He threw the flags that he had in his hand, on the floor, then stepping over them, he came next to me. I knew he must have been upset and sad knowing that we will say goodbye to Tomas for good, but I wanted to be near him, to support him.

Together, we walked towards the beach. When we reached there, people were already gathered around the small boat, where Tomas' body was placed. I saw Gertrud staying next to the boat and looking down at him.

I went to her and hugged her tightly. She looked at me, and I could see the pain and suffering in her beautiful eyes. I didn't say a word, and I stood next to her. I watched as people approached and said their goodbye to Tomas.

When Viktor came, he kneeled next to the boat, then placed his hand on his lifeless body.

'I pray we meet again, dear Tomas. Until then, go to the gods and tell them about our fight. When we will join you up there, in the world of gods, we will laugh and celebrate for days, and we will forget about how much we suffered today.'

He looked at me, then he continued.

'May the gods take great care of you, since they have called you so early to be amongst them, I know how much joy your presence will bring them.'

Valtyr kneeled beside the boat, and so did I. Gertrud looked at us and nodded her head. While we said our farewells to Tomas, all the soldiers had gathered on the beach and prepared the torches.

It was dark outside now, as we started to push the boat, quietly, into the cold water. I gasped when the water went up to my waist, then I looked at the soldiers handing us the torches.

We took a step back, and watched as Gertrud threw the first torch in the boat, followed by Viktor. I threw the last torch, and as the waves were taking the boat, further away, into the sea, I looked at the flames growing bigger.

'Goodbye, my dear husband. May the gods take care of your soul.'

I hugged Gertrud, then we turned back on the beach and watched as the burning boat was floating further away from us. Viktor placed his hand on Gertrud's shoulder, while Valtyr stood next to me.

I felt the tears falling on my face as I looked at the flames dying out.

Tomas was now gone, but he will live in our hearts, and in our memories.

Gertrud took a step back, then turned towards us. She wiped the tears on her face slowly, then looked at us.

'Tomas would not like it if he saw us weeping on the beach, let us wipe our tears now, and tomorrow we will all celebrate our new king, and our great moments. Let's pick up our broken hearts, keep our heads high, and look ahead to the future!'

We walked back toward the gathering hall, and we looked at it, while the people of Jotun already arranged it. Some locals have approached Valtyr and addressed him.

'Valtyr the Warrior, we want to assure you that we are happy and relieved to know that Magnus is dead. You are welcome into Jotun, and we support you ruling Kulta, our kingdom. We know who your parents were, and we still remember how King Ketiln, wanted your father, Bjorn, to be the next one on the throne after him. We welcome you, and all your friends here. This is your home; Jotun had patiently waited for you to be ready.'

I smiled, feeling touched by the warm welcome of the locals. I knew about Valtyr's past and how his parents were murdered, and today it felt like the gods have stepped in to make things right.

The man turned towards me, and spoke again, this time softly.

'Astrid, our seer, you are welcome here, and every family in Jotun will open their doors for you. May the gods protect you, and may the gods bless our kingdom, from now on.'

As soon as he finished speaking, the raven entered the hall flying and landed on my shoulders. The people of Jotun saw it, and bowed their heads, in respect.

Soon, I saw women entering the hall carrying pots of food, and buckets of wine. We all sat at the table and started eating. Valtyr sat next to us, and laughter and happy voices filled the hall, while the warm flames dancing in the middle of the room, were giving us warmth.

After everyone had finished eating, Valtyr was the first to move on the benches near the fire, in the middle of the hall.

I followed him, sitting on another bench, and so did others.

I looked at Valtyr, seeing how tired he was. All of us were tired, it had been a long day, and my body was hurting. My heart was broken, but once again, I had another reason to look forward to tomorrow, as the future of our kingdom was now in Valtyr's capable hands. I trusted him to do the best for the kingdom, and for the people.

'Friends, tomorrow we will celebrate, and after that, we will start bringing the kingdom on the right path. Step by step, we will correct everything that Magnus did. Now, we will all rest.'

One by one, people walked away from the hall, and Valtyr stood up.

'Gertrud, Viktor, let us find the bedroom. It has been a long day.'

We found several, and Gertrud claimed one as hers, and so did Viktor. When Valtyr opened another door, he showed me the bedroom that Magnus used before.

'Come Astrid, we will sleep here. I asked someone to bring us some water so we can wash, and the bedding has been changed.'

I followed Valtyr into the room, and after I closed the door, I saw him removing his clothes. He signalled for me to come closer, and he took out my body armour then my clothes, one by one. He kissed me gently then he helped me to wash my long hair, then I slowly washed my body, while he was looking.

He handed me a big, clean cloth, and I used it to dry my hair and my body, then wrapped it around me. Returning the favour, I helped him to wash his hair, then I watched as he was washing his body. In the soft candlelight, I could see the bruises on his body, and I helped him clean some of his wounds, then it was his turn to inspect me carefully and clean my own wounds.

'Tonight, we rest, my lovely. Your body is bruised as well, and you need to sleep, just as much as I do.'

I followed him to the bed, removed the cloth that was covering my body, and laid down, into his welcoming arms. His body was hot, next to mine, and covered by the luxurious furs, all the warmth had made me sleepy. I placed my head on his chest, and fell asleep quickly, lulled by rhythm of Valtyr's heart.

***

As soon as I felt the rays of sun on my face, I opened my eyes. Valtyr was still sleeping next to me, and I caressed his face, slowly. I felt his arms tightening around my waist, then I saw him smiling.

He looked at me sleepily, then kissed me slowly.

'Good morning, beautiful.'

His voice sounded so sleepy, yet so deep, that it tingled something inside of me. Suddenly, all I wanted to do was hearing him moaning my name, but I tried to keep my head clear of such cheeky thoughts, so early in the morning.

'Good morning, handsome. Valtyr, do you remember the very first time we met, that I had a vision?'

'Yes, I remember. So, what happened in your vision?'

'Today. I saw myself putting a crown on your head.'

'Then why didn't you join me when I asked you? If you knew this was going to happened, why you refused to join me?'

'Because of my grandmother. I was afraid, and I didn't know you. I wasn't sure what was going to happen…'

I tried to explain further, then I saw him frowning and he interrupted me.

'And like an idiot, I forced you to join my camp, and wanted to have you chained to me, and all this time you were afraid for your life… I'm sorry, Astrid.'

'You are forgiven, Valtyr.'

I hugged him, then I kissed him. He placed a finger on my forehead, then pushed my head back, gently.

'So, you are going to place a crown on my head, today?'

I nodded, looking confused at him, not understanding what he meant.

'Lady, you are going to throw a lot of responsibility on these poor shoulders. I will be responsible for the whole kingdom, until I die, or someone decides to chop my head off, and I am supposed to accept this and allow you to put that crown that will make me, for life, a servant of this kingdom, without you, at least trying to seduce me? Not even a little?'

His innocent smirk made me laugh, so I decided to join his little game, and got on top of him quickly, then whispered in his ear.

'I beg for your forgiveness my king, I will make sure that you're properly seduced before, so you accept the crown willingly.'

I nibble gently on his ear, then felt his hips rising and moving slowly underneath me, just so he can let me know that his manhood was already deeply seduced, and while he was moving gently, I helped him as well, so right now he was penetrating me, slowly.

'Valtyr...'

I moaned his name, feeling him moving underneath me and inside me. The way he filled me made me tilt my head back and dance with him, to his own rhythm. I leaned forward, just so I could suck and nibble his hardened little nipples, and I smiled when I heard my name from his mouth, moaned in his raspy, sleepy voice.

I straightened, and I continued in my own rhythm faster and harder, while looking him in the eyes and holding tight onto his hips. I was making love to him now, and he just purred between my legs, while his hands were busy massaging my breasts.

Valtyr was the first to tilt his head back and this time, he whispered my name, while he held on tight to my waist. I followed him, squeezing his hips gently, then I collapsed on his large, warm chest.

His heart was beating frantically, just like mine, and I felt his fingers playing gently with my hair. I wished I could stay here, in this bed, all day, but today was important, and I moved next to him.

Valtyr looked happy, his large smile illuminating his face, while his eyes shined. I felt loved, and I felt his presence touching my very spirit and bringing happiness in my life.

'Alright, alright, I'll take that crown.'

I laughed, then I watched him getting up from the bed, and extending his hand, inviting me to get ready, with him. We got dressed in the same clothes as yesterday, with the body armour on, and I did my best to clean the blood from his clothes, then he returned the favour, and quickly cleaned my clothes, as well.

I watched him braiding his hair fast, then he turned around to look at me. I nodded, then felt him braiding my hair, in a similar style to his. When he finished, he placed a delicate kiss on my neck, and I felt my back arching towards him, instinctively.

I turned around and hugged him tight, then we left the room. As soon as we reached the hall, I saw Viktor approaching him, then noticing Gertrud, I allowed them to speak, so I could talk to her.

'Good morning, Gertrud. How are you feeling?'

I saw her looking at me, and I could read the sadness in her eyes. She was smiling, but her smile had no joy in it.

'Good morning, Astrid. I feel like shit, but at least, we have something good to look up to. I cried last night, then I went to Viktor's bedroom, and he held me in his arms, then I cried again. After that, he started crying and I cried again with him. I think Tomas would have whopped our arses if he saw us like that.'

I hugged her, hoping that in time, she will find the strength she needed, for herself and for her son. I knew that Viktor would watch over them, and I promise myself to always check on her.

People were in a frenzy around us, trying to prepare everything for the crowning ceremony.

While Valtyr and Viktor were talking about how they could quickly organize the kingdom for the time being, I turned to them.

'Valtyr, we need to make sure that Fjill, our neighbouring kingdom, supports you. Write a letter to King Arne, let him know who you are, and what happened yesterday in Jotun.'

'I have already sent a group of riders to each village in our kingdom, but I haven't considered to send one to King Arne. I will do this, before the ceremony.'

I nodded.

'Do you think that the soldiers will accept you as their king?'

'All the soldiers are summoned here, in Jotun. I took care to send the groups in their own village, so they will be the ones replacing the soldiers that Magnus has hired. The ones coming here, well, they will be building the boats and ships that were burned yesterday, and for some time, or at least until I can make sure that I can trust them, they will work continuously as fishermen and hunters. After that, we will make other plans, but for the time being, I want to bring them all here, so I can understand whether they were loyal to their king, greedy, afraid for their families, or just straight up evil and corrupted like Magnus.'

I liked his plan, and I like the way he was thinking. I nodded, knowing that the kingdom will be well taken care of by Valtyr. I loved his modesty, and his wish to meet the soldiers personally, so he can make his own opinion about them. Viktor looked at him, just as proud as I was.

I stepped outside the hall, taking a small walk towards the beach. To my surprise, I saw people walking around busy, laughing, and praising the new king, and the mighty gods that decided to punish Magnus.

On the doors and in the windows, people used tree branches with green leaves to decorate their houses, and it felt like the Jotun was welcoming Valtyr with open arms.

The sea was quiet today, and I sat on the cold sand, for a few moments. I looked at the gently waves and hoped that Tomas was welcomed by the gods.

I was missing my family, and I could not wait to tell them what happened. I knew now that one of the groups sent by Valtyr will reach my village as well, and I prayed to gods that they will soon find out that I was alive.

I stood up slowly, then I walked back to the hall. On my way back, I saw people greeting me, and it warmed my heart to feel so welcomed here. I could feel the hope that rose inside people's hearts, especially when everyone was acknowledging me with a warm smile. Magnus was gone, and with him, the constant fear was gone as well.

As I reached the hall, I heard the bells ringing loudly in the city, and I saw people starting to gather in front of the building. Something good was about to happen, and I knew that we were all ready to have a new king.

Soon, the crowd was so big, that it was barely any space left. Valtyr was now waiting on the steps on the building, with Viktor and Gertrud on his side. He was looking at me and smiling.

Inside of me, something healed when I saw Gertrud holding the true crown of Kulta in her hands, one made of iron and wood; iron, the metal that swords were forged from, and wood, so precious for building the world around us.

I was glad that Valtyr chose to have this crown on his head, instead of the one made of gold and gems, that Magnus was proudly wearing.

Gertrud took a step to the side and motioned for me to join them on the stairs.

I walked and stood between her and Valtyr, facing the crowd that was looking at us. I saw Valtyr getting closer to people and when he lifted his hands, the whispering stopped.

Gertrud gave me the crown, and I held it in my hands, knowing that soon, I will be the one to place it on Valtyr's head.

'People of Kulta! Yesterday, we entered the city, having only one thought in our minds: to remove Magnus from the throne, so we can stop his cruel ruling. Uknown to us, the gods themselves had come here as well, and they were the ones to decide the fate of Magnus, his group, and his mercenaries. We will never forget, that for the first time in many winters, the gods have come amongst us and delivered their answer to cruelty. Today, I stay here, with all of you, hoping for better days to come. I don't want anyone to live in fear, and not have food to feed their families. I will make changes, and I will always be here, for all of you; I will listen to you and do my best to help you, as a king is intended to. Starting today, we are all allowed to pray in peace to our gods, and Jotun and all other villages in the kingdom, will have the altars and the servants of gods back. The leaders of the villages will now have to make sure everyone is taken care of, and I will personally travel to each village to make sure that things are changing for the better.'

Valtyr looked at the people nodding, and I never felt so proud of him.

I saw the admiration that everyone had when they looked at him, and I saw the men bowing their head in respect in front of him, while the children were looking at him completely mesmerised. He was the king we all waited for so long.

'I will never forget that the king is in service of his people, and not the other way around. I am here to serve for a better kingdom.'

He turned to look at me, and I felt the need to say a few words as well.

'Valtyr, from today you will be known as Valtyr the Warrior. The gods have stood with you and your army, against the corrupted men that were leading us before. I pray they will bless you with a long life and wisdom to take the best decisions for us, your people.'

Valtyr came closer, and just as our elders did, he kneeled in front of me, the seer representing the voice of gods amongst people, and I placed the crown on his head.

'Long live Valtyr the Warrior, our king!'

I shouted as loud as I could, and I heard the others shouting with me, as well. I had tears in my eyes, but this time, it was for the gratitude and calmness I felt knowing that we were all in good and capable hands. I knew that Valtyr will make the right choices as a king, and I hoped that the kingdom will bloom under his rule.

'We have fought and cried for our fallen men yesterday, today is time to laugh and celebrate our bright future!'

And with that, Valtyr had started the celebrations. I watched as people started to take the tables and the chairs from the hall, outside, and soon, more were brought.

Preparations for food were made, right in front of us, and baskets with cups were brought. I saw Valtyr opening a barrel of wine and handing cups to everybody.

To my surprise, I saw a group of women and men approaching us, and I could not tear my eyes away from the funny boxes in their hands. I heard a woman singing, then the men started to make lovely noises from the boxes. Music!

I remembered my grandmother telling me a story about bards and musical instruments, but I never had the chance to see them before.

Now, people were holding hands together and formed a large circle around the ones playing music, and they started to dance, and they kept spinning around. Another circle was formed, and I joined them as well. I saw Valtyr, Viktor and Gertrud joining us, and I laughed like a child when we started to spin quickly, in the opposite direction from the smaller circle that was in the middle.

When the music changed, they changed direction as well, and so did we. We were moving in the rhythm with the music that was played, and I realised, looking around me and seeing so many people that whole Jotun was here, dancing and laughing.

Chapter 13
Astrid
Shattered hopes

The sun has just set, and torches were lit all around us. The party continued well into the night, only that now we were all seated at tables, and we had already eaten and drank plenty of wine.

I pulled the cloak on my shoulders; it was cold tonight, but thankfully, with the fire made close to the tables, we were keeping warm. People were dancing and laughing, and I watched as Valtyr was now dancing with Gertrud. She seemed to be in a better mood, and I was admiring her strength, and how she managed to pull herself up, again and again.

As I was looking at them, I heard the raven in the distance; then I saw, in my mind, the flight of the raven above us. It was weird seeing myself from the raven's eyes, but I got used to it.

I saw the raven circling the party from above, flying over the city, above the main gates, and showing me the same area of forest where we waited, only the day before, to start our fight. I saw the raven landing on a tree, and I heard his cawing.

The raven wanted me to go there, in the forest, away from the party. I wasn't sure why, but I will not doubt or make the raven wait. Thankfully, I did not have much to drink, since I wasn't used to alcohol, and I already ate, so I wasn't tipsy, and the cold air was keeping me awake and alert.

I stood up, and realising that Valtyr and Gertrud were still dancing, I looked for Viktor to let him know that I would be away from the party.

Viktor was near, so I went to him. I didn't want anyone to worry about me, so I thought it would be better to let him know.

'Viktor, I must go away from the party for a bit. I'm not sure how long, but if Valtyr or Gertrud asks for me, let them know that I'm alright and I will be back.'

'Do you want me to come with you? It's dark now.'

'No, Viktor, don't worry about me. When I'm finished, I will come back here.'

'Is it the raven, Astrid?'

I nodded, and Viktor understood. I left the party and went to the main gate. It was open, but it was guarded by our soldiers, who recognised me, and allowed me to exit without a question. Just like I saw it in the flight of the raven, I headed for that specific portion of the forest.

As soon as I got closer, I heard the raven cawing, guiding me closer. But this time, when I reached the spot that I saw in my mind, the raven wasn't waiting for me.

Instead, the same god that I saw in the cave was right here, in front of me. I gasped, not expecting to see him ever again, and I looked again at his alluring face, and his tall frame.

I was so surprised that I found myself staring at him, dressed all in black, with a black cape over his shoulder, and his long, silver hair down. His hair was shining in the moonlight, and I could not take my eyes away from him.

My heart started beating faster, as I was wondering why he was here, in the human world. I was so worried that something bad was about to happen, especially when I realised how quiet he was; almost like he was preparing me for something bad.

He took a few steps forward and he came face to face with me. I had to tilt my head back, to be able to look at him in the eyes, but I wasn't afraid of him. I felt like something important was about to happen, and my hands started shaking.

'I'm sorry, Astrid.'

As soon as he said that he lifted his hands and placed them on either side of my head, gently. I didn't understand why he was sorry about, but I had the urge to close my eyes, then I had the vision.

In front of the gathering hall, there were many people gathered. I saw myself sitting on the stairs, facing them, while Valtyr was at the base of the stairs. I saw a beautiful woman, with long blonde hair and blue eyes walking towards Valtyr, smiling at him.

She seemed to be so much smaller than him, with a small and delicate frame; she looked like a princess and her long hair was braided in an intricate model. I wasn't jealous of her, or her beautiful face and delicate features, and I decided that she was one of the most beautiful women that I have ever seen in my life.

I saw her facing me, then Valtyr coming next to her. I saw myself talking, but I couldn't hear what I was saying. I saw them smiling and me, and soon, I stopped talking and I saw horrified how Valtyr turned towards the woman and kissed her passionately. I saw people throwing flowers up, in the air, and I saw everyone laughing and clapping their hands, like they were celebrating something.

My face was serious, and I wasn't smiling. I was looking at the pair and I looked... sad?

Why did it looked like I was officiating a wedding between Valtyr and another woman? No, no, no, this couldn't happen...

I opened my eyes, just to look in the black eyes of the god.

'Please tell me this is not going to happen...', I begged him, feeling my voice breaking.

I felt tears falling on my face, as I was waiting for an answer from him.

'Your visions have always come true, Astrid. I'm sorry.'

I felt my heart breaking as I heard him telling me what I already knew. I screamed, and I fell on my knees, with my head bowed.

Why would Valtyr choose to marry another, when he just asked me to marry him, a few days before?

I cried my soul out, and I felt the god lowering himself, then hugging me. I hid my face in his cloak, as I felt him supporting me.

'This is his choice, Astrid, but you don't know the reason why. Marriages between rulers are sometimes made in favour of the kingdom. Cry now, let it all out, but after this, I need you to pull yourself together. You must know about this. I'm sorry for you, seer, I can tell that you care deeply for him.'

I hear the god talking softly to me, like you'd talk to a child to calm him down. While I was trying to stop myself from crying, I felt him pulling me back to my feet, and I saw him turning to face me, with his hand on my shoulder.

Oh, the irony of it…

I hoped that Valtyr would always make the best choices for his people, not realising that one of his choices will break my heart.

I look desperately at the god in front of me, not knowing what to say, feeling so hurt that I wanted to run away in the forest, and never see Valtyr again. I wanted to disappear, and cry in peace.

'Astrid.'

Hearing my name called by the god, broke me away from my trance and I looked at him, waiting to hear what he had to say.

'I am Zanos, the god of souls. Since you met me in the cave, I have been watching you, as a raven, and as a wolf, so I can protect you if someone tries to harm you. I will be at your side for some time. You can talk to me, even if I am in my raven form or in my wolf form, but do not say my name out loud; only you are allowed to know my name.'

I nodded, barely feeling able to talk. I was thankful to him for watching over me.

'Thank you for protecting me so far. I am grateful for your presence around me', I added, wanting to express my gratitude for having a god protecting me.

'You are welcome. How are you feeling now?'

'I'm… My heart is broken. I cannot believe that Valtyr will marry another woman. I love him, and it hurts me, what I just learned…'

I could barely find my words, but I noticed that Zanos understood what I wanted to say.

'You must pull yourself together, Astrid. No one knows about it, yet, and if you are going to argue or act differently towards him, he will not understand why. You must go back there and not tell anyone about your vision. Soon enough, everyone will know, but it's important to let him make his choices. I will be around you; if this is too much for you, let me know.'

'I wished for Valtyr to make the right choices for the people in this kingdom; we have suffered too much when Magnus was ruling. I have never realised that he will have to take a decision like this, some day. I'm shocked, but I understand it, in a way; if this marriage secures the fate of the kingdom, what matters if one heart is broken, in front of hundreds of people that have suffered for so long?'

I lowered my head, looking at his feet. Even when I said it, it makes sense, but it felt like I was taking a dagger, and willingly stabbed my own heart with it.

I looked up at Zanos, and I saw his pensive expression.

'To think that I was avoiding humans before. Now, I look at you, and see what you are going through, and I cannot understand how you people manage to move on with your life. You are so frail; I could break into pieces with my own hands, but at the same time, you are so strong... I will be by your side. Take your time to calm yourself, and when you are ready, you should go back to the party.'

I saw him walking towards a tree, then the raven came back flying towards me and landed on my shoulder. I instinctively caressed the raven with the side of my face, like I did so many times before, then I gently caressed its head with my fingers; I heard the raven cawing softly. I had to remember that this was a god, not just a raven, but I simply realised it a few moments too late.

'I'm sorry, I got used to touch you, I did not mean to be disrespectful. I will go back to the party now.'

I kept walking, but this time slowly, with the raven still on my shoulder. The image of Valtyr kissing another woman was etched in my mind, and I wish I have not seen it. I felt like someone had beaten every inch of my body; I tried to tell myself that maybe he will change his mind, or maybe, something will happen, and my vision will not come true.

Soon, I reached at the main gate, and I saw the soldiers bowing their head at me, showing respect towards me, as a seer. They greeted me, and I answered back, then I started to walk slowly towards the party.

When I reached, people were still gathered at the tables, but the dancing had stopped. I saw Valtyr talking with Viktor, and I felt that dagger twisting in my heart, and I could barely breathe, looking at him.

I never realised, and it never crossed my mind, that one day, I will not sleep in his arms anymore, and I will not be able to kiss him. One of these days, he will kiss me for the last time, and he will have no clue. I knew it now, and wish I hadn't...

'Astrid are you alright?', Gertrud asked me, looking concerned at me.

I looked at her, then I nodded. I wasn't sure what to tell her...

'Don't tell her about the vision', I heard Zanos' voice in my mind.

I almost jumped when I heard him, forgetting for a moment that he was seated comfortably on my shoulder. His presence gave me the strength that I needed to carry on and pretend that I did not knew what will happen, but I needed to reassure Gertrud.

'Yes, it's been a long day, and I had to go to the forest to bring the raven back here. I think the night has ended for me.'

'I agree. Yesterday, we fought, today we celebrated. I'm in great need of a long sleep, as well. I'll go and tell Viktor that we're going to sleep.'

I nodded, thanking her. It was better for me like this. Everyone wanted to talk with their new king, and people seemed to be in awe, looking at Valtyr, while I felt drained of energy, and I was in desperate need to lay down, and be away from him, for the moment.

I saw Gertrud whispering something to Viktor, then she came back to me, and we headed to our bedrooms. I bid her good night, and I gave her a hug.

'Have a good sleep, Gertrud. Better days are coming for all of us, we just need to hang on a bit longer. Be strong, your son cannot wait to see you, and most probably he found out by now that you are alright.'

'I talked with the group that Valtyr sent to Helga, his aunt. I asked the men to not say a word to Petur about his father, so I can be the one that will let him know. His father died fighting against Magnus, so Petur could have a nice and long life. I know that his future will be better with a king like Valtyr, ruling over Kulta. Goodnight, Astrid, have a good sleep.'

When I entered the bedroom, I realised that the raven has left my shoulder, but when I looked at the window, I saw the raven outside, with his back turned away from the room. I took out my clothes, then I hide between the quilts and the fur on the bed.

I could only think of the vision, and I cried, thinking about what I had to face, soon.

Will Valtyr fight for us, or he will give up easily, and marry that woman?

***

When I opened my eyes, I turned my head to the side and realised that Valtyr was not in the bed with me. I could see the contour of his head on the pillow, and I hugged the pillow close to my chest, burrowing my face in it and feeling his scent on it. I placed the pillow back, then I started to get dressed.

Without Valtyr, it was harder to put my body armour back, but I managed, eventually.

I braided my long hair quickly, then I took my belt, and placed the sword back in the hilt. I wasn't planning to fight anyone, but I started to get used to feel the weight of the sword, since I had to wear in the camp all the time; it was giving me reassurance, and I like it to have it with me.

I took a deep breath, then left the bedroom. In the gathering hall, I saw Valtyr talking with Viktor and Gertrud. When he heard me coming, he turned towards me, and hugged me, in front of everyone.

'Good morning, Astrid.'

'Good morning, King Valtyr', I answered and smiled, feeling proud of him. No matter what will happen next, I still admired his strength and courage, and now, he was my king. I saw him smiling back at me.

'So, what we are going to do today?'

'I was talking with Viktor, Gertrud, and our men about how we can organise ourselves to make sure that the kingdom is ruled wisely, then we received an answer from King Arne of Fjill. He wants to meet me and talk with me about a possible alliance between Kulta and Fjill.'

I barely stopped myself from gasping, realising that this is how is going to happen.

Will this be the meeting that will lead to Valtyr marrying another woman?

'And what decision have you took about it?'

My voice seemed to shake a bit, but Valtyr did not noticed.

'I will take the trip to Fjill with you, Viktor, Gertrud, and some of my men, while others will stay here and watch over Jotun, for me. We will come back quickly from this journey. We must secure an agreement between us and the kingdom of Fjill, and I want Kulta to be more open to other kingdoms, especially its neighbouring kingdom. We must make friends, since the news of what happened to Magnus will travel now, and everyone will know about it.'

I nodded. I missed my family, and I wanted to see them. I wondered if I should head back to my small village, instead.

'What's happening, Astrid?'

'I miss my family, and I want to see them soon', I told him.

Valtyr frowned, realising that I left my village for some time already, then he turned towards me.

'When I sent the riders with the news, I made sure to tell the one heading to Frostheim to look out for your parents, and let them know how brave you are, to tell them everything that happened since you left your village, and that you will soon visit them. I thought that you would want them to know that you are alright.'

'Thank you, Valtyr.'

I smiled at him, feeling gratitude for his gesture.

At least, my parents will know that I was alright, and I will see them soon.

'Astrid, you are our seer, and the seer is free to go and leave, as it wishes, everywhere in this kingdom. I understand that you must follow the requests of our gods, but if you can, please come with us to Fjill. I want King Arne to meet you, and I want him to know how the gods were here, in Jotun, and they delivered justice.'

'Of course, I will join you.'

'We will make the plans, then we will fetch some clothes and food for the road, and we will start riding soon. If we are lucky, tomorrow morning, we will meet King Arne.'

I nodded, then at his sign, I joined them at the table. They saved some food for me, and I ate slowly, while I was listening to Valtyr, Viktor and his men making the plans for the following days.

I saw the silver wolf entering the hall, and the shocked expressions of people. The men were moving away from the wolf, afraid of his unusually large size. The wolf came next to me, then laid down on the floor, at my feet. I felt him placing his paws on my feet, and without realising, I reached underneath the table and stroke gently his silky fur.

I stopped as soon as I remembered that the wolf was Zanos, and his fur was the same shade of silver like his hair. It was him, sitting next to my feet.

People were staring at the large wolf, and it became so quiet in the hall, that I could hear my own heartbeat. People of Jotun were speechless, but the one that knew, were used to the presence of the raven and the wolf. Valtyr looked amused around him and giggled.

'Come on people, she is our seer; the gods are protecting her. Astrid and any animal or creature accompanying her are welcome to come and go as they please; this is the way it used to be before, and we will respect our seer.'

The men in the hall relaxed visibly, but some were still looking at the wolf. They continued to make the plans. Soon, I saw Gertrud entering with some clothes in her hand, and I stood up and followed her to her bedroom.

The wolf followed me, and once we got into her bedroom, he laid on the floor again, with his back turned to us, giving us some privacy.

'Finally, I found some clothes for both of us. Look, I even found us nightgowns and some warmer cloaks.'

She showed me the beautiful black cloaks she found, a nightgown, then the black pair of trousers, with the black shirt. The clothes were beautiful, and I was grateful to finally have some clean ones, for the journey to Fjill.

'Let's wash now and change for the journey. Viktor had already found clothes for him and Valtyr, and when we come back from Fjill, we will stop at the camp in the mountains, take our clothes, then come back to Jotun.'

Gertrud started to get undressed straight away and washed herself. I looked at her, then I looked at the wolf that was sleeping on the floor. For a second, I wondered how much Zanos heard and saw, but that was a conversation for another day.

I got undressed and washed myself as well, and after that, I almost moaned when I felt the nice touch of clean clothes of my skin.

'Thank you so much Gertrud, you are such a nice, thoughtful friend.'

'You're welcome, but stop moaning, otherwise Valtyr will break the door. I'm not sure that he will like hearing you moaning, without him.'

I laughed, then I look at her. Gertrud was laughing as well, proud of her joke.

'You know, Astrid, that night in the cave... was one of my best nights after Magnus kidnapped me. I needed a long time to feel like myself again, and I am grateful to have met you.'

I looked at her, feeling my face blushing, when I remembered the moments we shared there.

'I'm not sure what's going to happen in the winters to come; I am happy as well for meeting you. Thank you for what you've showed me and for the moments we shared.'

I hugged her, and while I started to braid her hair, I decided to tell her about the vision that I had with Tomas; I had to get that out of my chest.

'Gertrud, I had to tell you something and I am not sure that you will like it.'

'What?'

She turned around to look at me, worried about what I had to say.

'Before the battle, I had a vision with Tomas, and I saw how he died. I told him, and I asked him not to come to Jotun, but I couldn't convince him. I feel guilty about it, I should have tried harder to...'

Gertrud stood up, turned to face me, then place her hands on my shoulders. She looked determined, while I felt guilty.

'Astrid, look at me. You know why Tomas hated Magnus so much. I knew Tomas, and I knew him well, and nothing that you might have said to him could have convinced him to stay away from Jotun. Don't blame yourself, you warned him, but trust me when I tell you, you could not steer him away from Jotun.'

She hugged me, then turned around to allow me to braid her hair. When I was finished, she stood up and smiled at me.

'Let's go now, soon we will have to start our journey to Fjill. Is the wolf coming with us as well?'

I turned to look at the wolf still sleeping on the floor, and went to him, and touched his fur gently.

'It's time for us to go.'

I saw him turning his head to look at me sleepy, then yawned, and finally stood up and stretched its body.

We exited the bedroom, and went to the hall, where Valtyr and Viktor were giving indications to the soldiers. Valtyr looked at me smiling.

'Are you ready, ladies? It's time for us to start our journey towards Kingdom of Fjill.'

***

As soon as we exited Jotun, we started riding on our horses. The silver wolf was running next to me, and I admired the beautiful landscape around us. The snow was already melting now, and the spring will come soon and paint the kingdom in bright colours.

We continued for some time, then we stopped when it was dark outside. We dismounted the horses, and Valtyr looked at me.

'Viktor, start the fire, I will go with Astrid and gather some wood from the forest.'

Viktor nodded and started to place some stones in a large circle. He took some branches from the ground, then took out a small satchel from his cloak; and kneeled in the middle of the circle to start the fire.

I looked at Gertrud while she was tying the horses next to a rich patch of grass, and the soldiers that were with us started to place some quilts on the ground, so we could all sleep on them.

Valtyr went through the trees, further in the forest, and I followed him.

As soon as we were a bit further away from our temporary camp, I saw him turning around, grabbing me gently by the neck, and kissing me passionately.

I grabbed his cloak and pulled him closer to me, answering to his hungry mouth. I realised that it's been some time since I kissed him, and I was just as hungry for him.

I wondered if this was the last time we kissed, and I pushed him back gently so I could breathe a bit.

'Astrid, my love, since you put that crown on my head, I barely had time for you. I'm sorry, beautiful.'

I looked at him and his gorgeous face, and I felt a wave of sadness hitting me. Somehow, I knew that this were probably one of our last intimate moments together. I wish I could prolong them, but I had no choice.

'Don't worry, Valtyr, you are king now. You have so many things to do and I understand you. Now, you finally have the chance to do what it's best for the kingdom and for the people, and it will take some time until you arrange everything.'

'Come here, Astrid', said Valtyr, placing his hands on my hips and pulling me closer to him. I kissed him again, then I gently pushed him back.

'Valtyr, we need to gather some wood for the fire, otherwise we will all be freezing tonight. This is not a proper time for lovemaking, people are waiting for us.'

He nodded disappointed and came back to our task. I needed to concentrate on something else because I could barely manage to hold myself together.

The vision that I had was haunting me, and I had a feeling that the woman from my vision might be King Arne's daughter.

Tomorrow we will reach Fjill, and I was about to find out.

I wanted so badly to put a stop to this, but I couldn't. Whatever will happen next, this will be Valtyr's decision, as well. I wanted to be with him, but if he placed kingdom's interests in front of our relationship, then I had no choice but to accept it, and move forward.

Would he fight for us?

Chapter 14
Valtyr
The temptations of a crown

We finally reached Fjill. As soon as we crossed the border from Kulta into Fjill, soldiers of King Arne approached us. When I told them who I was, they informed us that we will be escorted to the king's gathering hall, so he can talk to us.

I saw the other men looking around curious, at how the houses were built here, in Fjill. The roofs were built at a sharp angle, and the houses seemed a little larger than the ones we would normally build in Kulta.

Back home, the snow almost melted, but here, everything was still covered in snow. I saw Astrid frowning and looking around her surprised. She noticed that everything was a little different here, beside the cold air.

'They build their houses so big, because the walls must be thick, to keep the warmth inside. The windows are small, and they build their roofs like that so the snow will fall off them easier. Otherwise, if they build the houses like we did, they would be cold, and the roofs would be damaged by the weight of the snow.'

Astrid came closer to me to listen what I was explaining. She was curious and looked around the city that we were in. We could hear a river nearby, but we did not have the chance to see it, yet.

'Did you see the fence surrounding the city? It's made of sharp, long logs. Why would they point one sharp long towards the sky, and one tilted like that?'

'Wild beasts, Astrid. They are trying to keep the animals from the forest away from their houses. That's why their fences look so unusual, there are many bears and wolves in these forests. They leaned the logs like that so it would deter the animals from attacking the people.'

'I wonder if they can grow vegetables here.'

'I know this from my father, he visited King Arne before; they have houses where they are growing vegetables and some fruits inside. Outside, the plants would freeze, but inside they can grow them. People eat a lot of meat here – animals and fish, the vegetables are hard to grow and saved for special occasions. It's cold and freezing most time of the year, so they do the best they can to survive.'

'It sounds like their life is harder than the one we have. At least, we have plenty of days of summer, while it seems that here, there is a never-ending winter.'

I nodded; Astrid was observant and smart. I looked at her, and I watched the wolf walking near us. When we reached the king's hall, we all dismounted.

As soon as we entered, I saw the wolf coming closer to Astrid. The soldiers that escorted us stopped and stared at the large animal.

'Is the beast coming inside, as well? Will he attack anyone?'

'That's no ordinary beast, it's the guardian of a seer. Wherever she goes, the wolf will go as well. He won't attack, unless someone tries to attack Astrid', I explained to the soldiers.

'You are a seer?', asked one of them, looking surprised at Astrid.

'Yes. Do not worry about the wolf. He will behave, and he won't be a problem.'

The soldier nodded, and we entered the hall.

The room was big, just like the one we had in Jotun. There were tables everywhere, and in the middle of the room, there was a large, open fireplace. In a corner, I could see two women stirring in the large pots; it smelled amazing, and I was hungry.

Six large benches surrounded the fire, and behind them, dominating the room, I saw King Arne, sitting on a big throne. Next to his throne, there was a smaller one.

King Arne was old, probably around the age that my father would be right now if he still lived. He had grey hair, a beautiful, noble face, and a long beard. He stood up when he saw us entering and he approached our group.

Behind him, I saw a beautiful woman, with long, blonde hair, following him. She seemed to be the same age as Astrid, and I assumed that she might be his daughter, since their faces seemed to be similar.

They were both dressed simply; the king had black clothes and a large, red cloak on his shoulders, while the young woman was wearing a black dress.

Her long hair was down and was framing her beautiful face. The long strands were going down to her hips, and they seemed to shine.

She was alluring, and her beauty made me look at her, a moment longer than I had wished. I felt bad, almost guilty of something, knowing that I was admiring this woman while Astrid was next to me. I looked at Astrid, and I saw her looking at the blonde woman.

Astrid was pale and looked like she just saw a ghost. I hoped that she won't be jealous on the king's daughter; obviously, she must think the same as me, since she did not seem able to take her eyes of the woman.

I turned my attention to King Arne, who was in front of me now, and looked at me, frowning.

I have only arrived here, why was he frowning at me?

'Welcome to my hall, travellers. I am Arne, King of Fjill. I heard from my soldiers that you are coming here from Kulta. Sit down next to the fire, and warm yourselves, you must be freezing.'

King Arne took a step forward, towards me, and did not took his eyes of me. He seemed to be intrigued.

'Sorry for my manners, I know I am staring at you, but your face seems so familiar; I'm sure I haven't seen you, but it feels like I know you.'

'King Arne, I am Valtyr the Warrior, son of Bjorn the Brave and Sigrid. Maybe you met my father; I know he travelled to Fjill before he died.'

'Of course! My days, your father was such a smart man, ahead of his days. I met him long time ago, and I wanted to bring him and his young wife here, in Fjill. I'm sorry Valtyr, I heard what happened to your parents. Sit down here, with me, so we can talk. Tell me, what is happening in Kulta?'

He sat on one of the benches and gestured for me to sit next to him; I did that, and I watched the young woman coming next to me. Viktor, Gertrud, and Astrid sat on the bench in front of us, while the soldiers sat on the other two.

'After my parents were killed, I went to my aunt, Helga, and she was the one that raised me. King Magnus had become corrupted and done a lot of awful things. Knowing what happened to my parents, after I've grown, I raised a small army of people willing to fight to dethrone him. Few days ago, we all went to Jotun, and we all fought against Magnus.'

'And what happened? You are alive, but what happened to your people?'

'King Arne, we have managed to corner Magnus and his men, when a pack of wolves came. The gods themselves have punished them, they ripped them to pieces in front of our eyes. Magnus is gone, I am now King of Kulta, and I want to be the king that makes the life of the people better. We all have suffered deeply under the rule of Magnus.'

'That's great news, I never liked Magnus; he was an awful, greedy man. He would have killed anyone to get what he wanted. I tried to warn your father that Magnus was jealous of him, and how much people admired him. King Ketiln wanted to make your father the next in line; I am happy to know that you are now a king.'

I saw Arne looking at us and smiling, glad of the news I bring him. He looked at my friends, then his eyes stopped on the wolf. He seemed to be curious of the wolf that was sitting on the floor, next to Astrid's feet. The wolf looked back at him, tilting his head a bit.

'How come you have such a beast with you? It's that your pet, young lady?'

'King Arne, this is not a beast from the woods. I am Astrid, I am the new seer, and since I have become seer, the wolf has been my guardian', explained Astrid.

She explained everything to Arne, and when she finished talking, she placed her hand on the wolf's head.

'A seer?! I haven't heard of a seer, in a long time', said Arne, turning to look at me. 'It seems that the gods are on your side, Valtyr. Your kingdom has been blessed with their presence, and now there is a seer, as well. Please Astrid, I will inform everyone that you and your wolf are always welcome in Fjill. If the gods will bring you here again, you can travel without any fear in our kingdom. I will make sure that everybody knows about you. Astrid, meet my daughter, Frida.'

When King Arne finally introduced the woman, I looked at her. Frida was next to me, on the bench, and up close, she looked even more beautiful; her beauty was alluring, and it was a sight for the eyes to be so close to her.

I looked at Astrid and I saw her bowing her head respectfully towards Frida.

'Let us move to the tables and eat something; you and your people must be hungry now', said Arne, gesturing towards the tables.

I followed him and waited for him to sit first. He chose to stay at the head of table, while I was seated naturally, next to him.

Frida sat next to me, while Viktor sat in front of me, across the table. Gertrud sat next to him, followed by Astrid and our soldiers. Across the table, I saw the soldiers of King Arne seating down, in front of my soldiers.

'Tell me, what are your planes for Kulta, Valtyr?'

I turned to Arne, so I could answer his question. I took a few moments before answering, trying to make sure that I would be clear enough on my intentions, but without revealing too much.

'I want Kulta to start trading with our neighbours, but I want to make sure that we also have a strong ally. Magnus has isolated Kulta for too long, while ignoring Fjill. I want our kingdoms to be at peace and support each other', I explained and waited for him to express his opinion.

'I knew your father, and I am glad to see that his spirit is alive, inside you, Valtyr. I agree with you. Magnus was an unwelcoming king, that wanted everyone far away from him, but I see that you are different. The fact that you have travelled here, to meet me, shows it. You are the type of man that I would marry my daughter with', he added, and I restrained myself from flinching or saying anything, knowing very well that I asked Astrid to marry me, few days ago. 'Of course, that will be a reassurance for the friendship between our kingdoms, but there is plenty of time to talk about this. Let us eat, first.'

While we were eating, I finally founds some moments to think quickly about the new situation that I found myself in. Arne was pushing the idea of marrying his daughter into my head.

As a king, that would have been a wise move, since it will secure a solid alliance between our kingdoms; but as a man who just proposed another woman to marry him, a few days ago, I wanted to follow my heart and have Astrid as my wife, instead.

After we finished eating, we were served wine, and I looked at Arne, trying to understand what kind of person he was. I could tell that due to his age, he had more experience than I did, but at first sight, he seemed trustworthy. I knew that he kept himself away from Magnus, as he did not agree with the decisions that he made, and I like that he admitted to having tried to tempt my father into staying in his kingdom; I wished my father would have done this, maybe himself and my mother would be alive today.

'Valtyr, you and your advisers must have had a long journey to reach us, in Fjill. I can offer you a spare bedroom, proper for a king, another one for your soldiers, but for your seer and your two advisers, I'm afraid that I will have to host them separately, into the house next to the hall.'

Arne turned to look at Astrid, to explain himself better, 'You see, because of the wolf, I want to make sure that you have a big room as well, and there isn't enough space here, in the hall. Is that alright with you?'

'Of course, King Arne', answered Astrid straight away, then she looked at me and nodded; she turned to Arne and continued, 'Thank you for thinking about the wolf, and giving us the comfort of your kingdom.'

Arne smiled straight away, looking pleased with Astrid's answer. To my surprise, I saw Frida standing up and excusing herself from the table.

'Please, excuse me. I'm afraid we had a long day before you arrived here, King Valtyr, and I am exhausted. I will go to sleep tonight, but I look forward to seeing you tomorrow.'

She left the table, and I saw her walking towards a big, wooden door, behind the thrones, where I assumed that the bedrooms were. I turned my attention back to the table and I looked at Astrid, who seemed to have noticed my eyes lingering on Frida.

Astrid looked sad. I saw her standing up and excusing herself from the table. Arne asked one of the women serving us the wine to show Astrid the house where she would sleep for the night.

'I wish to talk alone with Valtyr for some time before we are heading to our bedrooms as well. If that's alright with everyone...?', said King Arne politely, but firmly.

I saw Viktor and Gertrud standing up, and so did our soldiers.

The ones that escorted us here, took the rest of my men towards their bedroom, while Viktor looked at me.

'Valtyr, I think we will follow Astrid, and I will be heading to the bedroom tonight; I need rest. Thank you, King Arne, for your warm welcoming.'

Viktor turned to Arne and bowed his head shortly, while I saw the king smiling, pleased with his manners and bowing his head back at him.

Gertrud stood up and addressed King Arne.

'I thank you as well, for your warm welcoming into your kingdom, King Arne.'

She followed Viktor outside.

Just as Arne requested, the main hall was now empty, and he could speak to me, in private.

He turned to me, with a large smile on his face.

I wondered what he wanted to say to me, just between the two of us.

It had to be important, and I tried to remain still, while the men were leaving the great room, allowing us to have the privacy that King Arne requested it a few moments ago.

'Valtyr, I will be direct. I admire your father, and I can see you are just like him. Years ago, when you were a toddler, and my daughter was only a few days old, I asked your father to consider marrying our children, in the future. Now, that I see the man that you have become, I renew my proposition: marry my daughter, and I will support Kulta with army and gold. I am old, and soon I will not be able to perform my duties, and someone else will have to rule, instead of me. Unite the two kingdoms, send your trusted men here, and take care of Fjill, just like you would take care of Kulta.'

I tried to keep myself calm, but I was shocked at Arne's proposition. I have just become king a few days ago, and now I was offered more power. It was tempting, and Arne was right, in a way. Two kingdoms, united, would be much stronger together. Fjill had resources that Kulta needed, and Kulta could use a part of Fjill's soldiers, to defend Jotun, that had such a delicate position, next to the sea.

Sure, it would have been double the headache for me, but just as Arne suggested, I could always send someone I could trust to watch over Fjill, and I could check on them, from time to time. I needed to rebuild Kulta first, and having the kingdom next to us, supporting me, would have made my work easier.

Arne was looking at me, trying to read my expression. I did not want to give him an answer straight away; I needed to think over this, and I wanted to talk with Viktor and Gertrud as well. Astrid...

Oh, this will not be good news for Astrid; I would have to disappoint her, break her heart, and marry another woman. This made me want to consider my choice wisely; it was hard to choose between the kingdom and my own heart.

'Arne, I cannot give you an answer right now. Sure, your proposition is very tempting to me, to be honest, but I want to think about it and talk with my advisers.'

'Ha! That's a man after my own heart, one that considers carefully and doesn't rush into action. The night is the best adviser, Valtyr, I agree with you as well. Think about it. I admit, I have an interest in this, seeing my daughter well-married; but I also want to make sure that whoever rules after me, has the intention of taking proper care of Fjill; it's challenging to rule over a kingdom of mountains and almost endless winter. We could use some supplies from the south as well, as we struggle for fresh food, besides meat, and your kingdom could use the resources in our mountains. Why not unite the summer of Kulta with the winter of Fjill and exchange and enjoy the best from both kingdoms?'

Arne looked straight into my eyes, and I could tell that he was honest about his intentions. As I learned now, he only had one daughter, and after hearing his reasons, I understood why he wanted to have the support of Kulta, for Fjill.

It made sense, but that would mean for me to take a decision that I wasn't sure of, marrying Frida.

'That's what I wanted to discuss with you, before we go to sleep as well', said Arne, standing up, 'think about it, talk with your advisers, and see what they have to say as well, then you could all come back, and we can talk together about it; we don't have to rush it. Now, let's go to sleep and have some rest.'

'Thank you for your understanding, Arne, and also for having us into your home.'

'Come, follow me, and I will show you your bedroom. You would have some warm water waiting for you, and I am sure that everything you might need is already prepared.'

I followed Arne through the big, wooden door. In front of us, I could see a hallway, and to my left, two doors.

'My soldiers and your soldiers are down these doors. Ahead, in the hallway, the first door on the right is your bedroom, the one the left is my daughter's bedroom, and the last one is mine. Have a good night, Valtyr.'

'Thank you, Arne, have a good night.'

He left and I entered my bedroom. When I opened the door, the only thing I could see was the fire burning in the fireplace, and in front of the fire, the big, wooden bathtub filled with hot water. I saw a small chair next to it, that a had a bar of soap, and a white, clean cloth.

I stripped my clothes straight away and let them fell on the floor. I took the soap in my hands, then went straight to the bathtub. I went inside, then lay down, and closed my eyes, thanking the gods for this luxurious bath that I was taking right now.

'Well, that was really nice to watch.'

I turned my head quickly, to see who spoke.

On the bed, Frida was laying naked, with her long hair down. She stood up, took the big cloth in her hands, and opened her arms.

'Let me dry you off', she added with a giggle.

I looked at her and I took a deep breath.

Why didn't I checked the room before taking my own clothes off? I could have seen her.

I washed myself quickly then tried to take the cloth out of her hands so I could dry myself.

'Frida, you have to leave this room', I asked her.

'Why? I saw you, and you are the most beautiful man that I laid my eyes on. I want to have a taste of you', she added, checking me up and down.

To my surprise I saw her coming even closer to me, and she extended her arm and pulled my face closer to hers.

I thought for a second of Astrid and how hurt she will be when she will find out that I fucked another woman; but Frida was here, next to me, and her naked body was glued to mine.

I wanted her, and I would take her.

I kissed Frida back, then I watched her as she kneeled in front of me, then started to touch my cock.

She opened her mouth and started to suck at the tip, and I hardened instantly. She looked at me and smiled, then started to suck even harder.

I moaned, enjoying her mouth on me, then she started to move her mouth up and down and suck even harder. I looked down at her, and I placed my hand at the nape of neck guiding her. Moans escaped my lips as I was enjoying every moment of what she was doing. I stopped her, lifting her slim body and laid her on the bed.

I kissed her, then I started touching her breasts with one hand, while I sneaked another one between her legs. She was wet and she started to move her hips seductively, while moaning my name. I went on top of her, then started to penetrate her slowly.

Frida was moaning my name, and I started to move faster, in and out. I needed to fuck her, and so I did; I didn't have any feelings for her, but her lovely mouth calling my name was driving me insane. I buried myself deep inside her, while I was holding her hips. She tilted her head back and started to play with her nipples, while I was moving fast, in and out of her. I moaned again, and buried myself once more, deep inside her, feeling her small hand squeezing my shoulders, while I came.

I collapsed on top of her, and I realised that now, I just managed to fuck my way into a marriage that I wasn't sure that I wanted. I looked down at Frida; she was grinning at me.

Princess Frida, the princess that I just slept with.

I rolled off her, stood up and offered my hand, so she could stand up as well. I went and cleaned myself in the bathtub, then, I watched her as she cleaned herself.

'Frida, this shouldn't have happened.'

'Why not, Valtyr? I wanted you, and you clearly wanted me as well. You are a king now, and no matter who you had feelings for, you slept with me; you could have thrown me out of your bedroom, but you didn't. I see you're conflicted, but you know very well that a marriage between us will be advantageous for both kingdoms. Come to bed with me and let us sleep.'

She went between the covers, and I joined her. Frida was right, I could have stop her, but not only that I didn't; I enjoyed every single moment with her.

I had to speak with Astrid tomorrow and tell her what happened. I wasn't a lying bastard, and I had no intention to hide this from her.

I felt Frida hugging me, and I wished I had made it clear from the begging that I wasn't free for marriage.

But I didn't.

Chapter 15
Valtyr
The weight of a crown

When I opened my eyes, I saw that Astrid wasn't in the bed next to me, then I remembered what happened last night. I rolled out of the bed straight away, and got dressed quickly, this time not bothering to braid my hair. I had to talk with Astrid, and I had to find her now.

After I left the room, I went straight to the hall. I saw King Arne sitting next to the fire and talking to one of his men.

'Good morning, King Arne! Would you be so kind to point me to the house where the rest of my people are?'

'Good morning, King Valtyr', answered Arne with a smile, 'it's easy to find it; exit the hall, and it's the first building on the right. You will find them there, but I think that they might be asleep.'

'Thank you', I answered and bowed my head towards Arne respectfully, then I opened the door, and I saw the house on the right, just as Arne had explained to me.

I went and opened the main door.

The first room was small, but it had a fireplace, a table, and some chairs, and after I noticed the door on the opposite wall, I opened it. There was a small hallway that led me to another three doors. On my left, there were two doors, and on my right, only one.

In which one was Astrid?

I remembered something that Arne said about Astrid needing a bigger room for herself and the wolf, so I took a lucky guess, and I opened the door on the right, thinking that it should be the bigger bedroom; and I was right; as soon as I opened the door, I saw the wolf coming towards me and growling threateningly, showing its big and sharp canines.

'Easy there, big boy. It's me, Valtyr.'

The wolf looked at me, and I could swear that I saw the beast rolling his eyes, then went and laid lazily on the floor, in front of the fire. I saw Astrid sitting on the bed, already dressed.

'Astrid, good morning. Did you have a good sleep?'

She stood up, then turned to look at me. Her eyes were red and puffy, and it looked like she cried. I froze, wondering for a second if she had any vision with me sleeping with Frida.

'Astrid, what happened? Are you alright?', I asked her, not knowing what to expect.

I took a few steps towards her, and I looked at her sad face. She knew something; somehow, she must have found out.

'Yes.'

'Astrid, I need to talk with you.'

'Go ahead, Valtyr', she said, looking calmly at me, waiting for me to talk.

'Astrid, I have done something that I am not proud of, but I don't want to lie to you or hide it from you; I slept with Frida last night.'

'I know', she answered calmly.

'You did WHAT?!' I heard the shout behind me, and I recognise Gertrud's voice straight away.

I turned to look at Gertrud, and I could tell she was shocked. I looked at her, not knowing what to do.

'Please don't tell me that you were so stupid to fuck the princess', begged Viktor, behind Gertrud.

'Could you men stop thinking with the head between your legs and think with the one on your shoulders instead?!', Gertrud shouted angrily at me, with pure rage in her voice.

To my surprise, I saw her taking one of her boots out and throwing it straight at my head. I avoided it easily, managing to catch the boot in my hand.

Viktor looked surprised at Gertrud, clearly not expecting her to throw a boot at me.

'Gertrud, did you just throw your boot at him?'

'He's lucky that I don't have my sword with me!'

'That's enough!' I saw Astrid, coming between us with her arms extended.

'Astrid...', I said, trying to take a step towards her; but I soon as I moved, I saw the damn wolf placing himself protectively between me and Astrid and baring his canines, then growled at me, again.

'Gertrud, we all need to talk. You and Viktor step inside and close that door. Valtyr, move away from me, and go next to the fireplace. I don't know why the wolf doesn't want you next to me, but let's not make a scene. First, we talk, then we do what we must do.'

In a few seconds, Astrid managed to calm us all. I moved closer to the fireplace, as she asked me. Gertrud was fuming and looking at me like she would love to cut me in half, while Viktor seemed surprised. I gave the boot back to Gertrud, while she looked like she considered throwing it again at my head.

When I turned my eyes to Astrid, I saw her saddened but determined expression; while she was looking at me, she was avoiding making eye contact with me, but giving the things that I just admitted to have done last night, I understood her.

'Valtyr, what did Arne talk about with you, last night?'

'He wants me to marry his daughter Frida and to unite the two kingdoms as one.'

'What decision have you taken about his proposition?', asked Astrid coldly, still avoiding my gaze towards her.

'As a man, I don't want to do it, but as a king this is the best for the people in Kulta', I answered her honestly.

'You have slept with Frida last night', she continued with her voice trembling, 'and if you turn around, and walk away, he might be offended, which might create conflict with the only direct neighbouring kingdom of Kulta. We all agree that it's not wise. You have made your choices; and you must do what is best for your kingdom and your people.'

She took a deep breath. I could tell that she was tired, and she was sad about what was happening.

'Gertrud, Viktor, what opinions do you have about this situation?' asked Astrid calmy.

'My dear King Valtyr, you are an idiot, and you'll have to marry Frida, because you are an idiot. You slept with her, after you asked Astrid to marry you… I truly hope you'll regret this mistake one day', answered Gertrud angrily.

'If I was Arne, I would force you to marry the daughter, since you did not told him clearly that you are with someone else', said Viktor, looking disappointed at me.

I turned to look at Astrid, after I heard the honest opinions of my friends.

'Valtyr, I release you from your proposition of marriage towards me. From now on, you can consider any personal relationship between us finished. What you choose to do next, it's not my problem anymore, but as Gertrud and Viktor told you, it would probably be wise to marry Frida.'

I could hear her weak voice, and I wished I could undo my wrongs towards her, but there was nothing that I could do.

She was right, I had done something that could change everything I fought for, and now I had to face the consequences of my own actions.

'Astrid, what if you are pregnant with my child? We have slept together...'

'I am bleeding. There is no way that I could be pregnant.'

'Astrid...'

'From now on, I will be the seer to you. I believe I have finished the work that the gods wanted me to do, for the moment. I will go back to my village. I want one horse for myself so I can travel'... Astrid frowned, looking at the wolf posted protectively in front of her, then continued, 'two horses, I demand you give me two of your best horses so I can travel back to my village.'

'Astrid, I cannot let you to leave by yourself, at least wait for us, and we can all ride back together...', I tried to convince her, but she lifted her hand, interrupting me.

'Valtyr, you might be the king, but I am the seer. The rule is simple: I come and go as I please, and no king will command me, ever. I have the wolf with me, I will be fine.'

She took her sword, put the cloak on her shoulders, and left the room; stopped in the hallway, while the wolf followed her. I couldn't believe that she chose to travel alone, instead of coming back with us. I was an idiot, and I managed to hurt her so badly.

'I'll go and bring her the horses', said Viktor, leaving the room.

'I'll come with you, Viktor', added Gertrud and left the room, as well.

I followed them and watched as Viktor and Gertrud walked away. It was just me and Astrid now, and she turned her back at me. As soon as I wanted to take a step towards her, the wolf growled at me, again. I watched as she went out of the house, followed by the wolf, and I walked beside them, outside.

I saw Viktor and Gertrud coming back with two horses, just as she asked. Gertrud went closer to Astrid.

'Are you sure you will be alright to travel alone?'

'Yes, Gertrud, I have the wolf with me.'

I watched Astrid hugging Gertrud and Viktor, then took the reins, and tied one horse to the other one's saddle. She moved quickly, and in a few moments, she was up in the saddle and ready to go. She started to ride straight away, without looking back.

Right then, I saw Arne exiting the hall and headed towards us.

'Did I just see your seer leaving?'

'Yes', I answered, without giving him any explanations.

'Alright... Have you managed to talk with your advisers?'

'Yes, King Arne. Let us all go inside the hall; we have a wedding to plan.'

'Excellent!', exclaimed King Arne with a big smile on his face, not noticing that Viktor was frowning and Gertrud was looking at me like she would want to shred me to pieces.

Chapter 16
Astrid
The seer and the god of souls

I left and I didn't look back. There was nothing else that I could do, and seeing how Valtyr didn't choose to fight for us, I knew that I made the right decision.

Was I hurt?

Yes, I was.

I could understand, in a way, why Valtyr had chosen the marriage with Frida, instead of our relationship, but that didn't mean that my heart understood it, as well. I felt empty inside, and I wished I could hug him so he would chase the emptiness away and bring back the happiness.

I knew that he had to choose between us and everybody else in the kingdom, so he had to do what was best for the people in the kingdom. I felt selfish, putting my heart in front of everybody else, but there was a part of me that felt hurt because he did not hesitate, not even for a moment, to push me aside.

In a way, I wanted someone that would choose me over anything else, so if Valtyr gave up so easily on me, I did not want to fight for him either. I could not force him to do what I wanted him to do, and I did not want to be an option, waiting for some breadcrumbs; either I had his love wholeheartedly and completely, or I prefer not to have it at all.

I was still hurt, and I still wanted him next to me, but more than anything I wanted to feel safe again, in his arms, and I craved his presence.

However, I knew that I could never look at him again in the same way, and as I was riding next to Zanos, I did my best to soothe my broken heart. Thankfully, Zanos understood easily that I needed some time to think about what happened and had chosen to ride silently beside me.

As soon as we crossed from the Kingdom of Fjill, back into the Kingdom of Kulta, Zanos disappeared for a few moments. I watched his wolf form hiding behind the trees, then he emerged in his god form, and since then he allowed me to spend time in my own head. He understood that I needed some time to process what had just happened, and we rode at a slower pace.

It was almost ironic how I wished our kingdom to have a king that would do what its best for the people, and now I am saddened by Valtyr's choice. He did what was best for the kingdom, and my mind agreed with him, but my heart didn't. I needed some time away from him, and I knew my heart would finally accept his choice as well.

'How are you feeling, Astrid?', I heard Zanos asking me, and I looked at him.

He was watching me, waiting for my answer. I was grateful to have a god beside me, and I was surprised to see how understanding he was.

'Honestly, my mind understand why Valtyr had made his choice, but my heart... I feel hurt, and I want to be away from him, forget about us and move on.'

'You will; life is beautiful, and you will have a lot of other things to think about.'

I looked at him curious, wondering what would happen next.

Did he know something that I didn't?

I was scared for a short moment, thinking that something tragic might happen, but I chose to push that thought away from my mind.

I had a god beside me, I knew that I was as safe as I could be, right now.

'You have knowledge about what will happen next?'

'No, it doesn't work like that. Father knows, and he is the one sending you the visions. I have my own kingdom, and it has nothing to do with the future, but more to do with the past. I would like to tell you about a lot of things, but that is knowledge reserved only for gods. You are still our seer, and so far, I think you've done a great job.'

I smiled at him, bowing my head shortly in respect.

'Thank you, Zanos. I hope that gods are happy with me, as a seer. I'm so grateful for Father choosing to help us and deliver justice to King Magnus.'

I wasn't sure how I should behave around gods, or how I should address them, but I knew that honesty and respect would be my best choice.

I was curious about our gods, and I wanted to ask Zanos so many questions, but I understood that I did not needed to know everything.

Right now, I was more than grateful to have a god travelling beside me, and finally, I was about to see my parents, that I haven't seen in a long time.

I couldn't wait to hug them and tell them about the things that happened since I left.

'Will you still be around me after I reach my village?'

I looked at Zanos, waiting for his answer. I saw him smiling at me, then raising his eyebrows, while looking almost surprised.

'Why? Is my presence not wanted anymore?', he asked smiling, trying to look offended.

'Of course, your presence is wanted, I was only curious to know how long you'll be around. I am grateful for having the chance to have a god around me.'

'When it's time for me to leave, I will let you know. I am enjoying my time here and I am curious about you.'

'Curious about me?', I asked surprised, taken aback by what he said.

What was he curious about?

For him, I was just another mortal, and my life must look so insignificant, comparing to the immortal life of a god...

'Yes. Life of mortals is short, compared to ours, but you are experiencing so much in such a short time; and the feelings that you are experiencing are so unknown to me and so fascinating. Humas are fragile, but at the same time you are so strong. Let's take you, for example. You have helped in dethroning Magnus, you've learned that the man you had feelings for have slept with someone else, and now, you're licking your wounds, and going back to your life with the head held high; if anything, that's admirable.'

I never looked at my life this way. I guess that for me, there was no other way than forward; keep moving ahead and finding out, as I was walking, what was waiting for me. I was hurt now, but I knew that I would be better, once I got the chance to see my family again.

What happened between me and Valtyr was a nice story, that unfortunately didn't last as long as I thought it would. There will be other things happening, there will be so much for me to experience in life, that when I look back, I will only be grateful for every moments that I had.

'There is nothing else for me left to do, but to keep moving forward. I couldn't stay there and watch Valtyr being with someone else. I know that there are some women who accept to have their husbands sleeping with someone else, and even themselves, go and sleep around regularly. I would like for the man that I choose, to have him choose me as well, again and again. Maybe I am selfish, but I don't like to share. I'm really upset because he slept with Frida, but at least he told me about it...'

I saw Zanos looking intently at me, then tilting his head a bit, seemed to consider his answer carefully.

'But you slept with Gertrud in the cave, and you did not tell him about it', he finally said, making me realise that in a way, he was right.

'Yes, but there was nothing between me and Valtyr when we... I mean, I did sleep with Gertrud, but that happened before I slept with him, and... wait a moment, how do you know about THAT?'

I am pretty sure my mouth was hanging open right now, while my eyes must be bulging, and my face must be red. I remembered vividly what happened in the cave, and that was one of the few moments that I experienced that I wanted to keep only for myself.

How did Zanos know about the cave?

'Well, I was around you all the time, sometimes as a raven, sometimes as a wolf. I was in the cave that night, as well. I have watched everything.'

'I see', I barely managed to speak, feeling uncomfortable of how much Zanos knew...

I wished I'd realise when I did something that one of the gods will be watching me as well.

That was something that I will have to remember from now on.

I felt my face on fire, when I remembered about the things that happened in the cave, but I looked at Zanos, straight into his black eyes, and I did my best to keep my head high.

Love was a part of human life, and I did not want to feel ashamed about it. I was thankful that he chose to enlighten me about this aspect, but in a way, I wished he didn't.

'That night looked so intense and full of pleasure, so much pleasure that I felt jealous for not being able to join', Zanos said, while looking intently at me.

I felt my mouth watering, wondering for a second how it felt to make love to a god, how did his touch felt, and how he looked underneath the clothes, but I turned my head quickly, away from him, trying to look at the road ahead of us.

I wanted to say something, but I did not know how I should respond to him, so I chose to stay silent, instead.

I was trying to direct my thoughts towards the reins that I had in my hand, but in that moment, I knew it.

Zanos had awaken my curiosity, and if I had the chance to make love to him, I would, and without any regret. I only had one life, and I wanted to make sure that I could enjoy the few moments of happiness that I could get.

Love was not guaranteed, as I just learned, and in the end, if I have the chance to have a long life, these will be the memories that I will hold dear in my heart. I tried to come to terms as best as I could, with the fact that I realised that now, I was interested in Zanos, and in a funny twist of fate, I somehow understood Valtyr.

Life was short, and if you could have something that you wanted, you should have it. I did not agree with the part where his choice hurt me, but he made his choices, and I already cried too much about it, last night.

Today, I chose to leave it all behind me, move on, and if I could laugh, I would choose to laugh.

'Are gods experiencing love the same way that humas are?'

'Much more intense, I would say', answered Zanos, while I saw one of his eyebrows lifted, curiously, 'we are able to go on for longer time than humans, but otherwise, it might look the same. Just like humans, some prefer to have the same partner, while some prefer to have occasional meetings.'

I was curious if he had someone, but I wasn't sure if I should ask; we only knew how many children Mother and Father had, but further, humans were not told much more about gods. I just learned the name of the god of souls, recently.

'Have you chosen someone to be by your side?'

I heard my own voice, sounding insecure, but at the same time I was curious.

'I haven't realised that you are so interested in my love life', answered Zanos smiling.

He did not look offended by my question, but rather amused by my curiosity.

'Well, you do know a lot about my own love life...'

'I guess that's fair. No, I have not committed to anyone. You see, I am a possessive god; what's mine it's mine alone, and I do not like to share. While you humans have a short life, mine is, well... really long, and I'd rather choose wisely who I'm sharing my life with.'

'But doesn't feel lonely to rule the world of souls on your own, for such a long time?'

Zanos seemed pensive now, and he looked at me. I saw him thinking for a moment before answering me

'It didn't, until now. There are so many things to do, that I enjoy every moment of peace that I get. Lately, I must admit that I realise that it feels good to have someone around you, but this time away that I am having now, in the world of humans... This is a break from my own kingdom. I would go back to my kingdom, but I guess I will come and visit here every now and then. Humans are different, here in this world, but in my world they all seem to regret passing away and they wish to have experienced life a bit longer. It's different there, it's a different world and I haven't wished for companionship. I still have the other gods that visit me occasionally, and spend some time with me, so it doesn't feel lonely.'

'Do you like the companionship of humans?', I asked curiously, wanting to know his opinion.

'I wasn't interested in it, but now that I have spent some time in your world, I can understand why my sisters enjoy spending time here.'

'What do you think about humans?'

'I think your life is hard, and I am surprised of how resilient humans are. You never stop trying, and when I think that I have made an opinion about a human, there is still something else that I learn, and it surprises me. Sometimes, even I am angered by how evil some people are, and sometimes, I am touched to see how pure and good others are. I think that there is more to humans, than I originally thought.'

I looked at Zanos, thinking about his answer. He was right, some of us were good, while others aren't. I felt happy to learn that gods were just as curious of us, like we are of them. Mostly, I felt so grateful that gods have chosen to step in, and help us, when it was known that Father would not mess with the life of humans; sometimes he chose to interfere, and I was glad to have witnessed this moment.

I looked around us, trying to recognise the road.

I knew that Zanos was with me, but I couldn't wait to see my family again. I could see mountains ahead of us, in the distance, and I knew that those were close to my own village.

Zanos must have seen me looking around, trying to understand where we are. There had been hours since we started this journey, early in the morning, and I knew that we were still one day of travelling, away from my village.

'Do not worry, you will not get lost with me. There is a cave just ahead of us, and we will spend the night there. Tomorrow we will start riding early in the morning, and probably, the day after that, we will finally reach Frostheim.'

I nodded my head, feeling thankful that there was little time left until I will see my family again, and I had a god accompanying me on my way back home.

'Thank you for travelling with me and keeping me safe, Zanos.'

'You are welcome, Astrid.'

We travelled for some time, but this time none of us spoke. I enjoyed his company, and I wondered if he did, as well. Zanos was quiet now, and just like me, he was looking at the landscape around us.

As we were travelling further away from Fjill, it wasn't that cold anymore, but there was still snow around us, since we were close to the mountains.

I knew that the snow must have melted by now, around my village, and probably it wasn't so cold anymore. Thankfully, Gertrud had given me some food for the road, while Viktor has given me his small, magic pouch, so I could start a fire.

I had Zanos with me, so I wasn't worried about finding a shelter, since he explained me that we were not far from a cave.

'Astrid, we will ride away from the path so we can reach the cave. Follow me.'

I did as he asked, and soon, between the trees, I could already see the cave that he was talking about. When we reached it, we finally dismounted and my feet felt so numb, that I almost fell, but in a blink of an eye, Zanos catch me and supported me with his arms.

'I haven't realised that we have been riding too much today. I should allow you a few moments for a short break', said Zanos, while he was holding me.

'Thank you, it's already better', I said while grabbing his arms, so I could steady myself.

I looked up at him smiling, and I was touched by how delicately he held me. This wasn't an embrace, but I enjoyed the shorts moments when his arms encircled my waist, to help me.

He was looking down at me, curiously. To my surprise, he pulled me close to his chest and offered me a real hug. I embraced him back, enjoying his presence, next to me.

'You are tired, Astrid, and you need rest now. You go and tie the horses, next to a tree; I will bring some wood, and I will start the fire.'

I did as he asked, reluctantly, stepping away from him. I wished I could stay in his arms a moment longer, but I did not dare to prolong the moment. After I tied the horses to a tree, I turned to look at him, and I felt my mouth hanging open.

Zanos chose a smaller tree, ripped it from the ground, and with his bare hands, he broke the tree, again and again, into small logs. He took the logs inside the cave, and I followed him, dumbfounded. Quickly, he arranged the logs, then with a touch of his fingers, I saw a small flame seeming to appear out of thin air, and the fire was started, just like that.

I felt my eyes and my mouth opened wide in surprise, seeing him moving so fast, and after watching him doing everything so easily and effortlessly, I wondered how strong he really was. He broke that tree like it was nothing but a thin stick and watching the flame seeming to come to life from his hands was something that my poor mind wasn't ready for.

'Close that beautiful mouth of yours, seer; the air it's still cold and I don't want you getting sick. Being a god has some advantages.'

He was smiling at me, amused by my perplexed reaction, but I knew that he wasn't upset. I tried to compose myself, not wanting to stare too much at him.

'Astrid, do you have food for yourself?'

'Yes, I have some food and water, and I can share it with you. It's not much, but it's better than nothing.'

Zanos smiled, then came closer to me, and put his hands on my shoulders.

'I don't need to eat like you do, Astrid. I feel no hunger, nor thirst, but I enjoy the taste of the food. You eat what you need now, I want you to get some rest first. Tomorrow night, we'll stop somewhere else, and I'll make sure you have something fresh to eat.'

He stepped aside, then went and sat on the ground, close to the fire, seeming unaffected by the cold ground. I ate and drank some water, then came back with a small blanket in my hands, trying to figure it out how I could arrange the blanket and my cloak so we could sleep comfortably.

'Don't worry about me, Astrid. The cold doesn't affect me. Come and sleep in my arms, and you will be warm for the night.'

I watched Zanos opening his arms, and I went to him and laid down, next to him, on his own cloak. He wiggled around, then placed me on top of him. He opened his legs, so my own legs were between his, and pulled me closer to his chest, then using the blanket, wrapped me up. I felt him pulling the sides of his cloak on top of me, enveloping me completely.

I was wrapped efficiently and having the fire next to us, I felt warm and relaxed quickly. I could hear him breathing gently, and I could barely keep my eyes opened anymore. His arms were keeping me close, and I felt grateful to be in a cocoon of warmth.

'Go to sleep, Astrid. I want you to be well-rested.'

I closed my eyes and drifted to sleep straight away.

***

'Astrid, it's time to wake up', I heard Zanos's voice, while he was touching my face gently.

I looked at him, and I smiled, then I stood up slowly. The whole night, I slept without waking up at all, and now I felt well rested.

'Good morning, Zanos. Thank you for keeping me safe over the night.'

'Good morning, Astrid. You're welcome.'

After I stood up, I went outside the cave, and I could hear a small river, nearby. I followed the sound, and as soon as I saw the river, I kneeled and washed my face with cold water. Zanos followed me and did the same. We came back to the horses, and I untied them; few moments later, we were back on the road.

This time, the horses were moving a bit slower, and since I knew that tomorrow, I will be finally able to see my family, I did not rush them. We rode for some time, and Zanos break the silence first.

'We will stop earlier, tonight. I know a good cave, with a hot lake inside, so we can take a bath tonight. I would really like a warm bath, before sleeping.'

I turned to look at him, frowning. Which cave was he talking about? Was it the same cave...

He had a grin on his face, and I knew it was the same place. I felt my face turning red again, but at the same time the thought of that lovely, warm lake inside the cave was too tempting and sounded so good, that I could face the place, both of us knowing what happened there, just so I could have the pleasure to swim in the lake again. I really loved the thought of a warm bath right now, and knowing that it will happen later, made me smile with excitement.

'Ah, I see that you are just as excited as I am about that hot lake', added Zanos, his voice going a bit deeper, while he looked in my eyes intently.

I looked back at him, feeling a shiver down my back realising that we will both be naked, in that lake.

'I am', I admitted.

'Good', he added, and we went back to a pleasant ride, without talking.

I was lost in my own thoughts, and they were going in a direction that surprised me.

Why was I almost looking forward to seeing him naked?

Would it have been disrespectful to stare at a naked god?

What if I was simply admiring him?

Should I look at him, or should I turn my back, to show him respect?

Since when I was thinking like this about Zanos? I asked myself, surprised about my own thoughts.

Last night, I felt him underneath me, but I was so tired, that I only had a few moments of appreciating the warmth of his body before I passed out to sleep. I still had a chance to feel his incredible smell, just as I was falling asleep, and I wondered how it would feel like to kiss Zanos.

I looked at him quickly, wondering if he could hear my thoughts. I would have been mortified if he could, because I'm sure that none of the thoughts that were crossing my mind right now were respectful.

I wondered if he ever looked at me the same way that I did, right now.

I know that I wasn't exactly a beauty, but I have seen many men looking a moment longer at my curves, their eyes lingering a bit too much. Zanos had been close to me last night, but he did not try anything, and made no gesture that would make me think otherwise.

Probably he had lovers far more attractive than I was...

He already has seen much more of me than I wanted him to, I realised, but at the same time, I did not care about anything else. I could only think of Zanos, and how would it feel like to sleep with him.

I wanted him, I realised.

I wanted to sleep with Zanos, and I was looking forward to reaching that cave, tonight...

Chapter 17
Zanos
Closer

Astrid was riding quietly next to me, while all I could think about was her.

Would she come willingly to me? I needed her to choose me, and I was surprised by how badly I wanted her.

I told her where we would sleep tonight, and I saw her blushing, but now I was curious of what could happen. I've seen her seeming slightly embarrassed about the fact that I knew what she did in that cave, and after that, she became awfully quiet.

I wondered what she was thinking about; if she was thinking of the same things that I was. Last night, when I held her in my arms, I realised that she was hurt and tired, and I wanted to give her time to move over what happened in the morning, but I wondered if she loved Valtyr deeply.

When I saw her breaking down and crying in the woods, I felt like I was the one that delivered a knife to her heart.

Few days after that sad night in the forest, I noticed the changes in her and I was angry watching her being hurt for a man that I now knew, didn't hesitate too much before choosing another woman.

I was angry at him, giving her up so easily, using as an excuse the fact that he had to do what was best for the people of the kingdom; I was ready to burn a kingdom down for her.

Happily for me, Valtyr chose to walk away from Astrid, and now she was next to me, looking like she realised there was no point in dedicating her life to someone that gave her up so easily.

I looked at her quickly and inhaled deeply. I really hoped she wanted me, because I was not ready to give her up at all.

Even if she didn't want me as a man, I would still not give up being around her and I was ready to try to stay in her life, just to be around her as much as I could. Maybe she wouldn't want me, but I did not want to be away from her, yet. I wondered what Father would think of me, right now.

He had sent me on the human's world, so I could take a break from ruling over my world after hundreds of winters, and now I have finally met a woman I wanted so badly that I was ready to give up my own world for. He'll have to accept the idea, because I will not give up on Astrid.

She was so blissfully unaware of the plan that I was making in my head so I could seduce her.

If she chose to come to me, then I would make sure that her moans would echo through the cave the whole night, but now I had to wait and see what would happen next.

'Astrid, we are getting closer to the cave. Follow me.'

I took her through the trees, using a shortcut that I have noticed in my raven form. She followed me, without saying anything. For a second, I was worried about her being so quiet, so I turned to look at her, riding behind me. As soon as our eyes met, I saw her lovely face blushing again, and she avoided my eyes.

I turned around and smiled, knowing that right now, she was probably thinking about the same things that I did; let's see how bad she wants it...

As soon as we reached the cave, I dismounted the horse and went to help her. When I held my arms out for her, she moved quickly, then I offered her my support, knowing that her feet would be numb from travelling for so long. I held my arms around her waist a moment longer, looking down at her.

I wanted her, and I wanted her badly, but first I had to know if she felt the same way.

She had to eat something, I remember, and I had to prepare some wood for the fire.

'Astrid, tie the horses and I will make the fire.'

'Alright', she nodded and took the horses near the cave entrance.

I moved as fast as I could, without scaring her, and I broke another young tree into small logs, then, just like yesterday I arranged them nicely, like I saw the humans doing, and light them on fire.

Astrid came into the cave, and I saw her looking at the hot lake inside and seeming to think about what happened there, the last time she was in the cave.

'Stay here and warm yourself. I will be back quickly', I said, while I took the cloak off my shoulders and arranged it nicely on the ground, next to the fire, so Astrid could sit on it.

'You won't be cold without your cloak?', she asked me worried.

'No. I feel the cold, but it doesn't bother me. I could sleep on the snow, and I will be just fine.'

She looked surprised at me, then nodded her head.

I went outside, and saw the rabbit, further away from the cave. I didn't waste too much time, and sprinted for the animal, then I took it to a river nearby, preparing it quickly, leaving only the meat on the bones, and buried the remains. I went back into the cave, and using a thicker branch, I managed to suspend the meat above the fire, and now it was grilling slowly.

'I didn't imagine that you would know how to cook in the forest', said Astrid, looking surprised at me, while I prepared everything.

'There are a lot of things that I have learned lately', I said while looking intently into her eyes.

The food was ready soon, and I watched her eating while seeming to enjoy every bite she took.

She seemed to be so grateful for these moments, and I took a bite of the food.

Surprisingly, the meat was tasty, and I found myself smiling, just like Astrid.

There was beauty in this moment that I never thought I would appreciate until now. The simplicity of the human life was an experience that I never knew it will go straight to my immortal heart. They had a hard life, but they knew how to enjoy the simple moments, like this, and they were holding on to their best memories so they could resist in their darkest time.

Meanwhile, I was experiencing with Astrid, an intimacy that I never enjoyed before. Sure, I slept with women before, but to cook food for them, and sit down next to a fire, in a cave, was something that I haven't done.

Why did I feel so proud seeing her enjoying the little things that I was doing?

I could get used to her watching me carefully, staying so close to me all the time...

After she finished eating, she thanked me for the food, and when we stood up, she hugged me quickly, then turned around and took the rest outside the cave.

Finally, the moment I was waiting for has arrived.

I watched her coming back with a blanket in the cave, and arranging our cloaks and the blanket, so we could sleep for the night.

'Before we go to sleep, I would love a hot bat in that lovely lake. Join me if you want.'

I walked to the lake, took my clothes off, then placed them on a dry area on the rocks surrounding the lake. I didn't rush, but I knew that she was watching me.

I could feel her curious gaze caressing me, and I felt proud to have her eyes feasting on my body. I untied my long hair, then I finally entered the lake. I went in a further corner, where the water was up to my chest, then I turned to look at her.

Astrid was looking at me, like she was hypnotised by my movements; and I was astonished to see how much I was affecting her, but at the same time, I was shocked by the feelings that she was awakening inside of me.

I felt the pull between us, and in that moment I knew that she wanted me, just as much as I wanted her. She seemed so timid, but I watched her as she walked next to the lake, took her clothes out timidly, then placed them near mine.

I watched just as mesmerised as she was, how she untied her long and dark, silky hair, and I felt jealous of those beautiful strands that were caressing her curvy body.

I frowned as her round breasts and soft hips were hidden by her hair, but I quickly smiled when she moved the hair away, fully unveiling her naked body to me.

Knowing that she was allowing me to see her, I was grateful to have the chance to be in her presence, and more than anything, I was grateful to see that she was indulging my eyes with the view of her soft curves.

I wanted to know how her body would feel next to mine, I needed to feel every part of her, and I wanted to taste her irresistible lips; I wanted to feel the taste of her smile on my lips.

She finally entered the water and stopped when the water covered her breasts. I never took my eyes of her, wondering if she will come to me. I wanted to know, and I wanted to see her choosing me.

I needed to hear her saying that she wanted me just as much as I wanted her.

I opened my arms wide, and I looked at her.

'Astrid, come to me.'

I watched her as she moved, and finally, she came into my arms. I hugged her and brought her closer to me so I could look into her eyes. I tried to be as delicate as I could with her, and I barely managed to control myself and not ravish her with my kisses.

'Astrid, if you choose to be with me, you will be mine in this life, and after you die. I will not let go of you, and I refuse to share you with anyone else, do you understand?'

'Yes, Zanos. I want you now, I want you as long as I live, and I will want you even after I'm dead.'

As soon as she said this to me, I finally kissed her, and I tried to be delicate, but I was thirsty, and her plump lips were the sweetest nectar that I have ever tasted. I pulled her closer to me, and with my left hand I supported her body and lifted her up to my level, while with my right hand, I pulled her head closer to mine.

I moaned when I felt her hand in my hair, and the other one around my waist. She was kissing me back with as much passion as I had, and I was surprised of how right she felt in my arms.

In that moment, I knew.

It was Astrid; she was the women that I wanted next to me, she was the one that had my admiration and my immortal heart. I was enjoying every moment of having her in my arms, and I kissed her neck, feeling delighted by her moans, and the way she was arching her body towards me.

When she moved again, I felt her freezing in my arms, when she realised how hard I was for her. I looked in her eyes, and I saw her lovely face blushing. Her lips were a bit swollen, but her eyes were shinning, as she was watching my face, looking just as hungry as I was.

'Zanos, I want you', she said simply, and that was everything that I needed to kiss her again, then I took a small pause from her sweet lips, so I could look in the eyes, while I was adjusting her body to mine, and started to penetrate her slowly.

I watched her moan, as I was making her mine, slowly and deliciously, while enjoying every part of her. When I was fully inside her, I watched her as she closed her eyes and tilted her head back. I started to move slowly, at the beginning, to allow her to adjust to me, then while I was holding her in my arms, I started to move faster, enjoying her moans as she was holding tight on my shoulders, and I increased my pace, as I felt her arching her body towards mine.

I took her there, in the warm water, and I tasted every moan of her, like it was the most exquisite food that this world could offer me. I kissed her again, while I was moving inside her, I felt her body arching, and felt her nails scratching my shoulders, as she was moaning my name.

Her rapid breaths were music to my ears, and when she called my name, I watched her body trembling, then it was my turn to moan her name, as I was riding the waves of pure bliss.

I kissed her again, then pulled her into a strong hug, and enjoying the feeling of having her in my arms, while I was buried deep inside of her. She was panting, and I held her until I heard her breath calming down.

She looked up, at me, and I caressed her face slowly, then kissed her passionately. I hugged her, bringing her body close to mine again.

'You are mine and I am yours. I will find you in every world, Astrid. My precious human...'

She looked at me, and for the first time, I saw a smile bringing light to her features. Her face was radiant, her eyes were shining, and her sweet lips seemed tastier than ever. I felt my immortal soul warming to hers, and I knew then that I will always want to be around her; I couldn't stay away from her, and I didn't want to.

'Zanos, I would follow you in this world, and in every other world.'

I hugged her, then I took her in my arms, and I went out of the water. I placed her gently on our makeshift bed of cloaks and blankets, then we dried quickly, and got under the blanket.

Astrid was laying on her back looking at the fire, and I gently hugged her and placed my arm underneath her head, to support her. I kissed her soft hair, and I felt her relaxing next to me. I closed my eyes and felt an unfamiliar pleasure; to have the woman that I wanted for some time, in my arms, naked next to me, while we were warming next to the fire, in a cave full of secrets and lovemaking.

For a moment there was no time, no gods, no kingdoms. Just two souls, enjoying the moment. I thought how lonely my life was before I met Astrid, and I understood that even though I was happy with what I was doing, I always missed on something.

Having her next to me, I understood what I was missing on.

She turned around, to face me, then snuggled herself closer. I looked at her, looking so pleased and happy, and for a second and I smiled, thinking of a little animal, that she reminded me of.

'What are you doing, kitten? Have you found your spot now?'

'Almost', she said, then she placed her head near my throat, and I almost jumped when I felt her lips kissing my skin.

'And I was thinking that you are tired and need rest...'

I removed the blanket slowly with a grin on my face and exposed her round breasts, and without a warning, I went straight for her delicate nipples and sucked gently on one, while I was playing with the other one, and her little moans sounded like music to my ears.

I felt her body arching towards mine, and I started to kiss her soft stomach, smiling when I felt her hand pulling gently at my hair. I went lower, caressing her soft thighs, then slowly spread her legs. I heard her gasping, and I cackled, then I went straight for her most sensitive area, and I sucked, and I licked like there was no tomorrow, and I had a full platter in my face to feast on.

She moaned at the beginning, but I wanted more from her; I didn't stop until I heard my name being called by her sweet lips while her body was trembling with pleasure. I lifted my head and looked at the beautiful woman in front of me, spread on the blanket, then I kissed her neck gently.

Astrid's breath was raspy; she smiled at me, and this time, it was her turn to surprise me, as she pushed me gently on my back. I was so hard for her, but at the same time, I was curious to see what she had in her mind, so I laid down the way she arranged me, and now it was my turn to moan as she was leaving hot kisses on my neck, then she started to tease my nipples. I moaned when she placed her hands on my hips, then I felt her hungry mouth going straight for my hardened dick.

This time, I called her name as her lips were moving up and down my length and I was pulsing inside her mouth. It was my time to arch and moan, and I enjoying her hungry mouth while I felt like I was close to explode.

Suddenly she stopped, and I looked at her to see her grinning, then, without warning she went on top of me, and lowered herself slowly. She was wet and ready for my hardened cock, and I moaned when I was finally inside her, and she started to move, slowly at the beginning, then faster, until we were both moaning and panting.

I held her hips and kept rocking her gently when I heard her screaming my name and I felt her trembling in my hands. Soon, I was moaning again, and I smiled when my little human collapsed on top of me, exhausted.

'Happy now, kitten? Or you're still hungry for more?'

'Happy now, thank you', she answered, and I smiled as I realised that she was barely whispering the words.

I felt her relaxing and pulled the blankets on top of her, then I hugged her close to my chest, marvelling at how content I was to enjoy having her so close to me.

I realised soon that she fell asleep on top of me, and I smiled, feeling proud of her trusting me so much, and how comfortable she felt with me.

I didn't need to sleep, but occasionally, I liked to do it.

Right now, I closed my eyes as well, and after I scanned the area with my ravens, I placed a heavy ward on the cave; no one, alive or dead could have entered the cave, as the wards placed by me, were also an extension of my own energy, while I was sleeping peacefully.

**

'Precious human, it's time to wake up', I said softly, as I caressed Astrid.

She slept on top of me the whole night, and sometime after the sunrise I decided to finally wake her, as I knew we were close to her village, and it was time for her to see her parents again.

Astrid started to move, and she looked at me sleepily. Her confused face was adorable, so I kissed her gently, and allowed her to wake up. She realised why I woke her up, and she moved slowly, but she got dressed, while I did the same.

Soon, she was back on her horse, while she looked at me, waiting for me to do the same.

'Today I will accompany you in my wolf form. As soon as you reach your home, I will have to go away for some time, then I will come back as a raven. I won't be gone for too long, don't worry.'

'You don't want to show yourself to people?'

When she asked, I knew she meant her family, and I could feel a bit of disappointment in her voice.

'I will, Astrid. It won't be long; I will be coming back soon tonight. When I come back, I will let you know, and I will knock on the door. I want to introduce myself properly to your parents, but first, I must let Father know about the things that happened, as well.'

She nodded, then smiled at me. I kissed her, then I turned to my wolf form, and we started travelling. It didn't take long until we got closer to her village, and I saw her avoiding the village on purpose, and going straight for her house.

Astrid stopped at a distance when she finally saw her home, and she turned around and smiled at me. I nodded my head, and I stood and watched as she went to the house.

She tied the horses to the fence, then knocked on the door. When the door opened, I watched as Astrid's mother hugged her and pulled her inside the house. I knew how much my precious human missed her family, so I smiled to myself, delighted to know that she was happy, for the moment.

Now it was the time for me to meet my family, and I turned away from Astrid's house, then disappeared into the forest.

I found my way to the world above and went straight to Father. I knew he was waiting for me, as he would feel straight away when I entered his kingdom, and when I finally found him, I saw him smiling, and he hugged me quickly.

'Zanos, my son, is a pleasure to see you!'

'Father', I said, as I hugged him, feeling glad to see him.

'How are you, son?'

I looked at him, and I smiled, then I saw him smiling back, to my surprise. Of course, he already knew what I was up to, and why I wanted to talk to him.

'I see that the human world is growing on you, and you have a great time there', he added, with a big smile, that was brightening his face.

'Indeed, father. I have learned and discovered things that I could never imagine, while I watched over the seer. I have strong feelings for her, and I intend to be with her. However, as you know, I cannot stay all the time in the human realm and I want to ask you if you allow me to take her with me, from time to time, to my kingdom.'

'Of course you can take her with you, if you make sure she will come back to her realm when she has a vision. Every time I send her a vision, make sure she comes back to her world, so she can let her people know about my messages to them.'

'Agree. How is the rest of the family doing, Father?'

'Ah, they are keeping themselves busy. Mother is watching over the humans like a hawk, while Elia is helping her. Sera is in her kingdom, protecting her creatures, and Gurun... I am worried about him.'

'What is happening with Gurun?'

'I am afraid that his will is overpowered by the evil creatures that he is supposed to control. He will be the next one that I will visit for a while. We have surrounded Gurun with our love, yet he is still corrupted by jealousy and greed. I have trusted him to be able to withstand the poisonous whispers of those creatures, but I am afraid that he is letting them win.'

'You think Gurun will turn evil, like the creatures he is meant to rule over?'

'Whatever will happen with Gurun, we will find a way. Sometimes, you must fall in the darkest abyss, to crave the light and start rising.'

'Gurun has always felt envy and has failed to see the love that we all have for him; I know Sera is guarding the edges of his kingdom to make sure that he doesn't step into the human realm, but at some point, we will have to try again to make him understand.'

'I know, Zanos. Gurun has allowed his creatures to corrupt him, and he forgot about his role. I have punished him and enclosed him in his kingdom, but I will not leave it like this. However, I want to make sure that he is not too far gone; I know that deep inside him, lies the strength of the gods and he will be able to defeat the temptations of his creatures. I can only hope that he will understand. I will not give up on him, but before I start working with him, he must live to his own ways. I truly hope he will not make another mistake.'

I nodded, feeling my Father's worried voice. While I was upset with Gurun, for trying to attack me, I could feel the hurt in my Father's voice when he talked about him, and in a way, I understood. My brother had the strength within him to resist the temptations of his creatures, but he failed to control them, and instead, he was poisoned by their whispers.

'If you want my help, let me know, Father. Thank you for allowing me to take Astrid into my kingdom; I will make sure she returns to the human realm often.'

'You are welcome, Zanos.'

Chapter 18
Astrid
Envy

After Zanos left, I looked at my home from a distance, and I could feel my heart beating faster, while I felt the joy spreading through me. I missed my family, and I couldn't wait to hug them and see my parents and my brother, again.

I tied the horses, then went to the door, and knocked. My mother opened the door, and as soon as she saw me, she pulled me into a tight embrace. We entered the house, and I noticed that my father and Vilmar weren't there.

'They are gone into the woods, to hunt', said my mother as soon as she noticed that I was looking for them.

'Sit down at the table, Astrid, and I will bring you some food, then you can bathe and change into your clothes.'

I sat down, and straight away my mother placed a bowl of food in front of me, and she waited patiently for me to finish eating. I could see the relief on her face, and I could see the smile that was brightening her features, now that she was sure that I was safe and sound, she seemed so relieved to finally see me back home.

'How are you, my daughter? I heard people talking about the battle that happened in Jotun, and how Magnus was punished by the gods.'

'I am alright mother. I have learned a lot of things since I left home, and there are so many things that I want to tell you about. Valtyr and his men had taught me how to fight, and I joined them in the battle at Jotun. I had visions about the fight, and I saw the gods themselves punishing Magnus. After the battle, I joined our new king, Valtyr, on a visit in the kingdom of Fjill, and after that, I travelled back home.'

'What happened? Why are you saddened?'

My mother knew straight away that something had made me sad, and even though I didn't want to tell her initially about my relationship with Valtyr, I ended up telling her how I felt attracted to Valtyr, how I have slept with him a few times.

I also told her about his marriage proposal and how I decided to accept it; then I explained to her how I decided to end everything when I had the vision that Valtyr would marry another one.

I saw her face saddening, then, I told her about Zanos, without revealing to her his real name, I told her how I decided to be with him, and that I moved over from Valtyr.

My mother was surprised, and I watched her.

I knew that she wanted me to be happy, and I felt bad to watch her being sad, because of me.

'I cannot believe that Valtyr had slept with that woman after everything you've been through, together.'

'I was hurt, as well, mother. This is life, and things like this will happen. I had never thought that I will meet the god from the cave, again, but when he came, I decided that I want to be with him, even if I would see him rarely. Valtyr will be a good king, one day, but I wanted someone that will not sleep around, the first chance he has, I wanted someone that will choose me, straight away. I am not sure that I could have a family with a god, the way you have one with father, but I am grateful to have met him, and I would rather have a few moments of happiness with the right person, rather than a lifetime with the wrong one.'

'Astrid, if that makes you happy, then it makes me happy as well. I'm sorry you had your heart broken, but I am proud of you and your way of thinking. Life is too short to spend it with someone that isn't right for you. Look how much you've grown up since you left home, and how much wiser you've become.'

I hugged her and felt the tears in my eyes. I knew that she would understand me, and I was thankful for having her support.

'We were so happy when we heard that Magnus was defeated, and the new king wants to help the people in his kingdom. Mind you, now, after everything you told me, I am not sure that I like him as much, but I am grateful to have you back home. Will you stay a bit longer, this time?'

'I am not sure mother; I don't know how long I will stay, and I don't know what I will do next. If the gods send me another vision, and I need to travel again, then I will, but otherwise, I would love to stay home for as much as I can.'

While I told her this, I heard the door opening, and I saw Vilmar and my father entering the house.

'Astrid!', I heard my little brother yelling with joy, and he stormed through the house and hugged me.

My father was smiling, and he hugged me as well. I could see the relief on his face to see me back home, and I thanked the gods that I had the chance to come back and see them again. I missed them, and I was fortunate to be back home, again.

'I'm so grateful to see you again, Astrid', said my father.

This time, I hugged him back and thanked the gods that I got the chance to see my family again.

I was afraid that we couldn't defeat Magnus, and it would have broken my heart to think that if I hadn't managed to get back home, my parents would have been worried, wondering what happened to me.

We all took a seat at the table, and my mother brought us all some tea.

'Astrid, is it true that the gods came themselves and punished Magnus?'

Vilmar was curious about what happened in Jotun, and I was happy to know that the news of the battle had travelled and reached my village, and my parents knew that I was alright long before I managed to reach home.

'Yes. It was something like I have never seen before; a pack of wolves that came and ended Magnus and his corrupted men. You see Vilmar, Magnus had done such evil, that even the gods were enraged with him. We all stood aside and watched as the gods punished them.'

'And what happened to them afterwards?'

I knew Vilmar was curious, and I tried to explain to him the best I could, omitting the cruel details, hoping that I would not give him nightmares. I knew he wasn't a child anymore, but I didn't want to terrify him.

'There was nothing left of them', I answered in the end, after I thought of the best explanation.

I saw Vilmar nodding, understanding the gravity of the punishment chosen by the gods, and he seemed to be quiet, thinking of what I just told him.

'I wondered how evil they must have been to upset the gods so much', said Vilmar pensive.

I exchange a quiet look with my mother, both of us remembering about my grandmother and what happened to her, when she delivered the warning of the gods to Magnus. We never told Vilmar about her death, since we considered that he didn't need to know about that tragic day, because he was young and could have hurt him unnecessarily.

I knew that one day my mother would tell him, but I preferred to let her choose the moment. Vilmar only knew that our grandmother was a seer, and she died some winters ago.

The villagers were mostly good people, and none of them will bring up such a painful memory in front of children, out of respect, so my brother didn't know yet about the painful memories of our family.

As my father took a lesson from that day onward, he made sure that we weren't going outside our home without him or our mother being always with us, so there was no chance of Vilmar finding out about our grandmother yet, until my mother decided to tell him.

'I have always tried to protect you and your brother, Astrid. I prayed so much to the gods that you will come back home untouched', I heard my father admitting and it hurt me knowing how worried he must have been for me.

'I know, father, and I thank you for taking such care of us, but sometimes we must make our way, through danger and dark times. This is what turns us into strong people. I have trained alongside one of the best fighters of Valtyr, and now I can say that I have learned how to defend myself. I know you will always be worried for us, but it comes a time when we need to stop standing behind you for protection, and as you grow older, me and my brother will stand in front of you and mother to defend you.'

I saw my father smiling proudly, as he listened to me. He understood what I felt, and what I tried to tell him. They took care of us when we were little, and as me and my brother were turning into adults and our parents were getting older, it was our turn to take care of them and protect them.

I was grateful for having loving parents, that did their best to take care of us, and I wanted to be able to take care of them as well, as gratitude for them being so loving towards me and my brother. I looked at my mother and saw pride on her face, and I could tell that she looked worried for me, as the time passed after the battle in Jotun, and I haven't returned home yet.

My father stood up from the table and looked at Vilmar.

'I say we need to go and gather some wood for the fire.'

I stood up as well, wanting to join them.

'No, Astrid, you need to rest for a few days. Stay home with your mother, and I will gather the supplies with Vilmar. After you get some rest, you can come with me to the forest to hunt.'

'Thank you, father', I said, feeling grateful for my father being so considerate.

I watched him and my brother as they exited the kitchen, then I turned towards my mother, to ask her if she needed help with the food for tonight. She must have realised, as she gestured for me to sit down.

'You will stay on your chair and tell me all about your adventures, and I will bring the meat and the vegetables here, and I will chop them right here, on this table. Your father is right, you need to rest, and I am curious to hear more about your adventures.'

My mother brought everything to the big table, and true to her words, she started preparing everything for the stew in front of me, while I watched her.

'Astrid; Valtyr had cheated on you, do you think he will make a good king?'

I tried to think about my answer, as it was contradictory.

'He did come to me the next day to tell me about what happened. You know mother, he could have chosen to refuse the marriage, but he didn't. I think it's for the best, as he seems to match better with the princess, and the marriage between them two will make our kingdom stronger.'

'And what about your heart, Astrid?'

'Well, that's why I chose to leave straight away. I am grateful for him being honest with me, and I know that there are some couples that don't mind the other one sleeping around, but I have never agreed to that, and I don't want to be just one of the lovers, I want to be the other half.'

'I agree with you, Astrid; I would have done the same. And look, after you have finished your relationship with Valtyr, you have met him. You choose what is best for you, my daughter, and you don't have to justify your decisions in front of anyone. You know your own heart better than anyone, and you have a duty to yourself, to make yourself happy.'

I nodded my head, thinking about what she said to me.

I looked away, towards the window, thinking about her and my father, and admitting to myself that I wanted something like what they had. If I loved someone, I could not sleep around with other people, and if my partner was sleeping around, I wasn't convinced that he truly loved me.

Zanos seemed to think exactly like me, and I knew that he was a god, and I couldn't ask him to be all the time around me, but I was happy with seeing him when it was possible, if we both agreed that what we had was between the two of us only, and we weren't sharing our bond with anyone else.

It felt normal to me, but at the same time, knowing about Gertrud, Tomas, and Viktor, I could understand why other people had different opinions and were content with what they had. I was grateful to have experienced some unforgettable moments, but at the end of the day, we each had our preferences.

I remembered about what happened in the cave and smiled. I couldn't tell my mother about that, and I chose not to tell Valtyr either, since we weren't together when that happened, and I had made a promise to keep the secret about that cave. That night was almost like a dream for me, and it opened a way for me to accept myself and to love and cherish the moments that people share together, even when they are intimate.

People making love wasn't something to be ashamed of, and my friends have taught me to accept myself and love my body the way it was, and I was grateful for experiencing such intimate moments with people that I could trust.

I always felt that I wasn't pretty like some other girls from the village, but I looked at my mother and I realised now how much I looked like her, down to the same curves. I was proud to have her sweet and soft features, and for the first time, I saw my own beauty while I was admiring her.

In my eyes, she was perfect just the way she was, and no other woman was more beautiful than her, for me. She was content to have me home and I watched her as she was preparing the food, knowing that few days before, I wasn't sure if I will make it out alive. Today, I was here, seated comfortably in my own house, and those days when I was afraid, were far behind me.

While I was looking towards my mother, I saw the shadow appearing in the corner of the kitchen and I froze. From the shadows, a tall men appeared. When I looked at him and saw his huge frame and his red eyes I screamed. He wasn't a simple mortal, I knew it straight away, but when I saw him putting a blade at my mother's throat, I trembled.

'Well, finally I meet the famous seer. Hello, Astrid, now be nice for me and listen to what I have to say; if you come with me willingly, I will not harm your mother, but if you don't... well, I guess you can imagine what will happen next.'

'Astrid, run, don't listen to him', pleaded my mother, and I cursed the moment I chose to leave the sword in my room.

'Let go of her!', I shouted angrily and wished I had something around me that I could use as a weapon.

Worried, I saw my mother trying to stab him with her kitchen knife, but he pushed her aside, and removed the knife from his side, almost giggling.

'Seriously? A mortal weapon? You think this could hurt me, woman?'

He threw the knife to the side, then looked at my mother, pointing with his finger at her.

'I don't need to hurt you or your daughter to get what I want, but if any of you is trying anything again, I will make sure you will regret it.'

I could feel something almost mean in his voice and I gestured towards my mother to calm down. I looked at him again, and realised he was just as tall as Zanos, and his large and strong frame was like his; only that his hair was dark, almost black and his red eyes were terrifying.

When I realised who was in front of me, my jaw dropped. I should have known, since people knew about the gods, Father and Mother, their daughters and the only two sons.

If I knew one of them, Zanos, then he was the god of the world below, the world where the wicked souls were sent, after they passed through the world of the souls, and the life that they had was judged. He was Zanos' brother, the only god that was corrupted by the evil creatures that were meant to test us, for us to prove that we are worthy to visit the world above, the home of our gods.

'Mother, please stay put. He is a god, the god of the world below.'

I saw my mother shocked when she realised that I was right, and I saw him looking back at me, chuckling.

'Well, you are smart. I shall enjoy spending some time with you. Now, will you join me?'

He extended his hand, and I look at my worried mother, trying to keep myself calm. Before I took his hand, I tried my best to reassure her.

'Mother, do not worry, I will return home, as soon as I can.'

After I took his hand, the darkness circled around us, and soon, I wasn't in my home, anymore.

I was now facing the biggest castle that I have ever seen and looked abandoned and desolated at the same time.

There was no grass around it, only dried out trees, that seemed to make the landscape even scarier. Around the castle, there was a huge forest of scarry trees, no green in sight. The sky was red, and from the distance, I could hear growls and screams.

'Well, how do you like the world below, seer?', he asked with an arrogant voice, while looking at me with his scarry, red eyes.

'Your castle looks abandoned. If you fix it a bit, it will look better. The forest is scarry, your trees could use some leaves, and what is with the screams and the growls? Are those the evil creatures and the punished souls?'

I knew that he could kill me in an instant if he really wanted to, and since I was still alive, I decided to be as honest as I could. I saw him almost surprised at how calm and composed I was, but deep down, I was praying that Zanos will realise soon that something was wrong, and he will rescue me from his brother. I tried to scream his name in my mind and tell him that I was taken away from my world, but I remembered that he was the only one who could push his voice into my mind, I couldn't do it.

Would he be able to come and rescue me?

I looked at his brother, trying to calm myself and I kept thinking that if he really wanted me dead, I would have been dead already, so I decided to do my best to stay alive for as long as I could.

'Do you think that there is any point to decorate this place? The most wicked souls come here.'

'Could you change it? Could you make it look different?', I asked him, trying to make him talk about him and his kingdom, so I could make sure that he wasn't plotting for ways to kill me.

'Of course, I could change this world, and I can make everything that I want here', he answered back to me, his tone slightly menacing.

I tried to ignore the danger that I was in, and instead, tried to make him talk to me as long as possible, so he will not have the chance to plot my ending.

Was he allowed to bring mortals into his kingdom and kill them?

I decided that I did not want to know the answer, so instead, I tried to make my presence as pleasant as possible, knowing that I had no chance, anyway, to fight against a god.

'What happens in your kingdom? Are the souls sent here to be punished? And what happens if they regret their wrongdoing? Are they forgiven?'

It seemed that my questions had thrown him aback, and after a few moments of debating, he finally decided to satisfy my curiosity.

'The creatures that roam this place are like the ones in your world, only that mortals cannot see them. However, they whisper unspeakable ideas to the mortals, and some end up doing what they are being whispered. I know of mortals that have not been affected, and continued their life normally, and in the end, the creatures have started to haunt other people. When the souls reach here, I allow the creatures to do as they please. They torture them again and again, and eventually, when Father decides that they are truly sorry for what they have done, they are given another chance at life.'

'And you get to decide what happens to the souls, depending on what they have done in their life?'

'Do you honestly think that I care that much? I am stuck here, in this awful kingdom, forced to listen to their screams continuously. None of my family wants anything to do with me, and every time I see any of them, it feels like we are about to start a war.'

His voice was angrier, and I had to refrain myself from taking a step back. I was afraid, and the desolation that I felt since I came here, wasn't helping me.

It felt like his kingdom was void of life, and there was no drop of joy here. Understandable, considering that this was the kingdom where the wicked souls were punished, and every soul or creature here was the walking and talking evil, in different forms.

For a moment, I almost felt sorry for a god ruling over this kingdom of evil and desolation.

'Why is your family upset with you?', I asked curious.

'Well, I might have tried to decapitate Zanos.'

I felt my eyes bulging when I heard him. The way he answered was so worrying as well, just like you would tell the herbs that one would use in a stew; almost like he had no remorse for it.

Oh, I really hoped that Zanos was close to realise that I was taken by his brother, because he really scared me.

'Why did you try to kill him?'

'How come you mortals, don't know about this yet? I was angry, since he and my sisters got the best kingdoms. Look around, this place is awful, and I am surrounded by the most wicked souls and the worst of creatures.'

I could feel the anger in him, and I tried not to be scared.

'I'm sorry, I haven't properly introduced myself since you took me away from my world. I'm Astrid. What's your name?'

'Gurun', he snarled back at me.

'What if Father decided that you were the strongest of the gods and you will be able to resist the whispers of the evil creatures, so he sent you here, to be in charge of them?'

'I never thought of that', he answered pensively.

Maybe if I could encourage him further, I will managed stay alive, long enough for Zanos to be able to find me.

'Gurun, have you tried to organise this world? I mean, you could keep the creatures and the souls a bit further away from you, and make the castle look a little better. I'm not an expert at ruling a kingdom, but is there any way that you could ask Father for suggestions, maybe? Or even Zanos... I mean, since you tried to kill him, maybe it's understandable that he is angry with you, but don't you regret that you tried to kill your brother?'

'He has all the love and admiration of the family. Meanwhile, I'm thrown to the side, and they pretend that I don't exist. And I'm left here, to deal with this nightmare of kingdom. You just see, as soon as they will realise that I took you, they will come here and punish me.'

'But why did you take me from my world?', I asked him, feeling a bit safer as I have realised that if I was talking to him, he did not show any indication that he would want to hurt me.

'Isn't it obvious? I heard from the souls coming that there is a new seer, and I wanted to meet you, but now that I did...', he started, coming closer to me and inhaling deeply, scarring me with his animal like behaviour, 'you smell familiar, just like my brother, Zanos.'

I looked at Gurun as innocent and unknowing as I could. I prayed that the smell of his brother on me will not wake up and murderous intentions in him.

'Perfect... as soon as he will realise that I took you, he will come here and try to finish what I did to him.'

'And that is what you really want? You want Zanos to come here and kill you?', I asked frowning, knowing that this wasn't his true intentions.

It seemed to me that Gurun was doing the things he was doing just because he wanted attention from his family. I was wondering why he did not try to have a conversation with his immortal family, instead of annoying them with his impulsive actions.

'Have you ever spoke with Zanos and apologise for trying to kill him?'

'Why would I apologise? I'm not sorry, it's not like I could kill him since he is immortal. And he gets all the praise and love...', murmured Gurun, almost annoyed by my suggestion.

'What if Zanos would try to kill you? Would you like that?', I asked him, hoping that he would see the reason why the other gods were upset with him.

I came closer to him, and looked him straight in his scarry, red eyes.

285

'I don't think you want to die, Gurun. You want to live, and you want to have a great kingdom, but I think it's hard to be good at ruling this world, when the only gods that could give you any advice are angry with you.'

Gurun tilted his head and took a step forward. I didn't move at all, resisting his terrifying gaze.

He snapped his fingers, and I saw a big table appearing, with chairs next to it.

'Take a seat, Astrid. You might be smarter than I thought, and mind you, it is a pleasure to talk with you, rather than my family.'

For the first time, I smiled and took a seat and saw him doing the same.

'I guess that if you organise the kingdom a little better, it could be easier for you. Just like a king will do in the mortal world, give some of your responsibilities to creatures or souls, and make sure you just keep your eyes on them. And the trees around us have no leaves, I know this place is supposed to be scary, but what if you make them have black leaves? I mean, you could make everything like the mortal world, just make them black and red. It would match the sky here and uhm…. your eyes as well.'

I saw him laughing, and I wondered if it was genuine laugh, or the kind of laugh that would make my head fall from my shoulders.

'I cannot believe that I ended up having a discussion with the human that I took, instead of killing you. You know what, if Father and Zanos don't kill me, I will ask them to allow you to visit me again. Who knows? Maybe you are right, and a better décor and some order will cheer me up.'

'What if you talk with them and explain them that you need… maybe a little guidance… it might help if you try to apologize for what you have done, you know, for trying to kill your brother.'

'They won't forgive me, and now that I took you from your world, they will be angrier with me. What's the point in telling them that I'm sorry if I know they will not care?'

'Why don't try, at least? It's the same for the souls here as well, only that they cannot fix their wrongdoings. You can still talk with them, maybe that will make them change their mind.'

Gurun placed his face in his hands, seeming pensive.

Thankfully, the things that I told him seemed to make him reconsider everything and I knew that he wasn't that long gone. Maybe because he was alone in his world, he ended up doing the wrong things, just to get some attention from his family.

'You know what? I like you. No wonder Father has chosen you as a seer, you are one intelligent mortal; if my head doesn't get separated from my shoulders, I will definitely have another conversation with you.'

'I would like to talk with you as well, Gurun, but it would be really nice if you don't scare my mother or other mortals.'

'Yes, we started on the wrong foot, but I'm glad I planned to kill you to get revenge on Father; otherwise, I would have never met you. I will talk with them, maybe this will change things.'

I froze when I heard him, and with a small voice, I opened my mouth and spoke.

'You still want to kill me, Gurun?'

'No silly, I will do something better, instead.'

And to my surprise, hundreds of scrolls and feathers appeared on the table, and here I was, with the god of the world below, giving him suggestion about how he could improve his kingdom; of course, hoping that he will not get eliminated the moment Father saw him.

Gurun asked me to be the one to tell his family that he regrets his own wrongdoing in case his head gets separated from his head before he had the chance to say it himself, and while we waited for Zanos and father to come to his world, we discussed about the hierarchy of the evil creatures and what type of duties they could have.

Here I was, stuck with a god that initially planned to kill me, and I was casually giving him suggestion about improving the kingdom that he ruled over. When Gurun took my suggestion and made black and red leaves, and added some dark red grass, the landscape had drastically changed.

It seemed that even he was surprised, so he continued to change his castle to my suggestions, while I was drawing different room arrangements for him.

I had to admit that I was surprised by the pleasant discussion I was having with Gurun and I was very thankful to him, because he decided not to hurt me.

Chapter 19
Zanos
The wrath of a god

After I finished talking with Father, I returned to the mortal world, craving to see her again. My beautiful Astrid, she was in for a big surprise, as I have now received Father's approvement of showing her my kingdom and allowing her to understand better some things about the world that no other mortal alive, could possibly knew about.

I have seen how curious she was, and I could only hope that she would like my kingdom, and not fear it.

Would she find it bearable to live for some time in my kingdom or would she be terrified of the souls?

When I returned to her house, I took my form as a raven, and I flew above the house, then landed gracefully on a windowsill and peered inside the kitchen. I saw her mother crying at a table, and I realised straight away that something was wrong.

Where was Astrid?

I flew towards the front door, and straight away took my real form, hoping that her mother would not fear me. I knocked on the door, and soon, her mother opened it.

It was the first time I met her, and when I saw the tears running down her face, I knew that something bad has happened. I saw her gasping when she looked at me, realising that I was not a normal mortal.

'Where is Astrid?', I asked her straight away.

For the first time, I experienced something that I haven't before; I was afraid. I was afraid that something might have happened to Astrid, and I was running out of time, and I couldn't save her.

'The man with red eyes and black hair took her with him. She went with him so he wouldn't hurt me. Please, find my daughter and save her!'

'I will find her, Birta, then I will bring her back to you', I said, trying to reassure the woman.

I walked away immediately, then reached out for Father to send him the message.

'Father, Astrid has been taken by Gurun. I will meet you down there, in his world.'

I wasn't sure if he could feel the anger in my voice, but I was ready to tear my brother to pieces. It was one thing for him to try and kill me, knowing that I was immortal, just like him, but a completely different things to take a mortal into his world. I wondered if that would make Father as angry as I was, since it was our seer that was taken by Gurun.

And yes, I was angry because that seer happened to be Astrid, and I was ready to turn his kingdom of evil and corrupted creatures upside down, to make sure that she was fine.

I was already at the entrance of his world when I met my whole family there. Mother was upset, Father was just as angry as I was, and Elia and Sera were so livid that I could sense their rage, boiling just as hot as mine; Gurun was in for a bad day.

'How dare he kidnaps the seer from the mortal world, when I was the one that banished him to this kingdom?', Father was angry, and his voice was just as strong and loud as thunder.

I wasn't sure that I would get the chance to punish Gurun, because I could bet that he will be ahead of me.

'Gurun ripped the borders of my kingdom so he could sneak to the mortal world. He did not even try to talk with me, he went straight to the seer', growled Sera, understandably annoyed by the behaviour of our brother.

'Have we not tried to talk with him before? Your Father locked him in this kingdom, and yet he found a way to sneak out, and look what he has done... It's disrespectful, as a god, to take away a mortal still alive, from his world. Not to mention, our seer. Instead of respecting her, for being the voice of gods in front of people, he treats her like this...'

When we finally reached the castle where we knew Gurun lived, we all stopped in our tracks, confused.

His world looked a bit different from the last time we were here, when we tried to help him create it, and to our surprise, in front of the castle, I saw the big table that Astrid and Gurun were seated at.

In front of them, everywhere on the table I could see multiple paper scrolls spread, and Astrid seemed to explain something to Gurun, while they were looking at a piece of paper.

'GURUN!'

Even I flinched when I heard the booming voice of Father.

Astrid jumped from her chair, and I saw Gurun looking truly afraid, for the first time in my immortal life.

In a blink of an eye, I went and took Astrid away from him, and hid her behind my back, to make sure that she was alright, while I watched Father unceremoniously grabbing Gurun by his throat and throwing him on the table.

'You are a god, and you have taken a mortal from her world into your kingdom?! Who allowed you to do this?'

Gurun lifted his hands up, and I saw Father calming down a bit, to allow him to talk.

'I'm sorry I took her without talking with you first, but all of you, you left me here alone. I admit that I was bitter and angry, but I did not harm her. I wanted to, just to get a bit of revenge, but the seer... she is such a kind soul. I have been surrounded by evil souls and creatures for so long that I forgot what it feels like to just talk to someone, without them whispering the most wicked of things. I'm sorry Zanos, that I tried to kill you so long ago, but none of you had ever helped with anything. You just threw me here and forgot about me...'

I saw Gurun stop for a moment and wonder what happened to my brother. He was changed; I could feel it. There was no wicked intention coming from him anymore, just regret and longing.

'I was so jealous of you, Zanos... I tried to be like you, but my own family didn't like me as much, and I watched as if they adored you. I'm sorry I have been such a coward that I tried to kill you. I miss all of you so much, and I'm just tired of being here alone.'

'Why didn't you try to talk to any of us? Did you really think that kidnapping our seer was the best idea?', asked Sera, not seeming to trust him.

'And if I ask you, would any of you come to see me?'

'Of course we would have come, Gurun', I answered, and I saw him looking surprised towards me.

He was my brother, and I could feel him being honest.

There wasn't an evil thought to this, but I needed to make him understand that Astrid was a limit that he was not allowed to cross.

I took one step towards him.

'But if you ever take Astrid again, without letting us know about it first, I promise you that I will separate your head from your body.'

'I won't do it again, brother.'

Finally, I saw a side a Gurun that I always knew it was there, only that it was poisoned by jealousy.

I saw him getting up slowly, then turning towards Father.

'I'm sorry for what I did now, and in the past. I want to be better, but I need you and my family. I'm tired of being here alone, and I had time to think about what I did before, and how I behaved. Forgive me, Father.'

I saw my Father finally hugging him, and the tension that was present at the beginning, had dissipated. After that he turned towards Mother and he hugged her, as well, followed by my sisters. He came to me, and I hugged him back.

'Well, Gurun, it seems that I am about to spend some time in your kingdom, now. I helped your brother with his realm, but I think I will take a break and spend some time with you, as well.'

'I would like that, Father. I let the creatures roam free around here and torture every soul they get their claws on, but I think that they also got to my head. I could really use some help to organise my world a bit better. I have missed you dearly, and I wished I had behaved better in the past.'

He turned around to face Astrid, and I tensed. I placed my hand, protectively, around her shoulders. One single wrong move towards her, and I would be ready to tear him apart.

'I apologize, seer, for taking you away from your world like that, and frightening your mother. I will not do it again.'

Astrid nodded her head, and I relaxed. I dropped my head, but I noticed Elia looking towards me, with her eyebrow raised, questioning silently my protective stance towards Astrid, while Sera was smiling suggestively.

'I will return the seer to her world, and I will come back here again', I said towards my family.

I took Astrid's hand in mine and walked away. I did not try to hide my love for her from my family, and I wanted them to know how much she meant for me. I saw Father nodding, and we walked together towards the mortal realm.

This time, travelling between realms with her meant that I had to move a bit slower, but that meant that I had a bit more time with her, before returning her home, to her parents.

I hugged her closer to me, and I kissed her passionately, missing her sweet presence. I have been scared for her, and I never felt so much relief to see that she was safe and unharmed. I looked at her beautiful face, and caressed her soft, dark hair.

'I was worried for you, Astrid. I wanted to kill Gurun when I saw your mother crying and scared.'

'Zanos, he wasn't that bad. I think he really missed his family, but he did not harm me. Maybe all of you will get along better, in the future.'

'How about your family? Do you think that today will be a good time for them to meet me?'

I saw her looking shocked at me, clearly surprised by my question.

'You want to meet my family.... as in... uhm, introduce you to them?'

'Well, you already have met mine and now, they all know we are together, so why wouldn't we tell your parents, as well?'

I saw her blushing and she seemed nervous by the idea, almost shy.

'Astrid, when I came to your house to talk with you, your mother saw me. I would like to tell your parents that I have feelings for their daughter, but if you think it's too much for them, right now, I can wait.'

I would have been able to wait as long as she wanted me to, but I hoped that she would change her mind, and decide to introduce me to her parents, as her lover. I knew that only some days ago she left Valtyr, and I hoped that her hesitation wasn't because of him.

I tried hard not to let the jealousy eat me alive, while I waited for an answer from her. I didn't want to push her in any way, but I wanted her to know that I would been more than happy to announce to every realm, every creature, and every soul how much I cared about her, and that she was mine.

'It might be early, but I'm alright with that. I did not think to talk with them about you, yet, but I think my father will be happy to meet you, and not to mention my little brother.'

I smiled and hugged her closer to me, feeling relieved that she agreed. I did not want to hide our relationship from my family or her family, the ones that should know about it. I hope that his father and his brother will not be too scared of me. I thought about her mother, and how scared she was, and I decided to hurry up our journey to her house; her parents needed to know that she was alright.

***

As soon as we reached the house and Astrid opened the door, I saw her parents rushing to her. While her mother was hugging her, her father looked at me surprised and bowed his head. Her little brother was looking shocked at me, realising straight away what I was.

'Thank you for bringing my daughter safe, back home.'

'You are welcome', I answered straight away, although I was feeling bad, knowing very well that it was my brother who took Astrid away from her family; lucky for my brother, he didn't hurt her, otherwise everything would have been different now.

'There is something I need to tell you', said Astrid and I looked at her breathing deeply, knowing fully well what she was going to talk about.

I took few steps and stood beside her, and I saw the smile on her mother's face; she knew, and she understood straight away. I wondered if she talked with her mother about us.

'This is Zanos, the god of the souls, as we know him.'

'I knew it!', I heard her little brother shouting straight away and I turned towards him, and I smiled.

'Zanos, they are my family; my mother's name is Birta, my father's name is Orn, and he is Vilmar, my brother.'

I saw his father coming near me and I extended my hand; we shook our hands and saw his surprised expression, while he was looking at me. Orn was a good man, I could tell it straight away, but I could also sense that he was intimidated by me.

Her mother, however, seemed to be so happy to see her daughter safely return home, that she was completely relaxed and gave me a short hug, which made me smile. There was something so comforting in her motherly hug, that I knew straight away that she will accept me.

Vilmar came closer to me, looking mesmerised by my long hair and my black eyes. I knew that while I looked somewhat normal, there were so many things about me that were an easy giveaway that I was not human. He seemed to be fascinated with my appearance, and I extended my hand for a shake, and the boy shook my hand quickly, looking like he did not dare to touch me a moment longer than he should.

'Also, there is something else that I would like to tell you... I have chosen Zanos as my partner', said Astrid and I watched his father's reaction.

'I know, this is a lot to take in for the moment', I said while looking at Orn's shocked expression, while his wife and his son were smiling wide, 'and I hope that you will be glad about your daughter's choice. For the moment, I will ask you kindly to keep this between us. There might be too much curiosity in your family if other people find out, so I think it's best for the time being, if I would stay in my raven or wolf form, if other people are around us.'

Orn looked at me and nodded his head.

'Of course. There are enough people curious about Astrid, since it was revealed that she is the seer, but if people would find out that she is with a god, it will cause unnecessary stir.'

'I wanted you all, Astrid's family, to know about us. However, since I have duties that are not in this world, I would be gone often in my kingdom, and if Astrid can, she is most welcome to accompany me. I don't want you to be worried about her and if she is missing for days, I want you to know that most likely she is with me, and she is safe. If Father wants her to speak his will towards the people in this kingdom or another, then I will do my best to watch over her, while she is in this world.'

I saw her father nodding, and her mother as well. They understood me, and I felt thankful for their acceptance. Her mother seemed to have an idea, and I saw her moving away quickly.

'Let us invite you to a humble dinner. You are most welcome into our house', said Birta, and started to pull the chairs on the table, inviting me to take a seat, which I did, straight away.

Astrid sat next to me, and Orn and Vilmar sat at the table, as well. While Birta gave us all drinks and food, I waited for her to finish setting the table so we could all talk.

Vilmar was the most curious about the other gods, my family, and I told him about how Mother was created, and later, how myself, my sisters and my brother were born.

When I mentioned my brother, I saw her mother tensing, and I explained to her that she was the one that took Astrid, then I told them how I went with my family, into my brother's kingdom, and how calmly Astrid has handled the situation.

When I told her parents that I was ready to fight with my brother, but I found him taking notes from Astrid's suggestions, I heard her brother laughing, while her mother smiled, and her father looked proudly towards her.

'I'm sorry and I apologise in the name of my brother because he kidnapped your daughter and put you under such great distress. Luckily, he still had something left in his head, because I assure you, had he harmed Astrid, I would have teared his kingdom apart and him as well, along with it.'

'That is not your fault, Zanos. We are not responsible for what others do, but I am glad to hear that your brother has apologised for his actions.'

I looked toward Orn and felt surprised of how calm and understanding he was.

'I will always try my best to protect my family, but sometimes, there are things that we cannot stop from happening. It is up to us to pick ourselves up and do the best we can.'

I looked at him and nodded.

After we finished the food, I complemented Birta's cooking, and I was blessed with one of her charming smiles. I knew that Mother would like her straight away.

I could easily sense Birta's kind nature and once again I felt enraged at the human king who had butchered Faida, Birta's mother, in front of Astrid.

I remembered how Father has dealt with him and felt my anger dimming. However, the pain that he put Astrid and her family trough, was still there, and I felt saddened thinking about Faida, our previous seer.

'Faida is in the world above, with Father and Mother. She is reunited with some of her family there, and she is at peace.'

I saw Birta looking at me and saw the tears falling on her face. I covered her small hands with mine and looked at her.

'The pain that you feel in this world, will only be a distant memory in the world above. Each soul has its own path. Bless the memory of your mother, Birta, and when the suffering is overwhelming you, don't think of what you could have done differently, what happened years ago had nothing to do with you; remember your mother when she was happy, remember her love and be proud of her.'

'Thank you for telling me about her', said Birta, and I nodded.

Astrid was looking at me, then I felt her little hand on my knee. She was thankful for my kind words, and when I looked at her face, I could see a pale shadow of sadness, in her eyes.

'Thank you all, for your warm welcoming', I said and looked at Orn and Birta. I could see on their faces that their day was long, especially when they were so worried for Astrid, and decided that it was time for us to rest, including myself.

'Shall we go to sleep? It has been a long day for all of us', I said, and I saw them nodding.

Vilmar stood up and went to his room, after he bided us 'good night'.

'If you don't mind our simple house, you are more than welcomed to sleep here', said Orn while looking at me.

'Thank you for receiving me into your house, Orn', I said, and I saw him nodding.

When I stood up, Birta showed me Astrid's room, and I smiled. She didn't seem to understand why I was smiling, until Astrid explained to her.

'The wolf, mother. It was Zanos.'

'You were the wolf that pulled my Astrid out of the lake and kept her warm, until we found her?'

'Yes.'

'Thank you for protecting her.'

'I will always protect her, Birta', I said, and saw her smiling.

After we entered Astrid's room, Birta exited, and soon, I was left alone with Astrid. I turned to her and hugged her, keeping my arms around her soft curves, while I was inhaling her sweet scent.

'It feels so good to have you in my arms again, my precious human.'

I felt her arms around my waist, while she came even closer to me.

'It does. Your arms are my favourite place in this world, and all others.'

I kissed her gently, then stepped aside, while she was frowning at me.

'It has been a long day for you, Astrid. You need to rest now.'

She nodded, and I saw her turning around, then picking up a white nightgown. While she took her clothes out, I watched her, enjoying every inch of her that was showed to my eyes, then I kept watching and pretend to frown as the night gown covered her body.

Astrid looked at me, while I was taking my clothes off, and went straight to bed. When she came and lay beside me, the bed felt a bit small for the both of us, but I pulled her closer to me and caressed her head gently.

Soon, she was asleep, and I finally relaxed, knowing that my beloved human was safe, in my arms.

**

Astrid was asleep next to me when I opened my eyes. I listened to the noises of the houses and realised that her parents were awake, and they were in the kitchen, moving quietly, to not wake us up. I moved slowly away, and covered Astrid with the blanket, while I exited the room, and went towards the kitchen.

'Good morning, Orn. Good morning, Birta.'

'Good morning, Zanos. Is Astrid still asleep?', asked Birta.

'Yes, let her rest. She was away from home for far too long, and I know that the spontaneous, unwanted trip to the world below has drained her.'

'Of course, Zanos. I am so grateful to know her back home. I am preparing some food, but it will take me some time. Are you hungry? Would you like me to make something quickly, for you?'

'You don't need to worry about me, Birta. I am not bothered by the warm or cold weather; I don't feel hunger or thirst, like humans do. I can feel the taste of the food, and I can tell, your food is the best in this world, so do not rush for me. Take your time and prepare the food the way you like it.'

I turned my head to my right. I could already see the rider from the distance, through the eyes of the ravens flying around Astrid's home.

Now I have seen that he had taken the road that it will lead him here, and wondered if he would stop here.

While her parents have seen me, I did not want other people to see me; I quickly sent a raven to follow him up close, so I could know if he was coming to speak with Astrid, or he was just passing by.

'Is there something wrong?', asked Orn worried, while he was getting ready to stand up from the table.

'No. There is a lone rider, in the distance, that had just taken the road that is close to your house. Since Astrid is here, I am not sure if he is just passing by your house, or he intends to come here, with a message for her. When he is closer, I will know, and if he comes here, I will take my wolf form. The people cannot see my real form, it is not the time, yet.'

I saw Orn nodding, and while I talked with them about how their life was going and what happened with them since the previous king was punished, I realised that the rider was coming towards us.

I stood up.

'The rider is coming here, after all. I will take my wolf form. Orn, Brita, do not worry, I am here.'

I went to Astrid's bedroom and checked on her; she was sleeping peacefully still, so I took my wolf form. I sneak through the creaked door, and I placed myself strategically in such a manner that any visitor standing in front of the door, would have been able to see me easily.

Few moments after I laid on the floor, I heard the horse neighing outside, then I heard the knock on the door.

Birta stood up and answered the door.

I could see that the man had armour on him, and I could also see the sword. He was holding a letter in his hand.

'Good day! I am looking for Astrid, the seer. King Valtyr has sent her a letter.'

Chapter 20
Astrid
Moving forward

The vision that I just had woke me up straight away. Valtyr was getting married to princess Frida; and I had to admit that they both shined with happiness, and they looked more beautiful than ever, but behind them, I saw the person who officiated the ceremony and it was me.

I stood up and looked around the room confused. Zanos wasn't here anymore. I knew the difference between a dream and a vision, and I knew this one was a vision, especially when I remembered having the same vision, the last time I was in Jotun. I got dressed as quickly as I could and went towards the kitchen.

In the kitchen, I could see my parents seated at the table, while a man looking like a soldier was eating. I finally saw Zanos and frowned when I realised that he was in his wolf form.

'Is everything alright? Who is this man?', I asked.

As soon as I spoke, I saw the soldier looking at me, he stopped eating, then came and bowed his head and handed me a sealed letter.

'Good morning, seer. King Valtyr has sent you this letter and I am instructed not to leave until I have an answer from you.'

'Please sit down and finish your food while I read it', I said, knowing very well that he had a long journey ahead of him, back to Jotun.

I was curious to see what Valtyr had written to me, so I opened the letter and started reading straight away.

Once again, he apologised for having upset me, and was asking me if I wanted to be the person that would officiate the wedding between him and Frida, as he wanted to make sure that there was no hard feeling between us.

He asked me if I would come to Jotun, and I closed the letter, then placed it on the table in front of me and considered if I wanted to go.

Honestly, I didn't want to, but as a seer, I could understand that my presence was needed on such an important day in the kingdom.

Of course, I still remembered what happened last time that I saw Valtyr, in the kingdom of Fjill, but all those feelings were forgotten, and I could only hope that Valtyr would be a good king.

I knew that as a seer, it was my duty to be present when the king was getting married, and as a woman, I decided some time ago that Valtyr wasn't the man that I was looking for, so I moved on from any feelings that I had for him.

I looked at the man in front of me, that has finished eating meanwhile, and was waiting politely for me to decide what answer I would send to Valtyr.

'When is the wedding?'

'In seven days from now', he answered.

'Tell your king that I will come. I will start my journey tomorrow morning. Would you like to rest a bit before going back?', I offered, knowing fully well how tiring it was to ride for a long time.

'No, thank you, Astrid. I will return right now to Jotun and give King Valtyr the news. Many thanks for your kindness and have a great day.'

The man stood up, and accompanied by my father, left our house. I could hear the horse neighing, then the sound of its hooves hitting the stones on the road.

I looked at the wolf that was approaching me, and without realising, I gently petted his head.

I giggled as I saw Zanos rolling his eyes; of course I will pet you Zanos, if you present yourself in front of me as a gorgeous fluff, I will not waste the chance to pet you, I thought to myself, while I was smiling at him.

'Mother, I am sorry for staying such a short time at home, but as you heard, there is a wedding and King Valtyr will be marrying Princes Frida of Fjill. He wants me to officiate the wedding, and I would rather sit home with you; but as a seer, the gods want me to be there.'

'That's alright, Astrid, you will have time to rest afterwards. Let's pack your clothes', said my mother, understanding the situation I was in.

While me and my mother were packing, I saw Zanos entering the room, still in his wolf form.

'I want to take your father and your brother to the woods, for a hunt, but I'd rather join them as a wolf. Would you ask your father for me, my precious human?'

As soon as I heard his voice in my mind, I smiled, and I nodded my head, then went and talked with my father.

A few moments after, they went to the forest, and I was left alone with my mother.

'Well, let's start preparing some vegetables so we have something for a stew, when they come back.'

I joined her at the table, and I looked at her face. Something seemed to be troubling her, and I frowned, wondering why she was so worried.

'Is everything alright, mother?'

'Astrid, I'm thinking about you and Zanos... I know that ideally, women want to have a family, but this would not be possible with a god, or maybe it is, I'm not sure how a relationship like this would work. I'm thinking... are you sure that this will make you happy?'

I looked at her and I nodded.

'He makes me happy, mother. And yes, in the future we might not be next to each other all the time, but that is alright with me. It's not because he is a god, it's because he treats me the way I wanted... first time I saw him, I couldn't get him out of my mind, and I never thought that I will see him again. I am happy to be with him when it's possible, and I am alright not to have a normal family.'

'As long as you are happy, Astrid that's all that matters to me.'

We went back to cleaning and chopping vegetables, and soon, just as we finished, the door opened, and I laughed when I saw an excited Vilmar. My brother was beaming with happiness, and I could tell that this had to be one of his best hunting trips, so far.

'Astrid, you would not believe what we caught, come outside to see!'

When I went outside, I could see a deer, five rabbits, and a goose. Next to the animals, my father was smiling proud, and Zanos, still in his wolf shape was looking straight at me. My mother came outside as well and looked surprised at their catch.

'Oh, dear, we need to smoke some meat, there is a bit more than we need. Quick, Astrid, let us help them!'

Zanos went inside the house, then came back outside in his god form, and I could see the excitement on his face.

'I will help you, as well, Birta.'

'You are a god, Zanos. You do not need to worry; we can prepare the meat', said my mother respectfully.

'I want to help', insisted Zanos, and I saw my mother handing him a knife, and explaining to him how we would proceed.

Everybody started working, and while my father, Vilmar and Zanos were working on the deer, me and my mother took the rabbits and the goose.

'So, what will you do with the fur?' I heard Zanos asking.

'We will save it, clean it, stretch it to make sure it's going to keep its shape, then we will use it for clothing. We try to use as much as we can, and what we do not use, we will bury back in the woods. I'm trying to keep the teaching of my parents, to be respectful of nature, and with the animals.'

I saw Zanos listening to my father, almost mesmerized, and now my father was explaining to him how to prepare the meat for cooking and for smoking. I watched in awe as my father was teaching a god our humanly ways, and nothing felt more beautiful to me that this moment.

Even if Zanos looked so different from us, he seemed to be marveling at how inventive we were, and how we have learned to make use of everything that we had. I looked at him, helping my father to arrange the meat, so they could smoke it.

Meanwhile, I went to the kitchen with my mother, and we prepared the meat for the stew. My mother looked at me and smiled.

'This is such a lovely day. I'm grateful that Zanos chose to meet us and spend some time with us, that is nice of him. I trust you are in good hands, Astrid.'

'Me too, mother. I know things are a little different, but I know I'm in good hands with Zanos.'

The rest of the day went quickly, while I enjoyed the time I had with my family and Zanos.

Clearly, Vilmar was adoring Zanos, and kept telling him about our ways, and Zanos kept asking him questions.

I was grateful for the lovely time I had with them, and hoped that we would enjoy days like this again.

When we went to sleep, I was happy and peaceful. Zanos hugged me, and I nestled closer to him. I felt him caressing my hair, and hid my face into his neck, breathing in his lovely smell.

'I enjoyed this day, and there is nothing better than ending a good day with you in my arms, my precious human.'

'It was lovely. Thank you for this beautiful day, Zanos.'

***

Next morning, at the first rays of sun, I was already back on my horse, starting my journey towards Jotun, while Zanos was accompanying me in his wolf form.

He decided that it was not the time yet for other people to see him, so he would stay in his wolf form the whole journey. He was leading the way, and I was following him, on the horse.

I knew it would be a long journey to Jotun, but I knew that I was safe with Zanos.

For some time, we followed the main road, then I saw Zanos stopping and indicated me to go off the main road, and into the forest.

I didn't question his decision, and I followed him, through the forest.

I was wondering if he was giving me a break, since we had managed to travel already half of the distance from Frostheim to Jotun, and I considered if I should ask him to keep on travelling, but I knew that the horse would need to rest for a bit.

The silver wolf disappeared trough the bushes, just to return straight away, walking towards me. He stretched his arms, and I unmounted the horse.

'The horse could use a bit of rest', said Zanos while looking at me, 'but how do you feel?'

'I am alright, I don't feel tired at all', I answered.

'Good, because I have some plans with you.'

I was surprised by him, and smiled, wondering if he was thinking at the same thing that I was thinking about. When he leaned closer and kissed me, I kissed him back passionately.

He bent down, and I didn't realise what he was doing when he sneaked his left hand under my posterior, but then he gently lifted me up, and as I realised what was happening, I grinned and wrapped my legs around his hips, tightly.

His right hand was holding me close to his body, and I wrapped my hands around his shoulders, giggling when I felt him moving.

I moved my face closer to his, and started to kiss him passionately, while he was taking me inside of a cave.

I wiggled around then leaned on a side, and I laughed out loud when he realised what I was doing; I managed to get his trousers undone, and I knew that they must have already fell, around his ankles.

I saw him raising an eyebrow, then I kept grinning, while I moved around a bit more and managed to lift my dress, conveniently. I moaned when I felt him hard between my legs, and I kept moving my hips, slowly, suggestively.

'Are you trying to take advantage of me, woman? Hold on tight', he groaned into my ear, and I did so, grabbing onto his shoulders, like my life was depending on it.

I felt his hard cock penetrating me slowly. He grabbed tightly into my hips, and started to move inside of me, while I kissed him. I breathed harshly, then put my head on his shoulder, while he was fucking me at a fast pace.

I squeezed hard into his shoulders when I felt that I will melt into a puddle in his arms, then I moaned and screamed his name when the bliss overpowered me. He kissed me again, then let me down slowly, and I watched him with a grin on my face, while he bent down and lifted his trousers.

'I think I'm pretty good with riding, Zanos, wouldn't you say so?'

'No. I think you still need to practice, human. I offer to lay down on my back for you, so you can have some more practice.'

'Good. We're going to do that tonight', I decided, while I went to him and kissed him again.

He took me to a river closed by, and we washed quickly, then we returned together to the horse.

'What's wrong?', asked Zanos when he saw me sitting next to the horse, and not getting up on it.

'I was thinking that I might need to change to my pair of trousers; I cannot trust you while I'm wearing a dress.'

Zanos took a few steps to get closer to me, and I saw his grin, while looking down at me.

'You can trust that no matter what you are wearing, I will always find a way to make you moan.'

'Glad I can trust you with that', I added, and finally decided it was best to get up on the horse and keep on going, otherwise our break could take a lot more time than it should.

As the sun was setting down, we finally reached the gates to Jotun, and I was surprised to see so many things were different from the last time that I was here.

I could see more look-out towers, as I was getting closer to Jotun, and it looked like Valtyr has decided to strengthen the gates and add more towers throughout the city, as well.

As soon as I got closer to the gates, the soldiers recognised me, and moved out of the way, so I could pass, while they were welcoming me.

'Seer, welcome to Jotun! King Valtyr is expecting you, please follow us and we will lead you to him.'

Followed by Zanos, now back in his wolf form, I unmounted the horse, then walked beside the soldiers.

On the city streets, I could see that the houses were renovated recently, and there were so many people walking around, while children were playing and laughing loudly. There were more traders on the streets, that were now closing their stalls. Overall, it seems that the atmosphere was much relaxed now, and people seemed to be happier.

We reached the biggest building in the city, the former house of Magnus, now Valtyr's house. I could see a lot of benches around the building, and sitting at a big fire, in front of the building was Valtyr, Gertrud and Viktor.

Next to Gertrud, I could see a small boy, and I gasped when I realised that it must be her son. As soon as Valtyr saw me, he came closer to me and extended his hand.

I shook his hand respectfully, as he was our king now, and was surprised to realise that everything that happened between us was now forgotten, and I did not feel hurt in his presence, anymore.

'Welcome to Jotun, Astrid. You are always welcome here', said Valtyr, while he looked at me.

Gertrud came and hugged me straight away, and I returned her hug. I really missed her, and I was so glad to see that she looked much better.

'Astrid, I am so happy to see you again. There is someone I want you to meet. He is my son, Petur.'

'Hi Astrid, I am Petur', said the boy, I felt my eyes tearing, looking at a smaller version of Tomas.

I shook his small hand, then I turned to hug Viktor, who came closer to me, as well.

'Viktor', I said, then hugged him.

'Let us sit for a bit, and we will bring you some warm food', said Valtyr, then we all took a seat around the big fire. Zanos, as always, sat at my feet, and I felt relaxed having him so close to me.

'Valtyr, I can see that Jotun looks much better than the last time I was here.'

'I'm trying to make people happier. I gave them back what it was unfairly taken from them, and I intended to keep on making the kingdom better for everyone.'

'That's good Valtyr, people needed someone to care about them', I said.

'The army is getting stronger as well', said Gertrud, 'there are a lot of people who voluntarily came to us to be part of the army of the new king'.

'We are preparing Jotun now for the wedding of our king, but soon, we will get to work, and we will make the kingdom stronger and better', said Viktor.

'Are there any threats to the kingdom?', I asked.

'No threats, Astrid, but we want to renovate the Old Bridge, near Vatnar. It is time we start trading with other kingdoms, but before doing so, I want to be sure that we are ready and capable of defending ourselves in case we need it. First, we rebuild the whole kingdom, every city, town, or village that we have, then we make sure we have a strong army in case we need it, and only after that we will be able to open the gates to learn about the other kingdoms in the mainland, that we have separated ourselves from. For the moment, all that matters is that Kulta and Fjill are united.'

'I am happy to hear that, Valtyr', I said.

And I was happy for the kingdom, and for Valtyr. It made sense, the way he explained everything, and the way things were falling into place. Just as I realised some time ago, the best choice for Kulta was the marriage between its king and the princess from the neighbouring kingdom, Fjill, and it helped that Valtyr and Frida were attracted to each other.

'Astrid, I wish to talk with you for a few moments', said Valtyr, and stood up and motion for me to follow him.

I stood up, and I watch Zanos. I nodded my head, and he came and followed me.

When we entered the gathering room, I looked around and realised that everything was changed here to accommodate as many people as possible, not only the rich ones. I followed Valtyr to a smaller room, where he lighted a few candles and set them on a big table, that was surrounded by twelve chairs. I could see a lot of papers arranged neatly in a corner of a table, and some shelves on a wall, where more papers were nicely folded and arranged.

'Astrid, please, sit down', said Valtyr and I sat on the chair closest to me, and felt Zanos curling at my feet, again.

I watched as Valtyr sat opposite me, at the table, and looked at him. Just like Gertrud and Viktor, he also looked a lot better than the last time I saw him.

'I have been an idiot, and I want to apologise for what I have done the last time I saw you. Please, do not be upset with Frida, for the things that I have done. I should have done better. I should have told you that I was attracted to her, instead of sleeping with her.'

I felt Zanos tensing at my feet, and I reached underneath the table to stroke his fur, gently.

'You were an idiot, I agree. I am happy to see that you admit your mistakes, but let's not talk about this, in the future. The past is behind us, and the only time we need to talk about it, is when we are learning from our mistakes, and we do our best to not repeat them. I was hurt then, but I am not hurt anymore. I am with someone, and I moved past what happened in Fjill.'

'I am happy to hear that you are with someone, Astrid, I really am. Please, invite your partner to the wedding', said Valtyr, clearly relieved that I wasn't upset on him, anymore.

'It's not possible.'

'Do I know your partner, Astrid?', asked Valtyr.

'I cannot tell you more, Valtyr. You do not need to know more about him, just that I am happy.'

'I understand', said Valtyr, then stood up, and I did the same.

'Look, behind the gathering hall, there are some bedrooms. This one is mine', said Valtyr pointing to a big door, 'here is Gertrud's and this one is Viktor's; I asked the women to prepare the last one for you. Here is where the children sleep, here is where our most trusted soldiers sleep, so in case you need something, any of us will be more than happy to help you with anything.'

'Thank you, Valtyr, it's kind of you', I added.

320

'Astrid, I mean it now, you are always welcomed where I am, and I am sure Frida would say the same, and if there is something I could help you with, let us know. You are a friend to me, and our seer for the whole kingdom. I told people about you, and every door in this kingdom should be opened for you, anytime, anywhere.'

'Thank you, Valtyr. Where is Frida?'

'She is coming towards Jotun with her father, and should be here tomorrow, but for the moment, they will have the house next to this building prepared. Let us join the others back at the fire, soon, we will all feast to celebrate your visit to Jotun. I want us all to be happy tonight. The last time we were all here was painful, and I want us to replace those painful memories with new ones, full of happiness and joy.'

'I agree, Valtyr. It's time for everyone to celebrate. We have fought and we have suffered enough.'

Chapter 21
Astrid
For better and for worse...

For the past days, I had the chance to spend some time with Gertrud and Viktor and was relieved to realise that they were supporting each other continuously after Tomas passed away. Petur, of course, was missing his father dearly, but having Viktor in his life was making things easier for him.

Gertrud and Viktor were each other's support, and together, they made the best council that a king could have. I saw that Valtyr was always looking out for them, and taking care of Petur as well, teaching him everything that he thought the boy should know.

When Frida and her father, King Arne arrived in Jotun, things were a bit tense at the beginning, but soon, they felt right at home.

The soldiers that were accompanying them relaxed and were talking with Valtyr's closest soldiers, and while they were talking, Frida met the rest of the people, and I had a chance to speak with her as well.

Just like Valtyr, she asked to speak to me privately, and after she explained to me that she did not know about our relationship, and after I told her that I have move past the events in Fjill, the tension between us disappeared.

Sure, I realised, I could not move over as fast, unless I did not acknowledge that the feelings I had for Valtyr were not anywhere near as strong as what I felt for Zanos; I did not use Zanos to forget about Valtyr.

I never cared for Valtyr the way I cared for Zanos.

While I was physically attracted to Valtyr some time ago, my soul, my mind and body together, were mesmerised by Zanos. The connection that we had was much stronger than any connection that happened between me and Valtyr.

When we first arrived in Jotun, I felt that Zanos was tensed, but as the days went by, he relaxed, as he understood that I would never look at anybody else the way I looked at him. While he stayed glued to me during the daytime, at nighttime, I took advantage of the big and comfortable bed that I had in the bedroom, and not one single night went by without us being together.

Now, as I stood on the steps of the new altar dedicated to our gods, that Valtyr had ordered to be renovated in time for his wedding, I looked at all the people gathered to witness the wedding between King Valtyr and Princess Frida.

There was joy and hope in the air, and for the first time I felt them, as well.

Zanos was sitting next to me, in his wolf form, while in front of me, two steps down were Valtyr and Frida. Everyone was looking at them, admiring the king and the future queen, and I must admit, they were completing each other, and they were making a good couple.

I stretched my hands in front of me, palms up, and Valtyr and Frida both, placed one hand in mine.

In front of everyone, I united their hands, and while holding their hands together, I started my speech.

'Today, in front of all the people, as your seer, I am blessing your union, and pray for you to the gods, so you may have a long and happy life and lead the people with a good heart. I pray to the gods that you will be blessed with many children, and many years of happiness. Let us all celebrate the marriage between King Valtyr of Kulta and Princess Frida of Fjill. You are now the king and queen of Kulta and Fjill. May your reign be long and prosperous!'

I placed a crown on Valtyr's head, then a smaller crown, that was made to resemble the other one, but more feminine, on Frida's head. They both bowed to me, and bowed, respectfully to each other. Valtyr turned to the people, and lifting Frida's hand up, he announced the beginning of the celebration.

'Now, let's celebrate!'

And like that, the greatest celebration has started.

Straight away I could hear the music, and the fires were lighted. People started to dance and shout their happiness, while I smiled and looked at everyone around.

To my surprise, King Arne himself invited me to dance with him, and I accepted.

'Astrid, I have asked people to always welcome you in their homes. We would be honoured if you would decide to visit us', said Arne while looking at me.

'Thank you, King Arne; I will make sure to visit Fjill', I said, but without telling him when, as I was not sure if I could go, any time soon.

'You are a great soul, and I have seen how kind you are to my daughter. I am happy to see how just and brave young people are. They have managed to rise against Magnus, and now the kingdoms and its people are healing.'

'Yes, a lot of good things have happened recently, and I can only hope that many more will come', I answered as our dance ended.

I bowed respectfully to King Arne, then went to one of the tables, were Gertrud, Viktor and Petur were seated.

'It's good to have a day like this', said Gertrud, while she smiled at me.

I nodded, as I was sitting down at the table.

'It's time for you to celebrate as well', I said while I lifted a glass up, 'let us drink to new beginnings, hope, and happiness!'

They both raised their glasses, then I saw Viktor inviting us all to dance.

For the first time, I laughed and danced with my friends, without a worry in the world. We had been together in miserable days, when we did not know if we're going to make it, and now we were celebrating and dancing as much as everyone else around us.

The celebrations continued, even after sunset, and as the moon was up in the sky, I got another vision.

I was walking through the forest, with Zanos close to me, but he wasn't in his wolf form anymore. I stopped, and in front of me, I could see all the gods.

I opened my eyes confused and realised that I was still at the party. As soon as I started to look around Zanos nudged me gently with his nose. I looked down at him and nodded. We needed to walk from the party now and go towards the forest to meet the gods.

I stood up and looked for Gertrud. When I saw her, I went straight to her.

'Gertrud, I must leave the party. I don't know when I will be back, but do not worry about me.'

'It's alright, Astrid. If someone asks for you, I will tell them that you had to leave.'

Straight away, I walked towards the main gates of Jotun, then I continued walking on the main road, with Zanos next to me. As soon as we entered the forest, he switched to his god form, and I looked at him worried.

'You think that something happened, Zanos?'

'When you have the vision, Father told me not to worry. So, whatever this is about, do not worry.'

I nodded and continued walking.

Soon, we reached the same clearing that I saw in my vision. I looked ahead and I could see Father, Mother, Elia, and Sera.

Apart from Gurun, all the gods that we knew about, were here, in this clearing.

326

I bowed respectfully in front of them, then I took a deep breath and looked at Zanos. I hoped that he had an idea about what was happening here but knowing that I was in the presence of the gods, I decided to calm my breathing, and trust them.

Whatever I was about to hear, I knew that it was going to be something important, since they were all gathered here, and I trusted them, I knew that everything would be alright.

'Zanos, Astrid, thank you both for answering so quick and coming straight away to me, when I called you', said Father and took a few steps forward, towards us.

'Of course, Father.'

'Probably you are wondering why; tonight, I have decided to bless Astrid with a gift. Zanos, as you know she is mortal, and their lives are short, so, Astrid, you will be blessed tonight with the gift of immortality.'

I felt my eyes widening in shock, and my mouth was wide open. I heard loud and clear what was being said, but these words were not making any sense to me.

'Astrid, will you accept my gift?', I heard Father asking me.

'Yes Father, thank you. I accept your gift', I said still looking confused.

'Father, is everything alright? I know you, and it seems like something is troubling you', I heard Zanos saying, with concern in his voice.

'Yes, Zanos, I am alright. I don't like what is going to happen next, but I know it must be done. Astrid was born mortal, so in order for her to become immortal, she must die, first. After that, I can bind her soul forever to her body.'

'What do you mean, she must die? I cannot allow any harm to be done to her, Father!'

'Zanos, my husband had become immortal like that. It's the way it must happen', I saw Elia answering and I swallowed a bit harder, realising what was going to happen to me.

'Father, if this is the way it must be done, then I agree to it.'

I saw him nodding, then a shiny blade appeared in his hands. It was thin, and longer than a knife, almost as big as a sword. I looked at Zanos, who seemed to be more terrified than all of us, including myself.

'Zanos, you know that I cannot do it, since I will be condemning her soul to be gone forever. She cannot do it either, since her taking her own life will live a stain on her soul and sent her to the world below… It either can be you, Mother or one of your sisters… Astrid, do you have a preference on who you would like to kill you?'

'Uhm… I'm not sure. Will it hurt?', I asked scared.

'Yes. You will die as a mortal.'

I looked at Zanos, who looked back at me. I saw him for the first time struggling to say something, but he seemed to be frozen. I saw Elia stepping forward and taking the blade from Father's hand and coming closer to me.

'Zanos, Astrid, if you are both alright, I will do it. I know Mother cannot do it, and since I have done this with my husband, already… Astrid, are you alright with this?'

'Yes', I answered, this time not hesitating anymore.

'Lovely', answered Elia, and straight away, with a move so fast that I barely saw it coming, she pushed the blade straight into my chest.

I gasped, feeling the pain immediately, then I looked down, and I could see my own blood staining the dress that I was wearing.

I was feeling dizzy already, and I could only hear Zanos calling my name, then I felt his arms around me.

I tried to look around me, but it was harder to breathe, and as I was gasping for air, I heard a cacophony of sounds, and movements around me.

There were shapes moving fast around me, but when I tried to distinguish them, my eyes were too tired, so I finally decided to close my eyes, and allowed the darkness to embrace me.

Chapter 22
Zanos
… until death do us part

'Father, are you sure she will be alright?', I shouted while I was holding her lifeless body.

Elia came closer, and wiped away the blood from her chest, while I was throwing her nasty looks. I was shocked by how fast she killed Astrid.

'Don't worry, Father still got it. Trust me, Zanos, I have been through the exact same thing, and I know what you feel now.'

'Zanos, lay her body down. I need everyone to step aside, and keep quiet until I finish', I heard Father saying and I reluctantly stepped aside from Astrid.

Father got closer to her, and I heard him murmuring something while his hands were above her wound.

Strangely, I could not understand the language that my father was using, and I was sure that I knew every language and dialect from all the souls that had visited my kingdom.

Soon, I saw a light seeming to come from Father's hands, shinning for a few moments inside Astrid's chest, then disappearing completely.

I knew that I could trust Father, but seeing Astrid dead was something that I wasn't prepared for.

Father stood up, and I saw Astrid opening her eyes. I wanted to get closer to her again, but Father signalled for me to stay away.

'Allow her a few moments, Zanos. Do not be afraid, she is alright', then turning towards her, I hear him talking again, 'child, how to you feel? Do you remember what happened here?'

Astrid stood up slowly, helped by Father. I saw her looking at his face, then nodding slowly.

Then, she looked at me and smiled and I could finally breathe again and felt the weight on my immortal heart coming off; she was alright. She kept looking at Mother and my sisters, then towards Elia, again.

'I promise I will never upset you', I heard Astrid saying, and I felt shocked when I heard Father laughing.

As soon as he laughed, we all did, relieved to realise that everything was alright.

'Don't worry Astrid, I can't kill you anymore. You're immortal now.'

'Did it work?' asked Astrid surprised.

'Of course it worked', answered Father straight away with a smile, trying to look offended. He crossed his arms and looked at Elia and Astrid, 'you can try to fight each other if you wish so...'

'I trust you, Father, we all saw her dying, then we saw what you did', answered Elia.

She turned towards Astrid, then looked at her apologetically, opening her arms.

'Welcome to immortality, Astrid. I'm sorry that I had to kill you, but we both know that Zanos would not do it, and neither would Sera. I would really like a hug from you if you don't mind?'

'Yes, I understand why you had to do it', answered Astrid timidly.

I watched her as she turned towards Elia and hugged her. I was surprised at how calm everything was now, while a few moments earlier, Elia had just stabbed Astrid without hesitation.

Sera joined in and hugged them both.

'Thank you, Elia, because I know I couldn't do it. Astrid, I hope you will be alright soon.'

After that, Astrid turned towards me, and finally, I hugged her. Having her back in my arms, where she belonged, had managed to calm me down, instantly.

I looked at Father, while I was holding her, and I nodded my head. I knew he understood what I couldn't say.

And yes, Elia was right, and I nodded towards her as well; I couldn't stab Astrid, I wasn't capable of even thinking about hurting her. Within me, it was embedded a strong instinct to protect her.

I saw them walking away, while I was still holding her, and I heard Father, loud in my mind.

'When you have the chance, visit us in the world above, son.'

'We will. Thank you, Father', I answered him.

I loosened my hug, and Astrid turned around, then turned back towards me, looking confused.

'Where is everybody else? When did they go away?'

'When I was too busy holding you in my arms', I answered, then I turned her around back to me, I leaned in and kissed her like my life depended on it.

She kissed me back, and when she hugged me, I opened my eyes in surprise and stepped back.

'What happened?', I heard her asking, while she was looking surprised at me, not expecting me to back away from her so fast.

It worked. She had so much strength now, that she didn't know she could easily rip a man to pieces.

'You are much stronger than a human, Astrid. Come with me.'

Reluctantly, she followed me, while I took her close to the nearest tree. I looked at her and smiled, knowing that she was about to have some really good fun.

'Astrid, do you see this tree? Punch it as hard as you can, with your fist.'

I saw how confused she was, but she still did as I asked her. She put her little hand in a fist, and prepared herself to punch the tree, not having the slightest clue that she was almost as strong as I was, as an immortal.

When she punched the tree, she left a hole so big in the trunk that it broke, and we both watched it, while it was falling to the ground. I looked at the trunk, and realising that it wasn't too big, I grinned.

'Lift it up now, you can do it', I encouraged her.

She did as I told her, and laughing like a child, she casually threw the whole tree towards the clearing. She ran quickly towards it, then threw it back towards me, managing to break two more trees, in the process.

Just as she saw me doing, she came towards the fallen trees, and started to break it, branch by branch, and arranged them nicely, in a big pile. I watched her giggling and marvelling at her new strength, realising how it felt to be immortal.

'Just remembered, you are still not as strong as a god, but you could give a good beating to Gurun, if he ever upsets you', I told her, and I saw her whole face lighting up.

'That's nice to know, but I don't think I will do that.'

'I was just mentioning it, it's good for you to know that you can do it, if you want to.'

'Zanos, so now that I am immortal, what would happen if someone would try to kill me?'

'Well, if it is by poison, you wouldn't even know it, unless it has a strong smell or a weird taste. If they try to hurt you with a blade or a sword, you will be able to remove it yourself from your body, and the wound will heal itself almost immediately. You would be able to break that sword in half, easily, then break the idiot that tried to hurt you, in half, as well. That is, if I don't rip him to pieces, before you have the chance.'

'That's good to know', murmured Astrid, probably taken aback by the sudden aggressivity in my voice.

'Zanos, should we go back to the wedding celebrations, now? I wouldn't like Gertrud to worry about me.'

'First, let me give you my cloak because your dress is now stained and damaged. We will get straight to your room, you will change into another dress, then we will continue to celebrate with the others, if they aren't asleep, by now.'

She nodded, then watched as I turned to my wolf form, and she started to walk back towards Jotun. I followed her, but this time, I was relaxed like I never was before, knowing that she is immortal now. I knew that no one else could hurt her anymore, even if I wasn't next to her, she would be perfectly capable of withstanding anything.

To my surprise, the humans were still celebrating, but there were fewer left now, and just a few were still dancing. I accompanied Astrid while she went to her room and changed her dress quickly; then we went outside, and I saw her looking for someone.

As soon as she spotted Gertrud, she went straight to her and took a seat at the table.

'Astrid, I'm glad that you are back! Is everything alright?', I heard the woman asking her.

'Yes, Gertrud. Where is Viktor?'

'He went away, to put Petur to sleep. I don't think that we will be able to stay much longer. Valtyr and Frida left some time ago, so now people are left to celebrate for as long as they wish. I think I already had my fair share of celebrations, and I would really like to lie down in my bed.'

I was laying on the ground lazily, listening to Astrid and Gertrud talking, and I saw Viktor approaching. He looked like he needed his bed as well.

'Ladies, should we all have a drink and dance again, together? I am so tired that I could fall asleep standing, but I want to dance one more time, before going to sleep.'

Gertrud and Astrid got up, and they all clinked their glassed, then emptied them straight away, and they started to dance. While I looked at them dancing, I was almost considering joining them, but I knew I couldn't.

We would not show ourselves so easily, and I wanted to respect Father's rule. Usually, only people deserving, or people being tested personally by the gods should see us; and myself, Gurun, and Elia, had different worlds altogether that we needed to take care of, and rarely had the time to visit the mortal world, but in the future, I knew that I would do it more often.

After their dance was finished, I saw Astrid hugging them quickly, then I stood up and got closer to her, as I realised that it was time for us to go to 'sleep'.

I grinned, knowing already that this would mean that finally, her stamina would be matching mine; I could only hope that she will not break the bed, accidentally.

As soon as we got in the room, and she closed the door, I change back to my form, and took my clothes off, then laid on my back, on the bed, while her eyes were glued to me. I enjoyed every moment of her attention, and I smiled at my beloved immortal human, inviting her to join me in the bed.

I admired her elegant moves, as she removed her clothes quickly, then grinned when I saw her getting on top of me and felt her sweet lips kissing me. I kissed her back, and while I was doing it, I was hardening already, feeling her warmth.

She started to rock her hips slowly, and I moved slowly underneath her, and while massaging her breast slowly, I slide inside her, then moaned when my little immortal human started to move faster and stronger, making me tense underneath her.

When I heard her breathing faster and moaning as well, I gently started to nibble on one of her hardened nipples and placed my hands on her hips, until it was my turn to moan and whisper her name.

She stopped moving and laid on top of me.

'Zanos, it's weird, I still feel so full of energy... it's like I just woke up', whispered Astrid.

I lifted her up gently, then went on top of her. I kissed her neck, then looked at her.

'I know Astrid, and the greatest things is that we could keep going until the morning, the whole next day, and the following night and you still wouldn't be tired.'

I kissed her again, and when I heard her giggles, I looked up at her.

'My turn now, Astrid.'

Chapter 23
Astrid
In this world, above and below

In the morning, I started to pack the few things that I had taken with me. Straight away, Zanos stood up and started to help me.

'Thank you for being so kind, it's only a few clothes, I will be done in no time', I said, while looking at him.

'It's alright, Astrid, it's my...' started Zanos, but then froze and seemed to be concentrating on something else.

'Zanos...? It's something wrong?', I asked, tensing straight away.

After some moments that felt like a lifetime, Zanos finally answered me.

'Father was checking on us to make sure we were alright. Also, it seems that we have an invitation to a celebration... in the world above', said Zanos with a smile, while I breathed a sigh of relief.

'That's amazing! Of course, we will join the celebrations in the world above. I will try to arrange with Gertrud for someone to take care of my horse; I am sure that she will hold on to our bags until we return...'

'Ask her if it's possible for them to do you a favour and have a rider to take the horse and the bags back to your parents' house', asked Zanos instead.

'Alright, I will do that.'

'It's something wrong, Astrid?' Zanos asked me as soon as he realised that I was frowning a bit.

'I'm dressed in fighting clothes and have part of my fighting gear with me', I said, while pointing at my sword, 'wouldn't a nice dress be better for the world above? Should I try and find one?', I asked, feeling unsure of my black leather trousers, that were paired with the white blouse and the black leather blouse on top of it, then pointed towards my sword.

'Do not worry Astrid; we are not going straight to the celebrations; that will be a bit later, and if you do want a dress, I'm sure that my sisters will be more than delighted to help you with it.'

'Alright', I nodded and as I was heading for the exit, Zanos stopped me.

'Allow me to kiss you again, before I turn into my wolf form.'

I turned towards him, hugged him, and kissed him, devouring his soft lips. I should have felt really tired, considering that I barely slept, but since I opened my eyes as an immortal, I had an insane amount of energy, and even after what it was almost a full night of making love with Zanos, I wasn't tired all; the only thing that seemed to be affected was the bed, that had started to make some creaking noises towards the morning.

Once we got outside the room, Zanos was back to his wolf form, and followed me quietly, while I managed to find Gertrud. Bless her, she seemed tired, but for the first time since the battle she had a smile on her face.

'Good morning, Gertrud, how are you?', I asked while I hugged her.

'Good morning, Astrid. I feel tired', she answered with her voice raspy, 'how do you manage to look so well rested? I still feel like everything is spinning around me.'

'I had a really good sleep', I answered knowing very well that it wasn't the sleep, 'but I need to disappear again, and I need your help. Can you please help me, and make sure to send my horse and my bags back to my home, in Frostheim?'

'Of course, do not worry about it. There are a lot of groups of soldiers travelling back and forth inside the kingdom, making sure that everything is alright in all the villages; I will ask one of them to have the horse sent to your home.'

'Thank you so much Gertrud, you are a sweetheart', I said, then I hugged her again.

'Have a safe journey, and hope I'll see you soon, Astrid.'

I didn't announce to anyone else that I was leaving, since I hadn't seen other people waking up. It was still early in the morning, and I started to walk towards the gates of Jotun. I knew that once we reached the forest, Zanos will take care of the rest of the travelling, so it made more sense to just walk.

As soon as we reached the tree lines, and the forest was hiding us, Zanos changed to his god form, and turned towards me.

'Astrid, would you be alright with spending most of your time in my kingdom?', he asked, seeming almost afraid of my answer.

'Would I be able to travel back and forth so that I can see my family and friends?', I asked him.

'Of course, Astrid. I will speak with Father so you would be allowed to travel like us. You will be able to come and go as you please.'

'Yes. I am alright with living in any kingdom, if you are present, as well', I answered and looked at him, admiring his attractive smile.

'Astrid, if I am taking you to my kingdom, I will take you as a queen. Will you marry me?', he asked me, and I froze for a moment, then I nodded my head quickly, while I hugged him straight away.

'Yes, Zanos. I will marry you in this world, in the world above, in the world below, and in any other kingdoms or worlds that exist.'

I felt him hugging me back tightly, and we kissed. I didn't expect Zanos to ask me to marry him yet, as I thought that we both agreed that we are partners, but his proposal warmed my heart.

'I know, so this is exactly what we are going to do. We are going in the world above, and we are going to celebrate our union, then we are going to move everyone in your home, with your parents. After that, we are going to annoy Gurun and celebrate in his world, as well, completely uninvited, then the last celebration will be held in our kingdom. Is this plan alright for you, my queen?'

'I cannot wait', I answered quickly, knowing very well that I had the biggest, happiest grin on my face.

***

In the world above, Elia, Sera and Mother were more than delighted to contribute to the celebration, and of course, they took care of my dress. I was given a gorgeous white dress, that had hundreds of pearls sewn at the seams, and delicate flowers in intricate patterns, adorned with shiny crystals.

As the preparations went on at incredible speed, everything was ready, and the celebrations started much sooner than we expected.

In front of all the gods, Father gave us his blessing, then everything was packed quickly, towards my surprised and we all moved to celebrate, to my parent's house.

I was shocked to see how quickly they organised everything. Since my home was far from the village, we could celebrate everything without worrying that other people might find out.

My parents were surprised, but absolutely delighted to see the gods that they were praying to, in their house. After they went to sleep, Zanos insisted on moving the celebrations in Gurun's kingdom, which we did.

Again, everything happened fast as we travelled through the worlds.

I finally got the hang on how to do it, and I was now incredible happy and grateful that I had the freedom to move so fast, knowing that I could visit my family often.

Gurun was just as surprised as my parents to see us all.

'Father, you are all here… has something happened? I…', he tried to explain something, then stopped when he noticed me in the white dress, and then looked straight at Zanos, who was also dressed in white, his clothes matching mine.

'Brother, we are celebrating the union between me and Astrid, and we have all come to your kingdom, so we can all celebrate together.'

I almost gasped with happiness when I saw Gurun hugging Zanos, and from that moment forward, I knew that something that was broken before between the two of them was now fixed.

Gurun seemed to be delighted that celebrations were being held in his kingdom, and we continued there, what we started in the world above.

After some time, Zanos turned towards me.

'Should we move to our kingdom, my precious human?' he asked with a soft smile, and I nodded.

And once again, everyone travelled again, including Gurun, towards the kingdom of souls.

It was the first time I saw Zanos's kingdom, and I gasped at its beauty.

There was no sun, there was no moon, but it felt exactly like those few moments before the sunrise; everything was like my world, but the grass and the leaves were a darker shade of green, almost black.

I saw the animals that gathered in front of us, and Zanos told me about his guardians and how they took care of everything in this world.

As I was learning more about his kingdom, I admired the quiet beauty that was surrounding me. Elia and Sera admired his kingdom as well, while Gurun was learning from his brother, so he could make his own kingdom better.

After I became more familiar to his kingdom, we continued the celebrations here, as well. I danced, again and again, and I watched Zanos as he seemed to shine with happiness. Soon, I decided to take a small break from dancing, and sat at the table.

Father came next to me, and I saw him looking at me, then he touched my hand.

I closed my eyes, and I saw him; the little boy that was accompanying me had Zanos's silver hair, my green eyes, and most of my features. He looked up at me and stretched his little hands, while I laughed and picked him up, in my arms.

I opened my eyes, and looked back at Father, feeling my eyes watering.

'Is he...?', I wanted to ask, but I didn't have the strength to continue, as I was overwhelmed with emotions.

'Yes, he is your son', he answered simply, and I looked at him, my heart being filled with gratitude for the vision he sent me.

'Thank you for allowing me to see him', I said.

'It will take some time until then, but for now, go and celebrate your union. Make this kingdom better and stronger, and keep on helping the mortals, when I send you the visions. You and Zanos will have a happy life together.'

'Thank you, Father', I answered and following his advice, I stood up, and went towards Zanos, so I could dance again with him.

When he looked at me and our eyes locked, I knew that my now immortal heart, skipped a beat. First time when I saw him, in the cave, I was taken aback by his beauty, and the strength and power that he emanated, effortlessly.

Now, once again, I felt the same butterflies in my stomach, every time he looked at me, like he wanted to devour me.

'You are stunning, my queen. Immortality will not be enough for me to adore you and love you.'

He pulled me in his arms, and I hugged him.

'I love you, Zanos', I whispered, knowing that he could hear me.

'I love you too, Astrid.'

THE END

Author's note

For my other half, thank you for your love and support; I know you had fun reading this book [☺] .

For you, dear reader, thank you for your love and support and I can only hope that you enjoyed this book as much as I enjoyed writing it.

This book was inspired by legends from Northern Europe; this work of fiction is not intended to be an accurate representation of any culture or legends.

The author, however, fully intended to make someone's day better by sharing the story she created.

<u>More books by Liliana Lia:</u>

Dear Clara...
by Liliana Lia

Clara moved to Edinburgh to follow her dream of becoming a forensic psychologist.

Between her job at a delivery company and the University classes, she makes time to enjoy the beautiful landscapes of Scotland, with her friend, Emma.

Love? Love is not there, in her plans, but she meets someone.

While reading about missing people in the newspapers, she finds some connections.

Is Clara actually uncovering something or it's just a dead end?

Feelings and seasons
by Liliana Lia

Feelings and seasons by Liliana Lia, is a poetry collection, a metaphoric painting of feelings inspired by different seasons, from warm smiles to cold hearts.

Spring - the awakening of a soul
Summer - the warmth of my soul
Autumn- guarding my warmth
Winter - a cold heart

The Sorcerer
by Liliana Lia

I am young and I'm dying.
I don't know what else to do to save my life, so, advised by
the old witch living in the forest, I make my way towards
the castle of the most powerful sorcerer.
He can save me, but if I want to live, I must pay a price...

What have I done?

*

*'The Sorcerer' was initially published as a poem, in 'Feelings and
seasons', 2022. The author has decided to explore the beautiful
story she created and has turned the poem into a fairy tale novella.*

*Please note that this book is for ADULT AUDIENCES
ONLY.

Three
by Liliana Lia

Amelia cannot remember anything about her past; she is struggling to make sense of her life and uncover the truth.

Ophelia's father is missing after a car accident. She is stuck in a small city, trying to uncover what happened to her father.

Julia is living with her mother, having no power of decision over her life. Her mother is her guardian and she has to do what she's being told, in order to become legally independent.

Amelia, Ophelia, and Julia are all living in the same house. Three women, trying to untangle the situation they found themselves in.
What they don't know, is that their stories are connected.

Truth cannot be hidden.

Scan the QR code below to find me on social media:

Printed in Great Britain
by Amazon

55637503R00209